Natterjack

Natterjack

Niall Duthie

faber and faber

LONDON · BOSTON

First published in 1996
by Faber and Faber Limited
3 Queen Square London WC1N 3AU

Phototypeset by Intype London Ltd
Printed and bound in Great Britain by
Mackays of Chatham PLC, Chatham, Kent

A CIP catalogue record for this book
is available from the British Library

ISBN 0–571–17664–X

2 4 6 8 10 9 7 5 3 1

for Angela

Book One

1

There are numberless ways of being of service. This is one. I am a toad – a tired and retired toad whose skin and accommodation are both peeling – but still, a toad. Of course I choose! Accordingly I take – if you wish, give – the distinguishing characteristic of toadery to be that the toad performs his obsequious rites gratis and in full, unasked.

The object of those rites, the subject for these pages, is dead. How dead? If I have my corruption rates right, between a third and a half rotted. Please do not take my commas for gulps. My toadery always was singular and this brief life is in the nature of a modest mausoleum, of dankish stone but of the chastest proportions. I discriminate. I refine. And I have prepared for the task as widely as allowed by my present place – the dry joint of a geological ox-tail overlooking the slug-slick blue of the Mediterranean. I have fingered quite a few tomes, have re-read Aristotle, at least looked in on Zarkhuri. Why? Mostly nerves I think. Have you never had that feeling – a mix of hope and fear, a gap between gust and buffet – that you will find the master volume already on the shelf? Very well. Here is something from Cicero (in Book One of the *Tuscalanae Disputationes*):

> For a man to commit his thoughts to writing when he can neither arrange them nor bring any new light to bear upon them and, indeed, when he has no attraction whatsoever to offer his reader, is a senseless waste of time, and of paper, too.

I am not sure why, but this reminds me of a chicken, first strangled, then plucked, then gutted – and in particular, as it waits on the cooking tray, of that sad, pimpled flap of skin that hangs down at the rear.

But come, not simply because I found so little of what con-

3

cerned me amongst the duller classics – no, my memory worked better and more confidently than that – I realized, to look up at a ready example, that I would have been better off squinting at the night sky. I had begun the business as an antidote to melancholy; my results, mixed with a bumptious sort of nervousness, had been melancholic. Know your narrator. Diffidence turned to resolute patience. I looked up at those refreshing glimmerings and leafed on, though jotting down even as I did so a mnemonic, a pointer, a link.

And when I had put away the last volume and wiped the greasy dust and moth-scrag from my hands, what was my score? Two! Two footling references to a very beautiful country and its proud, quite decent enough people. And both by derisory, wintry way of the weather. Or did they have somewhere else in mind? I am thinking of those tricks played by bad hearing and unfamiliar tongues. No matter. I understood what I wanted. I have the formula here. The uniqueness that precision gives a soul. *My* MacBeth!

Distrust all metreless poets and study-bound geographers. For imagination is one thing and commodity should be another. I'll give you winter! The whooper swan whose mournful blowing can crack the ice. The frantic, fleeing blue hare whose spattered tracks resemble, whose spoor is, a mould for some wild flower. The trap snaps. The dripping blood slows and does not pierce the snow so deep; diminishing size, diminishing depth, dropping from magenta hole to tinctured crystal. The last drop never comes but breaks off crisply, later, on a stumble. The capercaillie makes a suspicious bustle, correct, and squawks. From the poacher's stretched lips, two streams of frosted breath rise up, antlered moustaches under the glacial moon. His feet sound like spades; claws, paws rustle at his belt. That's winter. A lip-cracking, ear-singing cold, fingers like aching sticks. The hills are like eclipses; the thin penumbra as drawn as your eyes.

But I said – didn't I? – that I'd be brief; briefer than winter at any rate, as sharp as winter's breath. Enough. Let me pick out one remarkable kind of day from winter's variety. There are perhaps two days in the whole year when all is stillness and to move in them, even smoothly on water, is to lend an inverted,

4

intimate heat to the effects of the cold. The amazingly long and narrow loch was edged with tiny, grey-pebbled shores and the hills, otherwise rising almost sheer from the water, had none of the marvellous ripple and colour I had been led to expect; have you ever seen the curve of an eel lying slack in harbour mud? Have you ever seen a drowned man's bruises? The water closer to the land was very dark, liquorice gelled, gelid, with here and there silver points. Overhead, a cloud, rust and cream smoke, mimicked the loch's shape. It began to snow. A flake would settle on the surface and the loch water seep up to show the texture of the crystal, hole it, make vanishing pincers of the rim and leave, momentarily, a black lick of water. All over the loch the process went silently on, a continuous ghostly stippling that made my fingertips itch.

The flakes were sticky and polished the shore pebbles to a gleam like port lights. The loch began to crack, the surface to thicken into ice. Larger patches of white appeared, stayed, slipped away. A grey shadow lagged behind the snow, came gradually lower, snuffed the hilltops. A sensation of the cold slowing and fluttering, as if someone clumsy but gentle were fluting in my face, had nothing to do with my emotions on seeing my parents' native country for the first time. Abruptly the cracking stopped. The snow began to layer and, as it turned in, the prow of the boat gave a two-note hum before, with a sound like a sharp belch, sliding on. I put a foot on the gunnel and was half-juddered down, half-jumped onto the jetty.

A scant huddle of persons, stuck about with snow, peered past me. A deep silence broken only by the thud of baggage lasted some time. I became very conscious of my auditory passages; a draught here, a stiffening of hairs and a creak of wax there. I was aware of panting, someone stamping his feet, even the faint crackle of the falling snow and then, puzzlingly soft when I considered the new clarity of the other sounds around me, a breathy version of my middle name. I looked about me and fixed on a very tall, very manly boy about my age, propped on a convenient rail and dressed with an extravagant disregard for the weather.

'Tahh. Tahhh,' came out of his barely moving lips like something at once infantile, baritone and despairing, that long escaping 'h' like a soul at the end of its tether, but completely contradicted by the ironic, smiling face and his unaffected scratching at the precocious swatch of hair revealed by his open collar. The bulky pebbles slipped and clicked as I stumbled towards him.

'Yes,' I said, 'my *second* name is Taha. But the first is Ronald.'

'And the last is Shearer.'

He smiled a little wider and clapped my padded shoulder.

'Come on,' he said, mouthing carefully, 'I am here to help you.'

The shingle in English. Mixed with agitated suspicions about my intonation and accent, my first impression of him was of an idle, intimidatingly well-made thug. Such large round stones under my feet.

'And you?' I said.

'What? Ah, forgive me.' He held out his hand. 'They call me MacBeth.'

My hand was already up. He gave it an amiable thump.

'Though pedants say Maelbaetha. You're a pedant?'

A snow flake snagged in my left eye. It stung painfully at first like a huge speck of grit, then dissolved and dribbled chill onto my cheek. Could I possibly have heard right? But by this time he had stooped, had picked up most of my luggage and was about to set off across the snow. What did I do? In a few strides he would have disappeared. I snatched up the remainder and natterjacked after him.

2

At that age, fifteen, one is still blessedly ignorant of the pain that lurks in translations. I do not refer just to language or to disjointed words. A foreigner is an extrinsic bastard. And while I have no wish to disinter a long-buried and otherwise insignificant unhappiness, I am nonetheless forced to admit that the first furl of my relationship with MacBeth was formed through the difficult contrast between my previous place of learning (with its splendid, supple light effects) and the dreary conglomeration of stone chambers, the colour of doused ashes, where I was to spend the next three years. The circumstances are also quite revealing of his early character.

He showed me to the cubicle allotted me, pointed somewhat confusingly in the direction of various parts and places, combined discretion with some necessary chore and left me to settle in. Alone, fatigue overcame agitation. I was stretched out on the coarse blanket when I realized how exhausting my journey and arrival had been. My eyelids twitched when the damp, musty smell of the place seeped through, apparently, to the inner side of my skull.

The sleep was dreamless. I woke with no sense of turning time. A scruffy, elderly man was staring dully at a crack in the wood behind my head. A birthmark, a port-wine shadow, a smear of ink appeared speculatively on his left cheek. 'So you're the Moor,' he said, picking at the wet corner of an eye and dragging a diluting finger downwards. He and his ac-ac-ac yawn petered out. Gone, his murmur, a previously unheard of mix of plead and growl, drifted back.

'No problems.'

I struggled up. I wondered, ignorant of the northern winter, if I had slept far into the night. I had never seen my breath issue *wet* before. I yawned rapidly, three or four times, a jaw trembling I could not control, and blinked about me at my surroundings. The difference with what I had left behind was thoroughly depressing. A miserable narcissism began drizzling in me as I stared at that grey wall until, my lower lip flopping and jerking, independent through cold, I saw water, greasy-looking drops, crawling out of one particularly dark slab. Any mason will shrug or tut. But this property, confined I believe to certain granite lumps which are properly called wet or weeping stones, administered to me an hallucinatory shock that hummed to the roots of my teeth. Through this, almost warm, came the coincident but distant beating of a gong. A moment after a voice called in, 'Dins, darkie,' and a torrent of howls and feet rushed past my cubicle. This was the start of my new life in my new, native country. I nosed cautiously towards the dining hall.

We forget youth's sly stupidities and hard knuckles. Such things as foreign accents, an ignorance of a very local culture, provide a motor for prejudice: I – son of a red-haired father and a mousy mother – became the exemplar of the Moor. I could not swim well; then Moors, all Moors, could not swim well. The reader will know this kind of relentless elastic deduction in which inanity and wit rub along. I remember with some ease a particularly odious wrangle: I had never eaten pork before and, having tried that meat several times in a number of fat-streaked forms, decided to let it be. But I had insulted the native porker. Yes, yes, all this is absurd but it was tiresome, sometimes unpleasant, to have the insult returned by those of the pig's party. You may imagine how amusing it was to find a piglet's head leaking gore and brains in my bed.

A look at the calendar long ago confirmed that my initiation lasted exactly a month, an extraordinarily long one for the time, with three or four robust, suilline jokes a day. After a week, I began to suspect that my tormentors thought I might be enjoying the business, particularly after a 'debate' in which some of my more spirited replies received gusts of what sounded like friendly laughter from the corral around me. However, it struck me that clowning simply encouraged the piggery, so I resolved to keep quiet and, while waiting the business out, to work hard at my grammar. Perhaps this policy of minding my particles and subjunctives was wrong. Certainly I saw a year later another arrival whirl at the first taunt and start punching his attackers. His face ended up a vividly coloured pulp but that was that; how appallingly easy it seemed, this battered face and liberty! But I have to say such never occurred to me and my matter was resolved differently, prolonged by duller, ingratiating boys. Ingratiating, I mean, to those who had joked first.

And then there was another corridor, another jokester's hand clapping pork fat to my face. A fraction before I could react, I was conscious of my ambusher briskly desisting, of, a moment later, a sudden crack as the parietal bone of his head struck stone. MacBeth gave me an expressionless wink, looked down at the heap attempting to rise from the floor (attempting a stunned grin!) and yarked him to his feet. That done, he walked on with me.

'Well,' he said, as I wiped my polluted face, 'I see they're still giving you a rough time.'

'I imagine it's normal.'

'Do you?'

There was nothing in this exchange to make me so but I suddenly felt incontinently grateful. I swayed. My eyes clutched at that ruminative, self-confident face before me, slid down over his massive shoulders, had almost swooned past his sternum when he spoke.

'I hear you're doing well academically.'

I looked up.

'Who told you that?'

It was definitely the first I had heard of it. But he simply shook his head.

'You should get out more. Explore a bit. Are you good at any sort of game,' he asked, 'that *isn't* chess?'

3

Now as it happens I am quite able to understand why a geographer might have his ignorance patronized by filthy weather, a bad poet bend truth to rhyme, storm to norm, rain again; yet it still strikes me as strange that not one word of summer should have drifted across the sea and settled on paper, especially as I myself, while strolling once on the sands, should have crouched to pick up and dust an Athenean tetra-drachm, a solid silver pebble with Pallas Athene on one side, a sprig of olive and an owl on the other, crudely marked, rather tarnished but exemplary for all that. What of the whitethroat? And the quiet water? The wild hyacinth? Strangest of all, why no sense of the north's summer light? I mean particularly the evening light, a wonderfully sustained fall towards darkness in which swallows, insects and bats hover and race and the flickering piecemeal mimics the patterns of a tired eye. But how soothing it is! What? Ah. Today amongst these mangey maritime hills used to be a holiday. Now suppressed. Deliver we still. Here they cannot knock briefly at the door. They must agitate the latch, a mechanical matching of want and grunt I dislike very much. Bah to the sluggish Mediterranean, thin milk, olive brine. Let's think back, worm in.

The waves sucksoothed the shingle. Let me just cover that bouncing yellow bird with some old sacking. There. No breeze, some hoarseness from across the sound. A long curve of white sand. I remember someone waxing on an island – fine beaches, leafy trees, fresh streams, bright birds – and I realized that there were hundreds within a few miles of us then, but for the untranslatable heat in his voice. Maelbaetha cleared his throat. A curlew called.

'Yes, yes. We'll go back now.'

The waves resounded after a long sigh, then poppled forward.

4

This is an intimate study: lamps, shadows and a first conversation that touched on pomegranates, sea urchins and the homing instinct of salmon, in the desultory and pleasurable way of boys before bed. MacBeth seemed to be some kind of good-humoured atheist, sat as near horizontal as he could in a chair, his head propped on his left hand while the fingers of his right slowly rippled, though occasionally, as at the salmon, he brought the digits together to represent, slow as a yawn, something of the creature's up-current strength. A pink tongue, an anadromous hand. It was then he shrugged. There was so little bedcap milk we thickened the water slightly rather than enjoining a sluice of clarity the other way; I stirred the white in.

Incidentally, I have never understood the passion of the genealogist, nor, having traced the relationship of a general, say, to a peaceable fisherman, been quite sure what the link might tell you – outside banal multiplicity, inside the character to be conjured up. I believe, from his shrugs, that MacBeth shared my attitude. Once, when we were at a quarry fallen into disuse and filled with black water, he told me that as children they had believed the thing to be bottomless and that if they dipped entirely below the surface they would disappear for ever. Who's they? Friends, cousins – why do you ask?

One side of the quarry rose like a miniature cliff, rather attractively marked according to the cut of the now weathered grain. Near the top a romantic bush had found sufficient fissures for its roots; the water was so still its reflection barely tremored. The rest was forest, ferns, wild garlic and monstrous toadstools. These nude-coloured fungi with their black gills had an impressionable, greasy dampness but broke with a crisp creak to let out a fresh bout of a smell he seemed to enjoy very much. The water itself, on a closer look, had a sluggish film in which some not very appetizing creatures were supporting their lives.

'You've been in?'

'A long time ago,' he said, palpating a toadstool. 'You know the kind of thing – dropping rocks into the water from behind a bush, girls screaming, pretending the monster had a grip on your ankle, asking if that was a tentacle. I always noticed though that the boys kept the crowns of their heads dry.'

'You too?'

'Oh yes.'

MacBeth stretched and gave a vigorous scratch behind his ear. 'Strange,' he said with a frown and a blush I had not seen before, 'how maternal injunctions carry on unchecked for years. It's only quite recently I learnt rowans are not fatally poisonous to humans.'

Rowans? The bright red berries of the mountain ash. I had known him perhaps seven months. His father had died when he was four. It was then he shrugged.

'I wonder,' he said.

He hoisted himself up and, after cocking his head at the quarry edge, tucked up his sleeve. I followed, watched him kneel and his hairy arm break the scum and slide into the water. He groped, smiled, eased something lodged under the bank and lifted.

A dripping jar of slimy grey earthenware appeared in his hand. 'Cold,' he commented. He grunted, straightened his thumbs. The top grated. He sighed and dried his hands. And . . . but here the lid came off easily, with a gassy crack. He shrugged. He peered inside.

'Clean,' he said frowning. 'Well.' And he tossed the jar into the water. I watched it fill and sink with a fat gurgle. MacBeth had slight difficulty with his cuff button. Too tight.

'We'll go now,' he said, already ambling along. He jerked a still whitish thumb. 'I rather wanted to see if I could manage to get the skeleton of a dead vole.'

If I looked surprised he did not notice.

'I wonder what got it?'

It seemed a rhetorical question and I contented myself with pushing out my lower lip in speculative sympathy; but he looked up.

'Any ideas?'

'Are you serious?'

'Why not?'

'Well,' I said, 'I imagine – you were rather young at the time – that this dead rat or whatever that you found was already in a process of corruption. In other words you simply locked up host and guests. Or you provided winter quarters for some of those things on the water.'

At this he shot me a sly smile and a look uncharacteristically gentle and I realized, warming pleasantly, the elation of friendship. He was very pleased. I shrugged happily and we continued our little ramble together.

5

Still, it would be dishonest of me not to mention that soon after my winter arrival I began to dream of Andalusia, or, as my nurse called it, Al-andalus. Not that this was adjacent to anywhere I had lived as a small boy. My nurse made it into a mirror image across the Straits of Gibraltar but the reflection was a marvel. The name Al-andalus is particularly stirring perhaps, like a crooned exhortation, round as a smoke ring. More liquid. And what thrill she could put into a name like Granada! At any rate, this I carried, this being a series of interconnected pools, a word I use in the context of colourful mental images to catch something of the rippling round comforts available to and developed by me, particularly after I found frost patterns on the inside of the dormitory windows, a myopic reflection of past and future, a rhythmic longing. Rather late in the day, with the clouds all glory behind me and trash and citrus skin in the swell, it struck me just how much I had worked on a simple infantile notion, had transposed my nurse's plangent chatter and warmth when I had woken from some obscure, violent dream. On such occasions my nurse used to say to me – 'My darling, we are all little Atlases, even this servant.' This triteness came in the gentlest of hoarse tones, while a lovely, swift hand would work at an airy version of a potter's beginning lump. Yes, I understood it represented a sphere but I wonder if you can appreciate the wailing dismay I felt once when – still with various shadowy shapes in mind, batwing states of incomprehension behind a centre as pale as the lemange, the hybrid fruit whose particles I used to pick and press and play with, each one like a juicy apostrophe – it occurred to me to experiment with water? In that element the little particles of fruit looked like limp flecks, made me think of the sea-horse, so fine and delicate and stately in water, disappointingly basic when draped across your palm. My father, a plump, freckled man, almost eye-wateringly kind, was obliged to travel a great deal. My mother, always delicate, was often indisposed. A pale acidic ache. The skin on a lem-ange is like the scarf-skin my nurse used to cut off my finger-nails. And I realized, by no means uncheerfully, that I was both luxuriating in and re-arranging my past to trade for present needs. My friend returned, wetcombed spruce with the swol-len, innocent red face of exercise and dejection. I put the kettle on again. He had a colossal bruise on his kneecap. He rolled up his trouser leg and showed it me while he recounted that it had hit a chin, that he had stopped, thinking he had hurt the other boy, and that the teacher had told him he should have kept running. I watched him with a certain detached exhilaration. There was, by chance, a solitary egg on the mantelpiece. It had a lovely patina but it took me a dreamy little while to discover what was familiar and pleasing and fragile about it. I cleared my throat.

'Kettle's boiling,' I said.

One of my dictionaries, its pages now brittle through age and heat rather than use, gives a definition of the word 'spawn' as an amphibian's unprotected eggs. It seems inadequate and quaint for spawn, reasonable for the words themselves. No shell, some jelly. I believe the number of spawn that grow to maturity is a model of scarcity.

And now I should like to indicate a remarkable and funda-mental aspect of my friendship with MacBeth. Remember translations. I am sure the reader will have regretted more than once the sight and sound of fine work draining into another language, seeing the brimful phrase puddled, the apt gurgled, hearing the dry tap thump. There is only a hapless art in translated words and this lumpen sentence is slated to have something intimate and strange to do with that marvel and the best that can be hoped for is the faint whispering of a foreign ecstasy – which conjures up as much a sense of loss as inti-mations of the original. No, I have not myself tried to translate written things; I am the one who had to undergo the trans-lation. Who'll argue about a word? I will. You *are* words. You cannot point and wink your way into true friendship. And merely the briefest consideration of what translation entails must give even the most resolutely stay-at-home reader pause, induce a slow lick of the lips. Never to be secure, your feet sliding, your hands fumbling. My point? That my friendship with MacBeth, at first puzzled, throbbing, tentative, was based, was conceived at the level of mother tongues. Yes, yes, his slippery tongue, my sorely treated mother, but it is sensibly easy I trust to see the aboriginality in this, of how understanding burgeoned between us in, I venture to say, ways unduplicable; for if I saw the light and perceived the meaning, he gained insights and perspectives from my grasp. A private glossary of his gleams and glimmers, my yearnings and qualms. He was able, that is, to recapture what had come to him naturally and unconsciously, could make out, through and off my explorations, something of what had made him. And that is a double sort of power.

Short essay subject: How can a people be imprisoned in a language? It is not a question, I assure you, that occurs to every boy. It is simple enough to imagine a simple language that lacks experience and concepts. Marginally more complicated is the insistent habit languages acquire. Traditional descriptions. And we had a teacher who frequently talked of 'pure' and 'corrupted' texts. Why so much moral health? But come now, we were boys. Is 'promising' really a helpful remark to put on an essay? I got a positive bark of laughter out of MacBeth when I showed him, 'As usual, most sensitively developed.' Have you ever picked up and guddled a tadpole? From toad and poll, a head? Hm? Cupped your hands with water and squirming little creature? I recommend it. Carefully replace the toadlet in the pond. See the small amphibians swim. See them begin to crawl, slither and hop. Frogspawn comes in lumps, toadspawn in a single chain. If words were little toad polls? If the lines on this page began to stir? If, say, poll sprouted legs and began to wassle its way down to here? Imagine for a moment the beginning wartishness, the slightly brown water, a trace of green slime by a tail, the plump infant toads vacating the page, a wriggling version of muddy sunbeams.

Of course the distractions I offered MacBeth sometimes toppled over, my smudged little ghosts of freedom and fantasy became over-fanciful. Sometimes too I was not entirely honest, in the sense that I would feign bafflement when I judged it might divert him to do so.

'But who are you supposed to be toadying *to*?' said another schoolfellow.

'What?'

I looked up. He exuded an indifferent chumminess and I remembered I had last seen him as a character in a play, in baize green tights, a saffron tabard and sleeves decorated like the crests on a newt, most measuredly and vigorously stripping the mucus from his throat.

'It's just a name that has stuck,' I said.

There was an element of self-protection too in this, since my bafflement was by no means always confidently feigned. Deprived of the da-da-da, the first steps in English, the contented stickiness of infant ability, I was inevitably unsure, an explanation MacBeth found more amusing than convincing I think, since he could not imagine, or did not care to, the extraordinary sensation, half-fear, half-thrill, of seeing a likely word loom up and having my tongue flick at it.

There are drawbacks, of course, inherent in any gift. I cannot draw at all ... At the end of my first school year I won prizes not only for foreign languages, live and dead, but also the English language one. The teachers should have spared me this last but were impelled by a childish, irritable sense of justice. In any case my relationship with languages is, relatively, facile. I have a tongue that delights in manipulating the mouth. It has nothing to do, I insist, with cleverness, says nothing whatsoever about the quality of the brain. I remember my father turgidly urging me forward to meet a self-important client's child, a gross, ten-year-old freak who ingested languages, kept count and, when adults were around, spoke with snotty aplomb backed by an asthmatic wheeze.

'No, no, you really shouldn't deprecate these talents,' said MacBeth that June with a certain asperity, to my mind as if I had been doing nothing of the kind.

Perhaps the timing of my story of the ten-year-old was tactless but I had found it acutely embarrassing to bob up and circle the stage, and I was upset with my friend's reaction. For it is one thing to study a foreign language at home, quite

another to be plunged into prolonged and unrelieved outland-
ishness. I have said something similar? No matter. Grasp what
it is like to exchange an hour or two a day for always, to have
verbal titbits turn into a staple diet. There were times I felt
miserably as if I were lying. I should have felt outrage. What
on earth did my parents have in mind? My nurse chattered
to me in Arabic, my mother affected a genteel but woefully
incompetent French and my father a contrite tri-lingual joshing. Imagine the sensation of uncontrol, the trapdoors, the
curtains, the dull echoes, those sleights of etymology, the scoot
and skite of all those verbs – get on, get up, get off, get over.
Consider the chaotic economy that claps a young cow to the
back of your shin. Some days *are* much better than others,
the tongue is wetter, the throat muscles swacker. But here I also
was, cut off but with memories, too many, of my mother's
sickly manner, too often in the small courtyard where the
oranges grew above her head – and could eclipse the sun.
Hélas! And what, *mon petit crapaud*, was she so sorry about? I
had a mild, reflex case of cultural chauvinism to deal with too.
I had seen bigger libraries in my previous life. These grew. I
took solace in the written word. At least the things lay still
(yes, they did) while I flicked at dictionary or reference book,
made notes, with the result, foreigners beware, that I became
familiar with the classics while slipping on common or garden
mud. I remember once, having given a chat on head-rhymes,
staring on being asked, 'Fancy a slug?' at a small, battered
flask. Those teachers who groaned at my uncultured class-
mates and lamented the decline in spelling and expression
quite missed the point. Imagine 'white elephant' from a
foreign point of view. Investigate the sentences in a grammar
book. Have them spoken, introduce a running nose, a thick
accent, a degree of idleness – and wonder. 'She is the most
beautiful woman in the city.' There are two problems. The
sheer philosophy of the thing, then usage. How many male
adolescents transform an impression, happy light, sly eyes, a
licked mouth and a soft erectile moan into a civic superlative?
All this should assist the reader to appreciate the difficulty
facing a transplanted young native with no hope of childhood

language and home, and the pleasure and relief I had rootling and rooted in my hours with Maelbaetha.

Since I am here I will also say something of MacBeth's foreign language ability. He never managed a good accent nor, for that matter, did he ever have much grip of any relevant grammar. But he could make himself sporadically understood on simple matters in two or three Romance languages. He combined grammatical economy (short sentences, one or two tenses) with longish, often latinate words, augmenting the business with dignified but still rather violent mimes. Mime the thickness of the sandwich you want. Now mime 'limitrophe'.

Finally, to put this matter quite in perspective, as we stood there gowned and clutching our prize volumes, we were at the stage where facility stumbles on childish matters, where tales are attractive but not always welcome, where the brain and tongue leap ahead of emotions and experience; pattering with Plato here, finding one's apple turned pear there. And this, it is simply the obverse, reinforces my earlier point on friendship and language – we were still moulding, still forming into patterns of thought and patterns of being. Mutually not mutely. Within a few minutes we were murmuring and laughing, gobbling strawberries and cream under an awning in the thick smell of covered grass. We went outside. For my part, I liked to uproot dry grass, carefully tugging, feeling the straggle and the form of tiny roots in the nerves of my fingers; sensuous, small vandalism.

6

When, as a boy, I was first called toad I had to look the word up. Having to read the definition made it doubly hurtful: Amphibian like frog but with clumsy and usu. warty body & not aquatic except when breeding. I could not, you see, understand the logic or temper behind the insult. For though I was aware that I had entered on an animalistic language of pigs and bitches, goats and cows, there was nothing I could see in my appearance or brain or habit to explain it. One should not speak too honestly – it is not even real honesty but rather the bewilderment and hurt caused by a brutal image. Such a hurt, such an epithet, is not in the end anything at all, is mere expressionism, a word effective rather than apt which owed its future currency as a tag to my puzzlement and distress and my woebegone consultative nature: I became a fixed toad because I stayed too long over reference books. I could have been looking at a celadon pot. And then, as is normal and quite unexceptional, toad became thoughtless, even affectionate and in one case I was asked how I spelt it and in another met with some disbelief that I had previously been called Taha the Moor.

I was once cornered in Rome by a young and very homesick priest who, nonetheless, evidently saw in me a subject for his vocation and tried to get off the sights and tastes and smells he missed so – memories of which rather touchingly interrupted and distorted his expressions – and onto me. Me, that is, trotted out on a deathbed, when the clauses and sub-clauses and declarations of intent which had brought me elegantly kitted out to Rome would be displaced by soiled sheets, white walls and fear. Faith flowers in the face of death. He accepted my dry invitation to drink something. Yes, two please. Please go on. He told me there was no such thing as a grown-up person, partly because youthful emotional hurt was the most lasting and formed, whether I liked it or not, the foundations of a considerable portion of adult life. This cock-eyed stuff brought back memories. I sat up. Of course, I said, I could recognize the ability of emotional pain – a constricted chest, a spasm of something like grief – to exist for years on its own almost intact, a leisurely belching circuitry that can puzzle at first rise – what's this? – but in my experience, after the age of twenty or at most twenty-two, this habit and hurt, the satisfied bitterness of *now* understanding, were up in the loft with an old shoebag of wooden building blocks and lots of cobwebs. Besides, wasn't he being a little simple? Youthful hurt was merely the earliest and often based on ignorance. Understanding pain as an adult could be worse. I was cheered. I had not spoken like that for years. But I saw he was not listening. He gave me a sickly smile. He told me he was appalled at and terrified of insects. Insects? What insects? In the loft. Ah, but surely spiders are not insects, I remember that from school. Spiders are our friends. They eat insects. He shuddered. He narrowed his eyes and peered at my number of legs out of his phobia. I blinked. Unlike me to be so insensitive. I murmured. And steered him onto . . . the berry tribe! Now there's a jewel for a country! Raspberries, blackberries, loganberries, strawberries. But my preferred berry is the gooseberry. Think of it. That ripple of ripeness, the seeds, the soft hairs, that warm amber jelly. I could see it take him, a leaping, melodramatic impulse to make me a bad man. He resisted. He swallowed. He said he really had to be going. It was a meeting in which my offer to pay for his beverage and his to pray for my soul came together; he had merely put his hand in his pocket to get out a small picture of a saint. Smiling, I shook my head and proffered my hand. He hoped – ha! – we would meet again and preferred to dab towards my shoulder as farewell.

In any circumstances the epithet toad has a rather interesting derivation. 'To eat toad' is of course multi-lingual – the phrase is remarkably widespread – and means the performing of an unpleasant, degrading or humiliating task: fictional old princes coming to terms with their sons' vulgar but rich fathers-in-law and dowry. In such cases I should have thought 'swallow pride' would do as well, if not better, and while there is some link between that self-esteem and another expression involving toad ('puffed as a') I confess, the thing is absurd and I am digressing amongst rank plants, wet pebbles and moss. You are, says the Frenchman, what you chew, swallow and keep down. In part and on the same lines this explains the cannibalistic shift in nomenclature with my amphibian. The other part, involving indignation and offence (because the pupil whistles an aria while blowing the dust off his teacher's shoes), is that a contemptuous mouth finds 'toad-eater' difficult to spit out. From that I suspect the non-diminutive 'toadie' derives; surround the mouth with a choleric face, strangle the tongue with rage and you can see why the phrase acquired an abrupt end. Mere 'toad' is altogether easier. The word has a strange, soothing effect on the utterer's adrenalin – chemical properties evidently.

'That priest,' said the man I was paying, 'is a disgrace.'

'Why?'

'Always toadying.'

'How?'

'Always sucking up to strangers for something to drink, something to eat.'

I shook my head. 'But that's sponging. And although we are both foreigners here, he is from my country.'

'It's not your responsibility.'

'I didn't say it was.'

I tipped him. I picked up my book and umbrella and stepped out into the street. It was a muggy day and overcast but the light still made my eyes water. For a moment I thought of abandoning my planned stroll – but why? I turned left where there was more shade.

7

I am trying to remember if I was ever interested in MacBeth's circumstances outside school; if I really wanted no reflections, no finding features or mannerisms of his spread about in relatives, his nose in an old uncle, his eyes in a dithering aunt. I take it that one of the advantages of fiction over historical memoir is the freedom with which a teller can, if a character trammels the story, perform a satisfyingly neat ablation. But I can hardly ask the reader to deny a mother. So.

Let me begin then by introducing, of all things, a cat. A spoiled Persian in a basket, brought to Donada's house by an elderly spinster cousin. The animal is one of those with great tufts of insecurely attached hair, insecure possibly because of the fat under the skin, floating stuff with what feel like soft orange pips suspended in it. A breathy smell of fish, then that of glands and old urine and, last, a helpless virtue, when it has turned right round and something small and puckered has rasped your face, an instant liking is announced. All that static makes the hairs cling to your clothes. The creature thrums into my lap, apparently, in the same style as with teeth, setting my pelvis on edge. The heat delivered into the crotch is strong and, in a truculent, half-hatch, half-cock way, demeaning.

For her part, Donada had a dog. For company or protection? I cannot believe I ever knew. Mutt and mog met promptly enough, mog opting for the nearest equivalent to a tree. Though brief, the encounter produced a broken antique vase and a number of deep scratches in an oak corner cupboard. The reason I burden my account with woof and spit is because I had gladly accepted my best friend's hospitable invitation and was thus a witness to the aftermath. (If I have omitted to say something of a maternal Uncle Hugh of mine, a timid, hugely obese person depressed into a generalized reluctance, to offend, to offer, it matters only because MacBeth then invited me to spend several holidays at his home.)

We arrived, cheerfully laden with the trunks and baggage of disbandment, at the gate, a stout wrought-iron affair flanked by some life-size but inexpert stone pineapples and six-foot walls. A track, its red mud ridges made brittle by frost, narrowed into the winter air and vanished in the grey-green-black of an old pine wood. Whether or not due to the proximity of his mother, I was reminded of my own and a foxfur muff she had had with which she had covered and needled my aching ears. But when could that have been? I was not allowed to manhandle my own baggage, for which reason I stood an awkward pace or two back. And that was it, the sensation of familiarity, chill and soft fur, came from stirred naphthalene, mothballs. I must have had the impression of ache and chill from my mother explaining what the muff was for. Pleased, I turned and saw something move about ten yards along the cement and greystone boundary wall. Curiosity pulled. The shadow began to yield up its contents. A first impression of trembling, of hunch and hung paw. I believe the creature was a brown and white pointer. What I saw were spectacular sores and that its ribs were so clearly marked that the patch where they had been stoved in looked soggy. I think it had at some time attacked its own tail. It was possible it had received a blow on the spine. The eye on the side facing me was almost entirely closed. I thought I was going to shudder but did not; instead, one of my own eyes fogged and I clapped a hand to it. MacBeth looked round. Squeamishly I pointed. He stared a while, nodded, suggested we go in. As we went, the wretched beast turned to watch, thereby exposing along one side of its head a loose flap of skin, a line of teeth and an eye like a black grape, bloomed, behind which a glistening fleck followed us. Very quietly it began to whine. The gate was louder. I do not know when whine becomes howl but my friend had to raise his murmur – 'They've overcut the topiary again' – as we approached the low, bleak façade. He had to speak up when he introduced me to his mother. Have you ever seen a drop of water in which a tentative artist has dipped a brush-tip of sky-blue? Her eyes were inquisitive and glassy at the same time. She was tall but stooped, sinewy rather than slim. I was proper, she embarrassedly gracious. We went into a chilly par-lour, sat far apart on hardbacked chairs and took a little refreshment (gooseberry purée in little white ramekins). Beside me on a table was a clump of dried, almost colourless lavender and a bowl of potpourri. This was also the first time I saw a frame of her accomplished, unpleasant needlepoint. She used to dispatch the lot as gifts and mine was a sampler, I think it is called, with far too much cornflower blue and black in the background. I think my wife has it. Donada insisted on calling me Mister Ta. Occasionally and with smooth illogicality she would put some question to Mister Ta – 'What's it like in your country? At this time of year?' – either ignoring the reply or correcting the answer.

'And when did you lose your poor mother, Mister Ta?'

'Six, nearly seven years ago.'

'Ah,' she said fondly, 'a mother's *age* is what matters.'

At the time I put this manner of hers down to a distracted anxiety because of the noise. Doubtless the threnody was blun-ted by those thick stone walls but even so the air was horribly keen with it. My kidneys felt spasmodically but acutely untrust-worthy so that I kept pressing my knees together and leaning forward, all discomfort and feigned interest. My nipples tightened, scraped against my shirt, tightened a pinch more. I kept finding the whine unbearable, providing as it were, my own crescendos. I do not know if dogs are the only creatures that can portray such a constancy of pain for such a time. Nor, of course, am I exactly sure of the minutes before MacBeth began to think of getting cleaned up after the trip, only that they dragged unconscionably. He asked if that was a new acquisition, yes, the dust-red bowl. Attractive. He stretched. He thought I might want to see my room and so on. I agreed at once and jumped up. He asked his mother what time we were all eating. And then, his fingers barely moving, his voice languid: would she mind if he interceded for the dog?

We all stayed stock-still a while, to that excruciating accompaniment, to the very faintest of flushes on the lady's cheeks. Was that a prim, middle-aged sulkiness? Bear with me a moment: for until then I had more or less unconsciously understood that I had been witness to an unwillingly taken but doubtless necessary prophylactic measure against a stray, very likely diseased dog, and had MacBeth said, come, let's put the poor brute out of its misery, I should at least have tagged along. 'Well,' said Donada's son and gently ushered me out of the room.

It may be asked what kind of adult can 'disown' an animal; after the visit of course, this was a private matter. It may be asked what kind of human being can have the uncomprehending offender placed outside the gate and then, when it tries to get in, have it repulsed by what kind of club-wielding gardener? The principle of property, an animal's sense of contract, a dog's concept and memory of crime, the cruelty inherent in sentimentality, many matters could be discussed, some furiously. Coming out of that room, however, MacBeth gave me a pointed but perfectly obscure nod.

A quarter of an hour later thick silence sighed and the next morning from my bedroom window I was to see MacBeth patting and playing with the dog. It had been stitched and patched up, cleaned and fed but was still a repulsive sight. And yet this pedigree friend was stiffly game and had a dreadful eagerness to lick his hand which made me wince, made me, a misplaced boy, almost nauseous with longing.

Of course I did not know then of the truly amazing recuperative powers of dogs. I could also, as a young and uncomfortable guest, just muster a theoretical and callow sympathy for pressures that might beset a widow; yet that business remained for me, made me, too easily perhaps, wary of his mother and think of her as harsh and self-pitying. Let us not get this wrong. From then on I was on a footing of what I can only call ignorant intimacy with Donada, heartily welcomed, frequently overlooked but sometimes enlisted in some problem, usually one in which I could know almost nothing, as when she asked my advice on how to 'liven up' the mosses and lichens on a forty-ton boulder she had as a feature in her garden. Who weighs these things the glacier brought? I know for a fact that she several times spoke of me with enthusiasm and coy respect and that I was certainly credited with the idea of a light brushing of liquid manure for that rock. But what had I done? I knew which chairs not to sit on. I was her son's loyal friend and then colleague. Nice word, colleague. But was that all? Have you never, lady or gentleman, leg or neck, shaved too hard? I have often seen the recipient of a remark start and stare at Donada and try to work out whether she was being rude, stupid or very decidedly bland – and then I would move in to assist. And as to canine fidelity and attempted felicide, I think Donada was somewhere unable, that her cruelty was the product of outraged shyness, an unloved cousin and the humiliation of being betrayed by an animal she had trusted.

8

Natterjack; a lovely, clumsy, plaintive, blinking sort of word. *Bufo calamita. Bufo* is toad, the common kind being *Bufo bufo.* And that *calamita* has nothing to do with calamity but refers to reeds; thinking reeds, whispering reeds and reed pens. It is a feature of the human natterjack *to be specific*. Within a fortnight of being called toad for the first time I had become, not an expert naturally, but expert enough for school. And of course the insult was silly, fatuous – and deplorable. What kind of fighting back is it to ask what kind of toad? My assailant let out a comfortable guffaw.

'How do you mean?'

'There are only two species in this country. The common toad. And the natterjack.'

'Tell me about the natterjack, toad.'

'My pleasure.'

'Take care.'

'Of course. Small, with legs so short it must always run. Skin is cream with a network of bubbled chocolate. Has a pale, egg-custard line or streak down its back.'

'Ah, then you're a natterjack.'

'Relief.'

'I don't follow you, toad. What's that?'

'Hate to be common.'

There was a sulky pause. 'I'm not sure I like your tone.'

'I understand, I do. But it is the way natterjacks are.'

Whether from confusion or fatigue, his grip slackened, enough for me to free my head from under his unsavoury arm. By that stage I had even developed a natterjack smile, a wide jerk of the lips that did not show my teeth.

Now I have had some doubts as to whether or not to include such brief, elderly memories. But then, why not? There is a local expression on heightened nerves as 'a flor de piel'. I have certainly never sought out the precise meaning, if that is flowering skin or the bloom on fruit or quick, yeasty stuff. I quite like the expression for that smart mix of fear, hatred and contempt I carried about as deep as my capillaries. And, besides, how we deal with difficulties is of interest. I would push out my lower lip to the left and make airy, sucking noises, which might have been for slippery Italian food but I gave over that I preferred writhing, linear hermaphrodites. Worms. And I think this passed for good, if disgusting, humour.

'What,' a frowning MacBeth was to ask later, 'was all that natterjack business?'

'Oh,' I said, 'a private thing. Like bed-wetting.'

His eyes widened. He laughed. Now *that* is the hallmark of the youthful natterjack; to feint at cancelling himself rather than the question, to startle into amusement, to secrete the name for future reference and development.

I did not, incidentally, tell that acrid-armed lout anything about the real natterjack's eyes. My naturalist here describes them as being like 'golden-nuggets'. With all respect, in an arrangement of plural lids and subtle camouflage, the first or outer lids are more like orbs draped in oily gold paint and intricately intricked with fine dribbles of Indian ink, too smooth, rotund and wet to give any impression of crevices. In the centre of this rich bulge is something like a small, solid bar or slot. A natterjack has mainly nocturnal habits, those veins of chocolate and that yellowish streak sit well at the base of reeds in the moonlight, and I should hate for any specially suscep-tible reader to imagine this page was not raised letters on paper but viscid gleam on maculate skin. No, no, natterjack is a colourful shorthand for my condition. I have heard the expression – be true to the dreams of your youth. And your fears? One of the first mistakes I ever made at that school, equivalent in its shock to that of lemange and sodden sea-horses, was to write 'freedoom' instead of 'freedom' in an essay.

'Oh, not bad, in a lowering sort of way,' said the teacher.

But how this stupid slip impressed me! Free doom! What patterns I saw in those words – more splanchnic than plan-chette.

'What a difference an "o" makes,' said someone nearer my age.

Who was it said poems were 'imaginary gardens with real toads in them'? A poetess, not that 'e', called Moore. Since I am a chronicler rather than a poet, I humbly prefer the antithesis; my gardens are real, my toads imaginary, my natterjacks pro-viding some correspondence to a fantastic way of holding on.

9

My schooldays, thank God, are almost done, but would not be complete without another incident involving my friend. You should imagine me at study during the silence time. My desk is contained in a sort of wooden stall, thick and battered, one side of which forms the headboard to my bed. I have laid a lap-rug and a square of smooth wood on the desk top to avoid my pen plunging downwards into holes gouged by previous workers. The light is wretched, the work a captiously set essay. Faith: dream or pragmatism? I turned. MacBeth's right index finger was placed vertically over his lips, was touching the tip of his nose. He had on but not buttoned an outdoor jacket and had draped a scarf round his neck. I mimed surprise and query. His finger came away sternly, jabbed towards his left and stiffened again warningly. His face was rather fierce. I pointed a doubtful finger downwards (what, *now*?) and in reply his digit rose towards his ear and his lips jerked cheerfully upwards. A touch of the manic there. I engineered myself silently out of my stall. He gave me a commendatory wink and, when I was free and upright, showed me the palm of his left hand and accompanied it with moues and nods (exactly right). Too late I realized I had left my own coat elsewhere; he was already by the door.

We had first to tackle a dog leg, easy enough, then a long, naked passage. I recalled the corridor after this, full of unpredictable bachelor masters, with some anxiety but my heart had barely begun to quicken – where were we going? – when MacBeth's hand shunted backwards and came hard against my chest. We were beside a grubby green curtain. A quick tug and an emergency door was revealed. MacBeth produced a thick key. A quick clack, the lock was easy, but the handle was another matter, seemed to be cemented with rust, and the effort to get that down made his forearm shake. I noted, in a kind of ignorant calm, that I was sheltering behind him. The handle groaned. MacBeth grimaced and leant briskly against the door. It gave, swung open. Uf! A dark flight of steps led down and round. Me first. I went down to the first turn while he closed up behind us. A moment later, with a brief baritone cluck to stifle my opening mouth, he was past. I pattered down after him, then along on flagstone flat, scuffling after his long soft stride. Another door, a chain of musty cellars, four glooms of mangled and broken objects, then out, right, and up a small, stepped well. There were two doors. A pause, a frown. Mac-Beth chose the one on the left.

It was raining lightly on a tiny garden, heathered and herbed, with climbing plants on every vertical, an unexpected and ingenious oasis in all that bleak stone. On tiptoe we jinked towards another door. While MacBeth was tackling the lock, this time with a piece of fine wire, my apprehension snagged on a central gurgle. Of course water and weathering had already blurred the little fountain but as I watched it seemed to crumble even more, lose all definition and most shape. I shut my eyes. I shivered. I had no idea where we were. 'Shh!' he said. As if I had been speaking! More darkness. Another passage, another cellar, this one empty, a dusty shaft of light from the broken part of a filthy pane, the smell of old coal, here casting an anxious shadow, abruptly a sweeping cloak. Then the warm smell, polish and food, of used places. He alarmed me by throwing one end of his scarf round his lower face like a highwayman. He listened at the next door, carefully turned the handle. A taste of luxury informed this corridor. Or perhaps – I had one hand clamped over my mouth, the other trembling round my right eye – all it had was furniture, picture-frames and curtains. I swallowed and followed. We had to pass a murmur of voices from which, 'Here, I'll peel it for you,' came to me shockingly clear. I skirted a delicate white rug, nerves making it like dandelion seeds and my shoes treacle-soled. The loud beating of my heart – a beat like the tugs maids give sheets – had done for my hearing. I was suddenly sure a fat glazed umbrella stand was about to waddle out and bawl and point. I started, cringed – and the skin kept crawling up my cheeks. Then quickly down another stone spiral, across a vaulted hall, up four broad steps. MacBeth cuffed hard at a thick bolt. He lifted the latch and fresh wet air was sucked in.

The rain was now heavy. The alley was paved but neglected. The grass that had sprouted in all the cracks looked mint bright. Rivulets of water bounced past us. My companion smiled. He took a couple of bounds and stopped by a bulging wall. I made to follow suit but slipped and landed hard on my hip and elbow. I scrabbled up hastily in case my friend had already swooped on. But no. The rain rattled on my skull and I had time to groan. He had his back to me, crouched by the wall, the rather coarse material of his trousers stretched tight round his muscular thighs. I had ample time to feel the extent of my discomfort as I hobbled over, was soothing my sodden and painful hip, when his hand came up and pulled me down. He had removed a ventilation grille. I found myself looking the wrong way down a hole in the wall. Since it narrowed as it went in I closed one eye. I was then peering at the innards of a stark bathroom.

I was struck with a lively disbelief, a kind of agitated wonder, so that when a sudden crack sounded, merely water shooting from holes in a pipe that ran along the ceiling, I started and gasped. The next was my friend's puzzled, gloomy face very close to mine and then a wink. Blinking, I was still in time to see steam rise towards the roof and for that cool surface to send the stuff curling down again. The steam was very thick. The discomfort was stony. The rain was heavy. I had just realized that the stone was not porous or whatever it is called but had mica flecks where I had seen holes, when my friend squeezed hard on my bicep. Only by squinting and peering was I able to make out some skinny white shapes in the interior, given life if hardly sex by their moving legs and some low black patches. And one gingerish. And the sight did not become much clearer but remained an abstraction, marbled, limbish, white and sheepishly crowded until we suddenly became navel high to a gross carrot-haired female and all I will say is that she turned, presenting us with an abundantly dimpled back.

My companion, however, was cheerful and gave my shoulder a tap before carefully replacing the grille and standing. We had barely walked two paces when a strident woman ordered someone to get back and wash properly. MacBeth stopped, smiled and listened. I could make nothing out in the consequent murmur and giggle. The rain huzzed. My friend's hair had flattened and tendrils hung over his forehead, there was a pale bruise on his left lobe and the water dripped from his chin. He pulled off his wet scarf and stuffed it into his pocket. I turned. A long strand of steam issued slowly from our ignoble slit and joined the rain. Inside the skivvies laughed, there was a sound of slapped wet flesh and an, 'I'll teach you, Eileen!' and MacBeth, noticing me shudder, softly clapped my shoulder and smiled again.

'It's enough to make you hoarse, isn't it? No, no. We can walk back quite openly now. The silence time is over. It took me two weeks to solve that one. You're my witness, eh? Don't forget.' And he squeezed his hands triumphantly. 'Fat Annie,' he crooned, 'Annie the Fat.'

An eager crowd was waiting for us.

'Did he? Did he?' they said, jostling round.

'Yes,' I mumbled and turned away. Only here I was stopped.

'Has she?'

'What?'

'An appendix scar.'

'I did not look.'

'Glued to her vasty tits?'

I slapped his face, something I registered by my stinging hand and his flush of pain and anger.

'Don't be a fool,' said another to the clod I had struck. 'Don't you know it was all about risk?'

I grunted. I had just remembered something completely unrelated, was feeling the hot, fat sweetness of unexpected revenge. The unslapped laughed low.

'Just look at toad's face, will you?'

And the slapped cocked an eyebrow over a reddened cheek and grinned.

'Off to your lonely stall, I suppose. Or do you want me to lend a hand?'

10

Perhaps I am depressed today but aspects of that dare, Mac-Beth casually counting his winnings, several wretchedly private tries at denouncing the exploitation of skivvies, reminds me of another, altogether later occasion, a wedding reception as it happens, which had been going on for hours when I took refuge near a bay window. Instanta I found a small bridesmaid sat almost hound-like on my feet and dutifully cast about me for some subject of conversation, to come up with that old story about the stubborn child who, having been read to long enough, first by mother, then by father, drives even the prince in the illustration to lose patience; with an expression of disgust he leans out of the book past the reading child and, in a gesture usually reserved for troublesome flies, flicks at the candle flame. Darkness comes down. The child is just in time to withdraw her hand before the book slaps shut. A moment later the weight on her lap vanishes and the book thuds onto the floor. Someone sighs and stretches. Weary feet depart, pause at the door and go off along the landing. The child puts her hand on the cool eiderdown. The front door slams and those feet grind on the chukkies beneath the bedroom window. A soft whistle, a panting dog. And shortly silence. I cleared my throat. An old granny leant towards me.

'Why,' she said, 'you do bring *passion* to your memories!' – a remark that made me, to my own surprise, laugh once out loud. I have never had much to offer children (a half-remembered story or two apart) and I saw that this one was quietly picking her toenails, her bottom parted and her chubby parts draped over the instep of my right shoe. I tried to move my foot discreetly, in a well-mannered fashion; but then gave up. Hup! I jerked my foot free. There was quite a loud thump of bone meeting wood floor but she barely glanced up before returning to her toenail.

11

When I was young I wanted the world to be covered in a wonderful, coloured Braille. I'd acquire a delicacy of touch, learn through whorls of finger and brain, attentively read out what I found. I once asked a botanist how his interest had begun; he pointed at the caliper on his leg. I understood and honoured him – he had a splendid collection of ferns and an equally splendid respect when handling fronds to show me their underside spores – and I was quite aware that, at best, I could acquire only small patches of knowledge and under-standing. That was fine. I enjoyed the notion of many possi-bilities. I enjoyed scholarly enthusiasms. I was not in the least combative. I had no idea of my roundish view skittling out others but had it, with a certain gelatinous tremble, incorpor-ate them instead. Of course I knew that at school my Braille had been, unwillingly, solipsistic, that, let me shut my eyes, I had spent too long queasily palpating the lumps and bumps raised on *me*. But that was why I was thrilled by the prospect of undergraduate life! Free of louts and odious tags! Free to read History, unravel old documents, decipher old codes, stare through glass at illuminated manuscripts.

And what did I find? A lackadaisical, ancient place and an aged tutor who kept character studies in napworn notebooks in which once black ink had faded to pale rust stains and nibmarks. He was an ugly, pulpous-lipped old fellow with distractingly long and dirty fingernails which used to pick at the scabs on his greasy, grey scalp where he had previously scratched too hard, and he would intersperse his portentously detailed knowledge of medieval weaponry, tortures and para-sitical illnesses with unwanted personal details – 'I never get a cold because I almost never wash.' But his sleeves were caked with old snot! And I wonder if the reader can glimpse through my eyes something of the startling sight of him, with every sign of relish, adding fresh lemon curd on top. 'Home-made,' he said, before inviting me to consider the effects of a battleaxe on a certain pretender's helmet and skull. I could not, as his sleeve waved, share his pleasure, a veritable chortle of gratification, in the rag tied round the head to hold the skull together – 'and his claim of course!' I do not know if he noticed what a fastidious young man I was, but he next asked me a question.

'Do you know what the verb "to baffle" means?'

'To confuse?'

'Yes, yes. But historically it means to turn a knight in armour upside down, hang him with a rope by his feet. Deface the arms on his shield. The Scots were the foremost practitioners of this. They'd give an English knight they'd captured a choice. Death – or be baffled. What do you think the English chose?'

'Baffled?'

'Quite. Of course to be left hanging upside down in full armour isn't that much fun. Even so. What was going on? Simple, the Scots had convinced themselves that bafflement meant a complete loss of honour. The English did not share this belief. So they would trot off home with rather a lot of blood in the head while the Scots looked after them, in contempt of course, but also rather in mourning as if for the ghost of a man. It's a nice example of the medieval taste for representation. Don't tell me the English knight lived to fight another day. That was literally immaterial to the heraldic symbolism the bafflers had constructed. The medieval mind conceived the world in allegorical terms. We are not so representative? I am not so sure. Do you see?'

The short answer was no, but I nodded and as a reward was sent away to further explore the point by writing three thousand words on scrofula. This entirely historical term for a disease now identified as tuberculosis, particularly of the bones and the lymph glands, aptly encloses in an ugly name centuries of pain, despair and divinely royal superstition. To my surprise he was pleased with my effort. He told me to go off and choose something on my own. University may be described as an opportunity to discover the nature of one's own mind. Let me put it another way. Natterjacks, though they have to run, are *slow*. I pottered happily off into gold mining at a time when it was more beachcombing than pick work, and

34

came across material for a small study of the fourteen miners imported from West Africa when a seam or strand of gold was found some twenty-five miles from our then location. Abutting my tutor's window was a curving run of what looked like idealized but now sooty and petrified tear drops. He read. He raised a despective eyebrow.

'Quite amusing,' he drawled, 'but lacks intellectual meat. I shall want something in addition.'

Now I had become quite used to considering myself a coward. This was unexceptionable, like the colour of my eyes. I mean, I did not consider myself a person who protested or fought back. Have you ever been furious without knowing it? Stiffly disguised rage even to yourself? I do not remember doing more than blink. At that intellectual meat, I think. My next work discussed early currencies. Specie. The leap of faith from a cauldron of victuals to some roughly circular bits of metal, to test, if necessary, between clamped teeth. Life values and a certain degree of trust. Pleasant maps with navigable rivers, simple roads, livestock tracks and coloured dots of overlapping coinages like pointillist bird sightings. I regret that I remember that I made the coinage sightings orange and green to exclude the colour-blind. A clammy-fingered, patronizingly expensive urologist then thought that I might, in consequence, have an interest in numismatology. Not at all. It is one thing with your trousers down to enquire as to how, when and with what variations coinage came to be accepted, improved and understood, another to have an interest in crude, bulbous profiles. I had consulted him because of a sporadic but acute urethral discomfort. It consisted of something like a painful lentil-sized gulp followed by an intense burning sensation. I do not know how other people contrive to forget their youth. It was not until the medical man, gently parping the end of his nose, asked me, 'Now young man, might it be advisable for me to consider the possibility of clap or similar in this case?' that I realized, through my blinks and that central, private pain, that I had come to seek treatment for a spasm of intense rage. He proffered me a tube of creamy white salve. How ashamed I was, how embarrassed! *Is* urine, then, the link between fear and rage? Or is it – I am no doctor – to do with muscles and glands? Does the word prostration derive from the prostate? I buttoned up and left. The tube, exactly the sort that contains white oil paint, I forsook as soon as I could. I think what most upset me was that my sensitivity, my hard-won delicacy, had when upset found its outlet in such a tubular and spongey setting. Errant boys and rigid fathers. Come, not *that* far back. But I spent some very miserable hours in a dark and cloistered quadrangle.

I do not know if it is interesting now to say that I did not immediately run off to see my friend. I chose to *remember* him, to reconstitute him in my mind. This was something I chose to do in life as I now do in death, so as not to trouble him, out of a degree of shame and pride, but mostly because of the discomfiture I experienced when seeking comfort in my schooldays. As when I first received a variety of complaints about the gibber and squeak emanating from my nightmares. Put simply, while I splashed desperately to keep from drowning, my noise kept others from sleep. Some threw books, some shoes or pillows, and a few, to help on with the drowning, would douse me with water.

'I've always had nightmares,' I told my friend.

'As far as you can remember,' corrected MacBeth.

'You never have nightmares?'

'I suppose I must have done. Nowadays my dreams tend to the paunchy.'

'The what?'

'Food,' said MacBeth, 'stomach.'

'Ah, so it *is* paunchy. Like belly.'

'That's what I said.'

He was about to go on to remedies, not a particular sleeping position or drink or drug or mental exercise but, as it were, animating the possibility of change. I would often see a person completely unaware of how they had been shaped and pointed from a sentient stone to a confident merman. I used sometimes, as in that quadrangle, to wonder whether this, the basis of a skill MacBeth was to develop to a prodigious degree, that of leading someone with a mix of suggestion, firm sympathy and a respectful invocation of choice, were not some special indifference or contempt of his. But I was, to use his verbal style rather than mine, very likely wrong. He was patient, observant and his interest in people combined energy and care.

I blinked. What I could not understand were my grounds for objecting so to my tutor. Why was I so flisty and indignant? Where was the justice in my antipathy? When it came down to it, why did I detest, far more than his unfortunate sense of hygiene, his use of words like 'heraldic' or 'symbolism' and 'allegory'? Whether I loathed it or not – I did – allegory existed. But had I really drawn from his drawl that he was a contemptible racist? And what possible difference could it make if the man *were* colour-blind? I groaned. I am not, I repeat, a person who swings naturally to self-justification. Rather the reverse. Now all this was, in a university quadrangle, chastening enough, I could recognize the virulent minutiae of my fear of him, but I could not quite say why I was afraid – it felt in any case more like alarm – and it did not occur to me to abandon my coinage. Instead, here is the self-justification of the natterjack, I worked dreadfully hard at it.

'Pooh, pooh, pooh,' went my tutor when he had looked it over. I smiled. There was nothing I had to say to that. By chance, the old fellow was about to lose his temper with another undergraduate, a poor, downy fellow whose paper annoyed him more.

'Rubbish!' he spluttered. 'Swine's argument!'

I looked up. It may have been the name-calling, may have been because it was not at me.

'Oh,' I said, 'surely not.'

'What? Don't' – banging his knuckles on his flabby torso – 'tangle with me.'

'For heaven's sake,' I replied. 'I've had arguments called toadspittle.' I think it was the toadspittle that did it. I fairly spat the epithet out. 'By an intellectual he-man who considered being a he-man more important than clarity. Or help.'

There was just a moment there I thought my degree was over, could see myself (quite cheerfully) walking down a long corridor. My tutor glared, raised a proud chin, but then fell to pressing a bunion-battered shoe against a chairleg, rhythmic as purring.

I can hardly think he considered me a worthy opponent but from then on, in an arrangement of doubtful sanity and, from my point of view, even less coherence, he would sometimes give me a mauling. Let me be impressionistic for once. He was a buffoon and a bully, an insidious monarch of scorn, of words, who would tear at me, a tadpole, with the ferocious jaws of a dragonfly nymph. The tadpole remains expressionless. Less impressionistically. With a small smile of spite, he suggested – 'since you appear to be fond of commerce' – ten thousand words on the Baltic amber trade. My role? Instantly at my most mincing and ethereal I pointed out that amber is properly fossil resin and that our word derives from ambergris, in its turn properly semi-digested food found in the intestines of sperm-whales, much used in perfumery. The Greek word for amber gives us the English word for electricity – adding up to a nicely coloured combination of the odiferous and the physical agent that binds the world together.

'Why,' said my tutor, 'you have a gift for turning words into proper worms.'

'Thank you. But I was merely considering the link between description and definition. Historical word casts.'

Some, that downy fellow for example, were made uncomfortable by these exchanges.

'But why do you do it? Why do you encourage him? You are barely civil to each other.'

'*Are* we civil?'

My tutor smirked happily. 'But your amber is etymological footnote.'

'Is that bad?'

'History is just a collection of footnotes?'

'In one sense it already is. All our characters are dead and shifted into a few feet.'

'Feet was that?'

'Earth, snails and linear worms.'

'Ha!' Though I am not sure whether this was confirmation or pleasure. And I admit, this type of grisly snippet was in a small store formed in a muttered backwash while walking, shaving or in the library. They would come out, sometimes with bits missing, when the first rush of adrenalin was over and I began to feel I was fading.

'I worry about your faith in the power of ideas,' said my tutor. 'How would you describe your kind of mind?'

'Suspicious.'

He beamed. 'You haven't thought of pursuing an academic career, have you?'

I gave him my sickliest smile. Then (not too consistently and certainly rather innocently after all my soured stomachs and sweaty backs prior to a southern Baltic export – ten thousand words on amber!) I went to my friend.

'Are you talking about old Angus?' he asked. 'The man without a handkerchief?'

'Yes I am.'

MacBeth nodded. 'Very well,' he said, 'why don't I meet you after your next tutorial?'

And so he did. Across the quadrangle my tutor saw us chatting together. He stopped to greet MacBeth, they exchanged a few pleasantries and then the old man, rather crudely to my mind, showed surprise that I was there.

'What? You know each other?'

This could equally as well have been my line but was his.

MacBeth's lids dropped. 'We're old friends,' he said firmly.

My tutor lowered his head. He looked mildly but pleasurably embarrassed. Those gross lips of his wormed out a soft smile. As he said goodbye his eyes slid briefly and shyly towards me. And even I could see, reader, that that was that. A bare minute had re-cast and settled our relations into something bland and accommodating.

'You look flabbergasted,' said MacBeth when the old man had tottered off.

'I am.' The reason that natterjacks, toads, gulp so is that they are obliged by their design to pump air into their lungs.

'And the amber?' I demanded.

'Oh, I'd show him what you can do.'

'Do you *know* him?'

'Not really. Same year as my father I think.'

'Ah. Did he have a crush on your mother?'

39

MacBeth smiled. 'Not that I know of. My father didn't marry till he was forty. Why?'

'I'm not sure.'

'More likely to have a crush on you.'

'I beg your pardon.'

'No, that's probably unfair. It's plump young minds he likes. I gather he calls you "that attractive little foreign boy". Oh yes, and he says you "promise well".'

Was he humouring me? It was disgusting to think of that old man flirting with vain classicisms. Had I really misread everything so badly? I found myself staring at a small easy circle from which I, apparently, was excluded. The circle doubled; I grew aware of my friend's green-surrounded pupils as he patiently waited for me to work the matter out.

'Bloody amber it is then,' I blurted.

He laughed. 'Come on,' he said, 'I have a favour to ask you.'

And we turned and walked side by side out of the quadrangle.

I think that what had most surprised and troubled me of MacBeth's career at university was its silence. I had taken it for granted that he would be sociable and admired, a leading, possibly even vociferous participant. Instead, he had renounced all sports with the instant finality of a chore relieved, passed by all societies and begun conscientiously and quietly with the Law. So I had no more standing on a touchline to do. And I would never again, as I had at school when the reserve cut his thumb, slither towards steaming backs under a very wintry sun and watch my friend jam the fruit into his mouth and give himself a gumshield of bright orange peel. A slight purple tinge on his skin, thin sweat, bulging neck vein. Beneath the empty plate my shoes, shine and mud. The glaze on the plate was bright and slippery. The players missed, the gnashed and pulped quarters skited. I picked them all up and went off the field, tacking from tuft to tuft. I would, however, always remember his splendid, young co-ordination, that ability, his big body, as he ran to scoop up balls of any size or shape, that sharp-eyed, quick-muscled skill with a racquet. Yes, he would always move well and elegantly but at university he shrugged the spectacular stuff off, set about acquiring skills he lacked, but, it seemed to me, had become impassive, self-contained, looming up one instant, with a flick, swimming away the next. It took me time – I said I was slow – to realize how relieved and contented I was that MacBeth should consult me.

Now my friend's usual voice was a pleasant rumble and whisper. But when he spoke up the rumble dominated monotonously. That night I accompanied him to a part of town I did not know, up a steep wynd of slippery cobbles to a dwarfish old doorway under which even I had to duck. Inside, in a snug, accompanied by saliva, halitosis and an increasing overlay of warm gin fumes, an elderly lady wearing a grubby black cape and a species of turban and who carried a long fruitwood stick bellowed at us fanciful anecdotes, theatrical memories and some tips as to breathing and voice projection.

'It's my dancing stick, dear. For beating out the rhythm.' She turned to MacBeth. 'Your companion seems a delicate young thing.' But there was something so good-naturedly stagey in her voice that I smiled. She smiled back and took my hand and, having glanced at knuckles and palm, patted it.

'You're not one of the legal brethren, are you, dear?'

I shook my head.

'Actors and lawyers, dear. Should be hanged.'

The energy in her voice was misleading. I saw that her face was an animated death mask, her forearm thin as my two smallest fingers held together. I was not sure she had any hair under the turban. Her touch had exactly the same feel as recently cast off grass-snake skin, a delicate, brittle and slightly oily smoothness. I am not sure why but I found her moving and attractive. Perhaps it was the way she treated MacBeth. He called her 'Madame' and she waved her stick at him. By the fire, sitting upright on a stiff-backed settle, amusingly like a heavy opera-singer suddenly suspecting and then listening to a possible throat infection, he tried to provide what she wanted.

'Widow. Window. Winnow.'

The effect was pleasant, he beetle-browed, his large hand uncertainly searching about his chest for tremors and tones, her stick prodding about his intestines and ribs – 'No, there man, there!' – his voice buffeting my ears in waves and syllables.

'What do you think?' he asked me.

'I would relax a little.'

We all started laughing and I remember thinking, yes, this will do.

For the mock trials the next day, however, he had got his mouth and chest round what he wanted; intrigued, amiable tone, confident laconic sentences. I admit, I did think the style too slow, with too many pauses, that it was uncomfortably near to insulting the intelligence of his listeners. But as a privileged member of the audience I saw and heard that he had in fact, with that very concise practicality of his, accurately allowed for the time, distance and other noises that speaking in public requires. And it was not until after the congratulations that it occurred to me how little he had taken from the night before.

'Tell me about your teacher,' I said.

'What do you want to know?'

'Was she a fine actress? Famous?'

He cocked an eyebrow at me. 'She's a good teacher. I went to her for a month. Yesterday was a sort of final clowning session. Her philosophy is a few drinks and a laugh against nerves the day before.'

At that age I had already started a habit I hesitate to call daydreaming. While someone spoke I'd find myself looking at a small scene, a kind of rent on curiosity, or a glimpse on a variation. It felt extraordinarily dispassionate and although I would be involved in the images I was also an idle, musing sort of witness. Here on that slippery wynd I came across a bundle in a doorway, bent and lifted a flap of black cape to find MacBeth's speech teacher underneath and much the worse for drink. I made to help her up. She raised her stick. Dull melodrama? No doubt. I looked up at my friend.

'Come on,' said MacBeth, 'let's celebrate.'

12

Did you, reader, *plan* your life? Make lines in it as the ancients, surely with some fantasy in their ingenuity, made lines between stars, conjured up nicely limited and terrenal forms as more or less fortunate mnemonics of their night-time bearings? Has the youthful reader plotted out an archer? Can the old man now trace a plough? In any case I have always preferred my stars reflected and softened by water. The still stuff will do but I like the sight of slow rings expanding towards a rim. I also like water-colours, under-tinged with leaf rot, green-speckled on the surface and certain delicate shades of slate grey and slate blue and there, in something as clear and gelatinous as egg glair, a ripple and cluster of stars.

Today was officially autumn, the equinox in September. Soon there will be a progressive procession of migrating birds. Noisy ducks in straggling saggital formation but also neat flocks of small birds. They form circular clouds which fold into a tilting black line as they wheel; for a moment the extremities of the line thicken, then the arrangement fans out again through a section like an hourglass into a disc. The remarkable thing is that the flock is not a rough sphere but is arranged vertically; that disc is almost two-dimensional. I am aware; some of the above is rather less verbal than may appear. Corpuscles and carbon, I sit now with a slow pulse in night and lamplit solitude. Well.

I was always, as I pottered about my life, conscious first of fear. The stuff has such aspects and varieties! It was through smell, for instance, that I grew to understand that fear has colours and contours. I have seen several times pale colours emanating from afflicted people – a man in a state of fearful shock managed a pale blue like that of a transparent jelly fish with a central system like an ink-blue clot. Concentrated round the face and head the emanation was about an undulating thumbnail wide. Another man, cornered in an untruth, tended to a colour like heated virgin olive oil beginning to give off traces and twists of smoke. Oh, and I remember a woman who was, for a human, a veritable aurora borealis; violet, pink and wisps of disintegrating green. I do not know, of course, if these were impositions of mine. The colours are very limited as to tone and that blue speaks of cold and that olive oil of unembarrassed urine which, given the circumstances, seems plausible enough. But come, this is not a confession, whatever devices I may borrow, and my portrait of the emotional anatomy of a human natterjack is more background than lens – except, possibly, for those readers whose mirrors sometimes lurch and soften. 'But let us progress,' as my tutor used to say.

Natterjacks, as the reader must know by now, are easily intimidated. My tutor, in that tortuous and insinuating silliness, had intimidated me all right – but I was, in what I suppose might be called practical terms, to learn more from another undergraduate.

There were times when a glimpse of him, or the suspicion that a shadow sweeping round a corner might be his, made my feet falter and my adam's apple sink. I remember once wondering how Lennox managed, as he walked between scythe and short goose-step across the quadrangle, to imbue even his feet with an element of menace. Ever so slightly shorter than me, he had disproportionately long legs and arms, a squat trunk, square-cut shoulders and a sardonic sort of necklessness. But it was not a question of height or build. Nor, though Lennox was the first person I ever heard described as a genius, was it a question of mental intimidation. The description seemed to me then both hopeful and overweening. The result, however, is that I went resolutely deaf and for the life of me can no longer remember what he was supposed to be a genius at. It was certainly something mathematical but I distrust a notion that he was furrowing or burrowing, or whatever the word is, new paths in probability. And let me be fair. Another genius of a mathematician was a flabby simpleton outside his matrices. No, my fellow was widely and sharply argumentative, enjoyed rising in debates, and what intimidated me were his eyes. His ruddle-tinged lids, dull, Siamese-blue pupils and whites the colour of peeled almonds contrived a degree of violence a weird iota short of a squint. Though he would sometimes, when someone else was talking, unite blink and grimace like a cat when its doze has been interrupted. To be plain. I knew very little of Lennox because I desired to know no more, an urge so strong I had to be insistently reminded I had met the person and his eyes before his reputation. In my very first week I had, through a tedious assumption, been inveigled into a chess match and had achieved a clumsy, long-drawn-out stalemate. My opponent snorted.

'What strategy do you call that?'

'Stubbornness I think.'

And Lennox cocked his head at me and stared, before shrugging and turning away to show a profile of contempt controlled. Over the next couple of years I sometimes heard he was nearby; that same intonation, incredulous and arrogant, would rise above the general murmur. Given warning, I avoided him, would veer off across square, street or hall. Otherwise ours quickly reduced to a passing relationship – except when, to his satisfaction, I shied when he played with the timing of his nod.

And now to the point of this. During the preparation of my dissertation I found I had cause to visit him in his rooms. The cause, a library book filched from my patch, both puzzled and irritated me. What possible interest could Lennox have in some arcane Church finances before the invention of double-entry book-keeping? It was so odd I insisted the record be checked. It was additional bad luck that the senior librarian, a man who had added an academic look to that of an old-fashioned grocer, appeared glumly to claim that Lennox was 'hoarding all manner of books'. My best course was to approach 'the person involved' direct. And would I mind delivering this sealed letter?

Reluctantly I found and climbed the right stairs, breathed in, stared at the numerals on the door as if they might shift shape – and then touched the wood so quickly and lightly I can find no memory of the sound. The memory is empty of scratch or tap. I can recall no peephole. The door crashed open at once.

'Ah!' he exclaimed, lifting his hands. There was then a brief pause – it would not have been Lennox without it. 'How delightful to see you! Do come in!'

45

I had stiffened. But he smiled, shooed me inside, sat me down by the fire and, with an outstretched hand, invited me to consider his table. At the end nearer me I could see a pile of scones, an entire ham, a bowl of hardboiled eggs, a dish of peach jam, a slab of unsalted butter and a slightly charred but hefty cake stuffed with dried fruit and topped by almonds. I wondered, but did not ask, whom the spread was for.

'I'm celebrating a decision,' he said.

I said and did nothing.

'Don't you want to know what? You will join with me, won't you?'

'Mm.'

My mummest reaction. He beamed. He began clattering about with kettles and pots and toasting forks. 'I have decided,' he announced, 'to give up my degree.'

I had heard similar self-dramatizations recently and was not about to protest or say that there were only a few months to graduation.

'I renounce. I am sick to death of sums.'

He skewered bread on a fork and with an inexpert fencer's flourish pushed it at the fire. 'What I want to do is combine logic and pleasure. Not the pleasure of logic but logic used to increase the pleasure of visual delights. Do you understand?'

'Perhaps not.'

Have you ever heard in the tone of a voice the equivalent to distressed chalk on a blackboard?

He smiled. 'It is for that reason,' he said, 'that I have determined to become an illusionist of renown. Do you take milk?'

'No thank you.'

It did not matter. He poured from high enough for the dribble to separate into single drops and plash into the tea. Lovely. Now where was he? Yes, he would live on a leafy island. And he would appear from time to time with his latest offering. There was something too, as he prised smoking toast off the fork, of a quiet native girl to wash his socks. I was not at all sure how to react to this surely banal twitter and milk, thought that was probably what he was after. It was only then, with a cup on one knee and a side plate of blackened bread on the other, that I realized I was captive. Lennox leant very close. His

46

eyelashes seemed extraordinarily thick and black and long. And was that transparent grease on his eyelids and cheekbones?

'Would you mind awfully?' he asked. 'Of course I am still a beginner and I find the finger exercises tedious and even painful. But it is not as if this were music, now is it?'

There was a fraction there when I was within a hairspring of jumping up, but that sank through the most cautious of shrugs into a silent, plaintive wariness. There are few things that make me more uneasy than so-called 'magic'. However skilled the practitioner, I feel embarrassment and shame that such time and ingenuity should have been spent on footling tricks. I twitched. Lennox giggled. 'I am rather limited,' he said. 'Light and eggs really.'

'What?'

He picked up an egg. 'Did you think it was hardboiled? It's not. If I drop this there will be a hash of yolk on my shoe. That is one of the attractions – an exhilarating possibility of humiliation. Perhaps you know what I mean? Ah, incidentally, it was your tall, upright friend who put me in touch with a retired conjurer. It is amazing! The tatty scaffolding behind the tricks. The second-hand dealing in antiques. Some of the tricks cost as much as a house! Quite a few of the best are cheap.'

He had now reassured himself of a hostile audience. But was that a trace of envy? And was he trying to imitate my manner and accent? He handed me a spoon.

'Use it as a mirror. What do you see?'

'Myself?'

'Which way round?'

'Quite.'

He put the egg on the spoon.

'Would you like to say some magic words?'

'No.'

'Abrarefract, abraretract.' He removed the egg. I was the right way up. On both sides.

'You may keep the spoon,' he said, 'as a token.'

I shook my head. He laughed – and made the egg disappear.

'Don't you want to know if the effect will last? It's an old Moorish trick.'

I looked down. Nothing. No reflection. No reflection. On both sides.

'Or is that illusion a little underdeveloped for you?'

I could skook at him now but let me, who has a fondness for wizards vanishing on their final performances in the briskest puffs of smoke, abbreviate. He was relentless. And I found myself getting stuck in a routine; of refreshing a tired grin here, accompanying it with a genteel palsy of applauding nods there. The longer it went on, the more he concentrated, the more *I* suffered. I could not even free myself of the side plate and wretched cup and saucer because he paid as much attention to me as to his eggwork. Helplessly, I began to count the eggs left, a visual snatching – which I gave up at half a dozen. I suppose the egg behind the royal blue silk handkerchief was performing a bellydance but it would have been better for a navel. I presume that was another egg that pumped in and out behind his shirt front – excited by a bellydancing egg? I similarly failed to see that the small end of an egg, however twitched, much resembles a rodent's nose. He could have painted his eggs. Added whiskers and a tail. True, the hickory-dickory business, sending it up and down his sleeve and even across his shoulders and down the other, was, as far as I could judge, well done. But the subsequent pin and egg sucking, apart from retelling me the eggs in the bowl were not hardboiled, was noisy and slow and had the air of an old raconteur forgetting he had already told that story twenty minutes before. Was he wearing some contraption to store eggs? Where had he secreted them? I blinked. My nerves had started to play a miserable trick on me. I had the most powerful urge to yawn. Accordingly I swallowed very frequently and, whenever a yawn threatened the back of my palate and began to pull on my nose, I swallowed again to force it, or at least a sometimes painful lump of it, downwards.

A sudden whirr. A rotund chime from the clock on his mantelpiece. I had been there that long! Or was this another of his dreary little tricks? He looked splendidly fresh. I felt disgruntled and dry. At least I managed to get rid of that plate and saucer. It was relief and privacy I wanted, nothing to do with urine. I found the bath nearly full of water and some old condensation on the window. I put out a finger and gently detached a drop of water from the glass. I had been frightened of him? I turned, was enjoying working up a thick lather on my hands, when I had the memorable desire to luxuriate in a vengeful, wide yawn. It began well but abruptly snagged; a belch tried to squeeze in and I was gripped by a horrible sharp pain. I contrived to swallow. The pain shifted slightly, then divided up and down and at last lessened. I blinked, breathed gently. A sound, a squeak exactly like a punctured rubber ball when it is squashed, I traced to me. My book!

'I'm sorry,' I said. 'Did I interrupt you?'

Then I hiccuped and threw up my hands. It was not even what I wanted to say. Lennox however turned those eyes of his on me. 'What a total fraud you are.'

I hiccuped again. I tried a little to look quizzical. I am not sure I managed. I mean, I was not intimidated.

'You're no Moor.'

'Well of course I'm not! Hic. My parents were merely expatriates over-anxious to blend in.'

'Where are they now?'

'Hic. Dead.'

'Recently?'

'No. Hic.'

'So they are stone cold, eh?'

I decidedly did not bother to reply. Instead, in my theatrical gesture of the meeting, I pressed my hand to my diaphragm and rolled my eyes to the left. And there was my book! Straightaway I marched and got it out from between an anthology of Gnosticism and a tome on Elementary Meteorology.

'*That* was the purpose of your visit?'

'Yes. I need it for my dissertation.'

'Ah,' he said, 'a friend must have left it.'

This was such an idle lie that I hiccuped again. What friend did he have in mind? I did not ask and passed over giving him the librarian's letter.

A further but by now perfunctory unpleasantness, he as a waiter trying to charge a hiccuping client for one stuffing of uncut cake, a hogsload of untouched ham, finished an experience I had no wish to repeat – and certainly not to anyone else. Exactly a fortnight later, his table similarly furnished with food, he killed himself in the old Roman fashion of turning his bathwater deep red.

Under the circumstances it was not difficult to cringe at the possible raggedness in a razor blade or at the prominence and elasticity of wrist veins. Nor to puzzle at the significance Thursday afternoons had for him. I even wondered if he had not played a library version of Russian roulette, as it were borrowing from a number of very casual acquaintances' subjects to encourage chance a little. And all that food, though I supposed items like the cake would keep. Less fancifully – I had lied to the librarian – I crumpled that letter and tossed it onto the fire. I also noted a number of overblown images, a hairless white knee rising from scarlet water for instance – though why that particular viewpoint? And had I shaved his leg for the composition? And of course I could also shudder when a background breakfaster decapitated an egg with one sweep of a serrated knife. And it took some shivering and brisk hand-rubbing to get into my next bath – how had they lifted that limp white shape out? Had they first pulled the plug and rinsed him off? And I managed a shudder, even in my own hot bath, when I closed my eyes and saw a slow drop of milk falling and falling to splash spectacularly in reddened water. I blinked. Come, I said to myself, this is agitated and sentimental tosh. But I remember now that underneath those intense but not particularly fitting snippets I felt, I think for the first time, a kind of brain twitch, a crawling disjointed progression like a back-broken earwig or horniegolloch.

Less susceptibly. More generally. I assumed a front of parsimonious pity, treated Lennox's absence as a lack, like a missing letter. Aha. Death is never a digression. Youth merely has the aspect of one. And then, in the style of youthful survivors, I worried more about the shift in my bodily gulps, about that rebellious yawn, about the private becoming helplessly public. Youth is suspicious self-concern? To the extent that I took time to wake up to the reactions around me. But how censorious my coevals were! How shocked and cruel! Lennox's genius had degenerated into miserable cowardice. Doubtless my aphorisms were fit for a callow and pompous limbo but I had never thought to take the self-slaughter as an attack on me! It was as if the twisted faces of his fellow students wanted to commit violence on a corpse, revive him to do him in again. Surely not. But then a fat girl told me she felt 'absolutely outraged' and when I squinted uncomprehendingly at her came up with the absurd but appalling formula – 'That bastard has outraged my *soul*!' No, I had never liked Lennox. Under no circumstances did I consider we were in some sort of brotherhood. But the girl's mad energy set me thinking on currents and directions. I needed, however – it was no more than a quiet moment, it involved one of those details my tutor liked to deride in regal tales for children – to observe a plain white saucer as it floated on soapy water. I prodded and pushed it. It stayed up. I twirled it. Still it stayed up. And then I embarked on a parallel or schematic coracle. It is a suitably thin-skinned, round, rudderless craft for the metaphor. I stirred water, felt almost immediately flabby and too large, but determined to keep on.

'What circumstances?' I was asked.

My heart beat gratifyingly fast. I refused to speak.

And from there it was easy to bobble and insinuate a very vague something and from there, on queries which may have had a touch of envy, to bobble faster. The senior librarian's confirmation that I had delivered his letter to Lennox provided a stabilizer.

'Are you sure about these circumstances?' demanded the boy's personal tutor after pigeonholing me.

'No.'

'Why not?'

'I may have been misled.'

'Take care.'

'Do you think I have not considered very carefully whether or not to speak with you? Answer me, because I could not find an answer. Why should I have kept away?'

'It's all right,' he said, 'it's all right. I suppose this has cost you. Well. I really have no choice. I must give you the benefit of the doubt.'

'Me? That's rich.'

'What?'

'I don't require doubt or benefit.'

'Require?'

'I don't require anything of this.'

The man blinked, decisively as it turned out, and the boy was given a decent quiet and misadventure.

Now all that I had insinuated was that Lennox had shown signs of instability and worry. Was this worry personal? It was difficult for me to think it was not. Somehow this chrysalized, he was an intelligent boy, into a fear of a possible brain tumour and I noted, with some bemusement, that when talking of tumours people often used their fingers so that the tumour took on something of a twisting caterpillar and, I presume, the suicide became an imago – the Red Admirable. Overnight a discreet murmur fluttered out to make the dead Lennox unassuming, shy, and too delicate to impose on others. Thus the university body came to terms with itself. I was, briefly, worried by what I had done, addressed myself in a mirror and sternly accused this natterjack of having abused good faith. But the accusation did not convince me. What good faith? Whose? What most exercised me was whether or not the university's desire for hush and hope would have reached the same conclusion in any case, whether or not the mood would have swung without me.

And MacBeth? He was not one for funerals but he attended this, incidentally rousting me out for it too. It was crowded with onlookers as well as mourners. The boy's mother was there, unexpectedly as fat as my own Uncle Hugh, draped in layers of black and so heavily powdered that her tears gathered dust. I did not quite see how MacBeth turned into her prop for the burial; after the cords had squeaked and the token earth had rattled on the coffin she murmured into his chest and he, looking over her hennaed head towards me, set off on a gloomy nodding. There was a combination of sleepiness and bizarre expectation in the air, perhaps due to the cold. MacBeth slipped her shoulder under his armpit and began moving her away, holding off the more insistent consolers. I had been stiff too long. I stretched in my coat. And it was only then that it abruptly occurred to me to wonder who had visited on the intermediate Thursday. For a ghastly moment I could see pale, pullulating patches on my hands; then I understood they were in the liquid over my eyes. I blinked. I swallowed. Clumps of departing mourners were revealing misty grave stones – and angels' wings, cherubims' heads and grim little temples. Then I saw a smile, a raised hand and various heads bowed to listen. 'What? At the weekend? Yes, of course.' I turned at once and began walking to the other entrance, having the path slap my numb feet, a little afraid of slipping, anxious to keep up my pace.

13

Stars and warts. I was amused today to wake on an image of my friend as a pale ghost standing on a slope outside a small Doric mausoleum beside a natterjack stretching up to see into a round, black pot. Or perhaps I was, with regard to his lack of colouring, just remembering that fat girl's muslin soul. It is pleasant to grow comfortable in the possession of his memory. But no, no. When slightly bored or impatient my friend's left index finger came up a fraction, his right lid down a little. He yawned and bit into an apple.

'What are you smiling at?' he asked.

I remember. I raise a cup of tea as I did then. Only here I am surprised by some bright external reflections – a side wall and eaves, a comely slice of blue Andalusian sky on the reddish tan liquid, all riffled by the exhalation from my nose after the thin intake of fluid. The pleasure of recapturing overlaid. But wait! Reader! In this white and dun place by the sea I do *not* move. A whirr above my head by the window frame and the merest breeze. A dragonfly! The span of its red-gold wings and the length of its body fit the liquid circle exactly. Three things: the rich fly, the white circuit of the porcelain rim and my own parted lips, comically stupid, fleshy with pleasure. The creature vanished. I cooled the tea, I emptied the cup. Warmth fanning my stomach. So.

*

53

My dissertation, so intensely worked at, was marked well though I was more than a little put out to receive a commendation specifically for the numerical apparatus attached to all those careful words. Somehow it made those words brittle, a judgement I soon considered fair. Imagine my surprise then when, quite out of the blue, I received on expensive, weighty paper a beautifully clear invitation to join a firm of fund managers which mentioned my work!

'Good!' said MacBeth. 'That's splendid!'

'Well! What impresses me is that they should take such trouble.'

At that age – it soon went – MacBeth showed surprise and concern by a twitch, a feint that just began either a wince or a wink.

'I sent it.'

'What?'

With one hand he picked up an apple, with the other pulled at an ear lobe. 'My mother, inaccurately I have to say, calls it the family firm. I went to see them myself a while back and they asked me if I knew anyone likely. You know how it is.'

'If I had thought of anybody it would have been Angus.'

'No. I think he might be disappointed you're not staying on.'

'Good.'

'Why?'

'Wondering why similes so often fail to graduate into metaphors is not the stuff of academics.'

MacBeth cocked his head, tossed up the apple and caught it. 'What are you talking about?'

And it suddenly, after a natterjack's delay, came to me that he had picked me, paid me an extraordinary compliment. Come, how many of your friends would you recommend for a job?

'I think I'm thanking you. You will be working there too?'

'Oh yes. And there's no need for thanks. Your dissertation was excellent. What are you doing this summer?'

'I'm afraid I've got to see my Uncle Hugh. Then I'll have to see when they want me to start.'

'Ah.' He sighed. He looked at the apple in his hand and bit into it.

'Are you all right?' I said.

'Yes. My mother is . . . a little nervous.'

'Oh.'

'She's not much of a diplomat.'

Indeed not. 'You've had a letter too?'

'Mm.'

I felt very cheerful. To recap. He yawned and bit into the apple again.

'What are you smiling at?'

'Pleasure.'

'In what?'

'Oh. In leaving. In the company.'

'Thank you,' he said. 'I find this part rather uncomfortable.'

I shook my head and smiled at him.

'Ah,' he said glumly, 'a *fit* of happiness.'

This made me grin, but seeing him frown slightly at his apple I suppressed it.

'I don't know why the hell I'm eating this,' he said and flicked the twice-bitten apple onto the coals, where it sat on the glow and smoke, for a surprising time nice and bright and crisp.

Book Two

14

'Now then,' said Duncan at our first meeting, 'do you like fishing?'

'Sir?'

Had I heard right? He mused a while at something rather to the left of me; an elderly, slender, beaky gentleman behind a large desk, most elegantly dressed, with thin white hair darkened by the stuff applied to it, an almost central parting and a baby's grey curl over one ear. Cream silk, hand-cut charcoal wool and little touches of gold, on his little finger, at his cuffs, across his midriff.

'I wonder,' he said in his fastidious voice. 'Have you enough stamina? Mm?'

'I think so, sir.'

'Oh yes,' he said as if in an aside. 'I believe in frank speaking.' And then, with the merest glance towards me, 'Yours is a very responsible position. I'll squeeze you! No doubt about that.'

'No, sir.'

'You're not the kind of person who complains about working overtime are you?'

'Not at all, sir.'

'No time limits here.'

'No, sir.'

His eyes passed me on their way to the other wall. He cleared his throat.

'Tell me,' he said, 'what did you really want to do?'

'Why this, sir.'

'Oh! That's very good.'

He then patted his manicured hands together, bare applause in the position of prayer. He sniffed.

'Now,' he said. 'First task for you. Why don't you go away and write a report of this interview?'

Do I have to say more of Duncan? Very well. I wrote two pages, a soberly expressed account of the subtle and instructive probing of a young man embarking on a much desired career. I also said something on guidance, the encouragement of self-discovery, time and context. I found I was trembling, almost faint from the idea of gambling. But what surprised Duncan was the speed of my effort.

'This is most extraordinarily prompt,' he said without much sign of pleasure. Having scanned the pages, however, he nodded and pushed out his lower lip.

'Oh excellent. Mm, perceptive. Though you know,' he said, 'you *inform* your sentences?'

'Sir?'

'Some have – how shall I put this? – an involuted quality.' He raised a finger. 'Most of our clients prefer the simple kind. One point one sentence.' He shrugged. 'Not much call for depth.' Duncan then took out his pen, initialled both pages and wrote: *If you have to sacrifice style for clarity, do so. Long-windedness is better than skimpiness. Thoroughness is usually of more value than speed. Steer clear of any sort of irony.*

To make sure I understood he tapped his finger on the last sentence and briefly indulged the bodily movements of a small laugh but with no other sign of the laugh at all.

Fittingly, his handwriting was a handsome, adapted italic, written with a supercilious frown and an uncomfortable neck, caused merely by his looking over half-moon glasses at the end of his nose. I was, while bemused, amused and deeply cautious, nevertheless learning. Duncan was, despite his parody of an academic with money handing back an essay, a disbeliever in direct instructions. My first practical problem was wondering what to do with those two sheets of paper. I filed them.

There were three of us as his assistants. I, at least, found him generally easy to work for. Fund management entails an imperative dose of mathematics but, at that time, in that firm, mathematicians were not held in esteem. It was the first time I had ever heard 'sliderule' as a despective term. Duncan much preferred to pronounce words like flair and panache than to talk of yields and returns. Of course he paid attention to figures and it is quite true that figures can be misleading and, in his phrase, 'ignorant of the future'. But I hardly thought that justified his description of a hunch-backed scheme as 'rather dashing and elegant', nor his enjoyment of the bizarre behaviour of some of the more exotic directors. One of these he called a 'swashbuckler', an absurdly affectionate term for a man clearly unbalanced, with a view of the relations between risk and profit both aggressively baroque and uncommunicatively mystic. Another, a legalist, *always* found a reason why something couldn't be done; worse, would not co-operate when overruled. Another was a chronic gossip, suffered verbal incontinence about his contacts and contracts, would tell quite the wrong person. Duncan indulged them all. On what were his decisions and vocabulary based? He once recommended to me the extraordinary formula for dealing with people of 'affable non-sentimentality'. But it was his swashbuckler who lost the money and the gossip, after a very shrill squabble, who was 'eased out'.

Not so incidentally, Duncan was the only person ever to call me by my given name which he pronounced Ranald – Spanish frog and old English currency. I don't know about any coronach. It combines that mix of slightly incorrect stickling, otherworldliness and a sense of his own separate worth that I regard as characteristic. His way of saying thank you was to pat the paper one had just slid in front of him. When particularly amiable he scratched the back of his own hand. He would even, first thing in the morning, give me advice on decorating my newly acquired flat or on using his tailor. Against that, he had little sense of economy and was surprisingly huffy when he found out at my tasteful little house-warming party that I had put up plain white curtains rather than the prohibitively expensive blue and green silk he had suggested. And he had a tendency to come in on a problem when it was already solved, driving departments almost to distraction with kindly, ignorant, excruciatingly long rehashes. And there was another, much more private business, when he would assume a sudden inability to go on. Wilful, perversely self-assertive, he would come to a dead stop. I soon learnt the signs. Smoothly, replete with whispered contemplations, I'd glide in but it was, as one of the other assistants complained – 'What are we? Waiters?' – essential to know whether or not he wanted a drink, a small joke or a change of activity. Making a gratified click of the tongue, he'd brighten up, hum appreciatively, settle down. Little bouts of office heroism. Here is a beverage grown cold. He points it out. Another? No, no, he'll make do with cold. His favourite verb was 'reflect' – 'These figures reflect well' – and his preferred adjective 'immense', usually twice. Immense pressures. When very put upon he sometimes mentioned a breakdown he had had at some unspecified time and which he usually, but by no means always, described as metaphysical. I never managed to understand what he meant, noticed more that he gave every sign of being immensely proud of it. I wonder if the reader can understand how chary this made me, of how I saw in it a fatuously complacent threat of irrational power.

There was something else. His self-regard had an overly prophylactic side, both in the style of instantly acquiring past experience when it suited – 'Oh yes, I wrote/ran/sculpted/acted and danced when I was young' – and in his pernickety toilette (someone came in weekly to snip and clip). He wanted to keep germs of mischance and misfortune off him, was too ready to see in clumsy happenstance and coincidence malevolent subordinates with wives and children and the normal run of debts. One of my two fellow assistants was sacked after a few months because his young wife had an ectopic pregnancy. Of course, this was not the reason given, the language used was dreadfully demure: incompatibility, new life, fresh opportunities. But I saw both Duncan's shudder of disgust and, a moment after, that not only natterjacks have more than one eyelid.

As I look back I am a little surprised, a little more depressed, at how we all bore with it. A wretched guest, Duncan was also a tyrannical if inept host. His house was enormous and gloomy, his kindness indifferently patronizing, his attention sporadic and fussy. Besides, I never enjoyed his snuffling sort of weekend humour, jokes and puzzles with matchsticks, aged board games, billiards and shove ha'penny. When I was first introduced to his family I was only a year or two older than his sons though he would always have them stuck in boyhood and urge me to give them advice. He had two, both with uninteresting interests which they would pursue and pout over in company. One was shamans and mushroom cults I think. The other? I see little chips of rock in cases. The first time I met them one was arranged with a book in a window seat while the other was waiting for me, seated at a set-up chess board. The elder, I remember, felt more important for being the elder one; I wondered when I would ever get away from black and white squares.

I much preferred their mother and am happy to say the liking was mutual. She was pert and smart, with a delightfully insinuating laugh and a taste for what she called 'racy stories'. Let us be clear, this is what *she* called them and there was never a hint of impropriety or coarse language. Even so, Duncan would show distant disapproval and then pursue some topic of his own, quite often pushing a little cake about his plate like a toy boat. And when he could see his way ahead, some time usually before he made much sense to his patient listeners, he would suddenly cram it into his mouth, swallow almost without chewing and then sit back, patting his fingers seal fashion, and expound. On winter Sundays I would squat near the fire – and his wife. Her way with their rather tasteless little cakes was to bite cleanly in the middle. I would appreciate the warmth of the fire and her mild maliciousness and she would slip the instep of one foot behind the heel of the other when pleased with my reaction.

My information is ageing but when I last heard of her she was still alive, still pretty but rather obese and quite gaga. These last two surprised me. But then it is nearly twenty-five years since I saw her and heard her out with sympathy and attention. On that occasion she did seem mildly physically uncomfortable and it took me a little while to make out the line from her shifting loins to my innocent and respectful flies. She then brazened out my observation, with tremulous vanity showed me the inside of her thigh. Forget human nature and widowhood – this was a wonderful sign of vulnerability and pride. I gave her a kiss when I left, a compromise between cheek and lips, her lips dry from hours of talking, her cheek greasy; not unpleasant. And then she lifted a hand – I do not know if this was her intention – and brought the heel of it gently and tremblingly against one of my eyes. Naturally I blinked; my lashes fluttered on her skin.

'Ah,' she sighed. 'Dear Duncan always said you were the cat's whiskers but rather a puritan at business. I was sure you would be sensitive to his loss!'

No, no, no, it was *her* sense of loss that I could feel.

15

At first sight, as she turned from a north-facing window to be introduced, Gruoch had veins of milk and bilberry blue and eyes as black as that malty stuff that had to be dug out of a stoneware jar in the winter term at school; as hard and sticky as toffee, the lump took minutes to dissolve. I would press it against the roof of my mouth and my saliva would become as thick as mucus and my throat would ache as if someone were holding down my tongue with a warm dessert spoon. I mean her skin had the translucent look of skimmed milk and her irises had no motes in them at all, they merely turned from black to tarsoap brown with the light. She had a habit of welcoming me with a nice amiable smile which would peak quickly into her cheeks but then slip distractedly back. A faint air of waiting about her, some tension at the corners of her lips and her eyes. Very tall, very slender, she would then tilt her head and her straight, chin-length hair would swing away from her face. Perhaps she grew to see me as a puzzling if innocent precursor. But enter MacBeth! She'd spring to, eyes gleaming – and if you have forgotten my icy black loch, remember it now. Her lips pressed in, a brimming pre-plosion that constituted the beginning of the smile she kept just for him. Her nose, a very slender piece of gristle not quite long enough for her face, would tighten and her hands would come up, one to push back her hair, the other, at about shoulder height, in a business I found wretchedly juicy and tender, to make a gesture like someone absent-mindedly sending a loose bracelet down her arm. There was a trembling hilarity in her welcome and a tiny, lateral see-sawing of her face before the lip-plumped kiss.

'Hello,' from him to me. 'Where's Lula (the diminutive stepson)?' to her.

I find these younger selves mendacious. I remember myself not slimmer, that is not quite the word when I now have a little belly like a buttoned soufflé, but suspiciously compact. At his wedding – let me pass over handing him the ring and so on – I looked like every moth-in-law's ideal best man. More than dapper. Varnished. Teeth gleaming, eyes gleaming, toecaps gleaming, hair gleaming. All partings and right creases. But I can also recall a set of delicate and competent fingers at my waistcoat, as if they were about to pull at an invisible string. To my extreme left Donada, despite her nasty letter to him, for once looked elegant and relaxed in nattier blue. Even Lula, sitting cross-legged, his head cocked to one side, looked charming and pleased. The couple themselves had their heads almost touching. A small satisfaction in that her garb soon dated horribly. It resembled an over-heavy nightdress of a colour as brilliantly fat as full milk at the top of the bottle. Leaning forward, I could just make out that her lipstick was smudged at the side of her mouth and that that was a tailor's hernia, a small show of white shirt where his waistcoat had come a fraction adrift and I think, it was the merest touch, that part of the reason for her smudged red had been left on his upper lip, a very thin rim of carmine after his knuckle had wiped.

Stop. My careful manners now look mean. My surprise that he should marry so early rather than that he married a twenty-five-year-old widow with an infant son now looks like distress. And by the time it occurred to me to think of MacBeth as a fatherless small boy, my mood was not of a kind to find it any sort of perception. No, it was after I learnt that Gruoch had even been a bud-breasted child of ten or eleven at the quarry pool among friends and cousins (one of whom was her first husband, another, little MacBeth!) by a forest of toadstools and a bush whose reflection took on a distinct tremor, that I could not stomach tracing all the many tedious times she and I had somehow contrived to miss.

'It's extraordinary! Do you remember Rowan?' she asked in her slightly hoarse voice.

'Rowan like the tree?'

'No. A dog. A rather friendly pointer.'

16

Now I tried, I did, to be congenial with my friend's wife. She had, however, an unfortunate newly married re-girlishness, tackled me with a robust intimacy, a desire to please her husband no doubt, that I found unnerving. They too had to go to Duncan's and I remember, almost a year after the wedding, Gruoch plumping down beside me.

'It's so boring being poor,' she said amid the purr and click of billiard balls. That purr, by the way, the crackle of ivory detaching from baize, irritated me almost as much as the callipers and angles and dog-leg lift that Duncan went in for. I blinked. 'But you're not poor,' I replied.

She gave me an old-fashioned look, which I felt annoyed enough to return. She sighed. She looked first at the bulbous legs of the billiard table, then at her own feet.

'I don't want to talk about that.'

Fair enough. I found that I too, though gloomily, was looking down at my own shoes. Suddenly she turned and her hot breath began hubbling and dampening my ear. I could not make out a word. I looked sideways. She was flushed and laughing, face up, throat stretched. What had she said? Was she pregnant? I considered it better to smile.

'Mm?' said Taha.

To my surprise she snorted and knuckled my bicep rather hard. 'You should see your face.'

This was unpleasant and embarrassing – or at least the sensation and taste of sweat on my upper lip was.

'Speak up a little.'

She laughed again.

'Stop it,' I whispered.

And she did. She raised her eyebrows at me. 'Well?'

'Well what?'

'Are you?'

'What?'

'Her boyfriend, of course.'

'For God's sake, whose?'

'Ah,' she protested, 'if you're going to be like that.'

It is difficult for me to portray the sharp-toothed, hot-eyed irritation I felt then. I almost slapped her, hard – but who she was talking about abruptly leaked in on me.

'Where did you get this rubbish?'

'Hah,' she said. 'I thought there might be some advantage in it.'

'Advantage?'

She made a tetchy sound. 'Don't be so prissy,' she said. 'You might be able to get something out of her.'

'My God.'

She got up as if I had just committed some tiresome grossery, sighed and headed for someone else. Her buttocks, dead-looking, rolled in her too-tight dress. I saw that the subject of our conversation was looking at me with a certain archness. I had begun an uncomfortable, soft smile when I saw the archness was plucked, her face pale and dull. I had never noticed, or perhaps been too polite to notice, that Duncan's wife had removed her eyebrows and substituted two thin black curves higher up. For a startled moment I thought she was blowing me a kiss but the thing was silent, a pout, a parting of the lips, a sign for me to watch – and then she called out to Gruoch. There was an indistinct murmur of fripperies. Then I heard a very loud sigh.

'Marriage is such an *intimate* business, don't you think?' bellowed our hostess, and she lay back, as if on a pillow. I should have thought that was enough but she was undoubtedly hurt. 'Especially twice.'

Gruoch, blushing, nodded but did not, I think, ever forgive her, referring to her more than once in my hearing as 'that witch of yours'.

To return however to more masculine concerns. A short while after Gruoch's whisper and knuckle, the remaining other of Duncan's assistant triplets sidled over to me with a plate of cakes – in that light they resembled an assortment of monstrous pupae – and, looking off, enquired.

'Don't you know it's dangerous to toady so?'

'Who to?' I said with as good a grace as I could muster.

He heaved his eyes heavenward. I grunted, grace going. But I later mulled over what he had said. I hadn't been called toad since school, and the word made me reflect on the link between classroom and office. There was none, unless I count variegation. And within a week I had leap-toaded ahead of him in a promotion which, incidentally or not, finished those Sunday afternoons sitting by the fire and Duncan's wife.

'I apologize,' said the fellow about a year on.

'For what?'

'It obviously works.'

'Speak clearer.'

'No, no. I learned my lesson. You'll see.'

It took me time to work out to what he was referring. But the action he was to show me, not pat proof but certainly a sad complement to his defeatist, endlessly apprentice air, was to abandon job, wife and two tiny daughters and run away with an under-age girl. But I do not believe he really knew that I would be the one clearing my throat among expressions like precociously mature or forward slut, or even the term, pronounced by our legalist with the kind of tongue smack I associate with dogs after they have swallowed a sweet, statutory rape. I was 'entrusted' with the matter. There was no more to be said. And I was rather lucky. The girl's parents treated me like a derisorily genteel debt-collector and triumphantly told me she would be marrying her man as soon as she turned sixteen.

Relieved, I adopted the pious fiction of resignation and had six months' salary sent to his abandoned wife. No one ever complained. He I was never to hear of or from again. But his wife soon remarried, just before, for some reason of her own, writing me a letter demanding her right to happiness. And why not? I arranged for her to be sent a small silver bowl as a wedding present and accompanied it with the usual sort of note, wishing her all the best and asking her to bear me in mind if there was anything I could ever do for her.

'Good bit of tact,' said Duncan later. 'Though I think we'll keep it off the record. Between ourselves, eh?'

'Yes, sir,' I said and nodded.

17

At last, after three muddled years, a whole world was settled in a day. It began discouragingly, with a sun so pale the naked eye could examine it easily. I thought it likely to rain and as we went along, I stiffly singing songs with his wife and stepson, having some difficulty because her singing voice was all flat breath, I was waiting, perhaps even hoping, for the first fat drops. In one of those sudden shifts however, for which that part is reputed, the weather changed. The boy shouted and on looking up I saw a thick blue sky like the glaze on an eel's back. A moment later the sun blinked and blazed, throwing a sudden heat on my face and making my eyes smart uncomfortably. I was just about to remark that it could all change back again when MacBeth grinned and pointed towards the sea.

In point of fact it had clouded over by the time we got down to the beach, a characteristic that was to last throughout the picnic, cloud and sun, with bursts of heat and chill alternating. I dislike sitting on soft sand. To the left of the little bay an enormous cliff head gave some privacy. It looked like a gigantic grey molar.

'Do you know this place?'

'No,' I said.

'I remember it from childhood. The tooth is hollow.'

'Let's go in,' said the boy.

'Too many bats.'

The other side of the bay was less stark, was arranged as a worn and rounded triple terrace. We huddled on grass-tufted sand and watched the breeze play patch and chill riff on the water. A sudden shot of sun.

'How about a swim?' said MacBeth.

I blinked. The boy was frightened of the water. Gruoch frowned.

'Come on,' he said, exposing his great chest. A mat of intertwined hairs.

'No, thank you,' I replied.

'Why not?'

'I burn.'

He gave the sky a squint.

'Well,' he said with a mildly disappointed look, 'that's one name for it.'

'Apart from the angle of the sun, there's the boy too,' I said.

He stood, thick and towering, looking amused and disgruntled. I picked up a twig and began a game of noughts and crosses to the accompaniment of sliding female clothes.

When I looked up from my several unavoidable draws the pale-buttocked pair of them were already knee-deep in water, a thin mist rolling in to meet them. A jiggle or two later both heads bobbed. Tugging at a tussock I grew conscious that I was being stared at. 'You're not happy,' said the boy.

'Don't talk relative rubbish. Would you like to build a sand-castle?'

'No thank you.'

I tried again. 'Well. Look for shells?'

Lula shook his head.

'I suppose,' I said, 'we could find some rock pools to explore.'

'No.'

I shrugged.

'That,' he said.

'What?'

'I thought we might explore that,' he said, pointing at the old molar.

70

'Bats your father said.'

'But you don't get bats when the puffins are out.'

There were two of these birds standing disconsolately on a rock just above the mist.

'Is that some kind of folklore?'

The boy shrugged and rested his head on one shoulder. As if in reply, the birds shot to the other side of the little bay and then back again.

'Do you mean the bats are asleep?'

The boy shrugged again.

We had to tackle some rocks first, sharp and slippery enough for me to cut my knee. The warm blood dribbled down my shin. My knee went stiff and a sudden surge of irritation in me had to be stifled. We arrived at one of the entrances to the cave and stooped to peer in.

There was cold damp dark to sniff. The noises were various – slapping water, a huzz and the rustle and twitter of those repulsive creatures at sleep. The boy looked up at me and suggested I go first. I groaned. I crouched. I waddled in.

I was struck at once with the chilly wetness that clung to the walls. Then by the extraordinary height of the ceiling, a disconcerting dome, its size emphasized by clumps of the shuffling, ragged creatures. A low arch gave to the sea itself and in front of me I could see the shifty gleam of round grey pebbles as in some interior beach. I am not sure whether sound, a soft slapping, not water, not wings, or glimpse came first but I was conscious with a sudden whirr that I did not want the matter settled into two oblivious white ghosts clutching at each other with such care and consideration.

I stumbled out again, startling the boy.

'What's the matter? Uncle Taha!'

I was about to speak, as short a lie as I could make it, when, to my own consternation, I began to weep. Regrettably, despite the extravagance of my limp, I found myself forced to explain why and as we went back I gulped the boy a maudlin mausoleum tale about my mother which would tighten the skin on my cheeks even now if I let it and which had the following result: a day or so later, Maelbaetha drew me aside and thanked me.

'It's good the boy shares these things. You must have loved your father very much. I can barely remember mine. He doesn't remember his at all.'

I nodded. I pressed my eyes. I had previously almost cleared from my retina that pale, undulating shape. Was camelopard the old word or outline for giraffe? I openéd my eyes to look at him and, I admit, to wonder again at his choice of married trysting place. But mostly – and I should say lovingly – I understood that he had forgotten some of my most basic biography.

As it was my ingenuity was further tested, now with sand, an hour spent constructing a famous battle, though the name was for convenience only, the boy blandly announcing his hunger from time to time, I another counter-attack or general's speech, while we waited.

They came out of the thin mist, he pleasantly shrunk and she, in a curious gesture of modesty, meant I suppose to cut the dribble, squeezed her body hair and presented me with a vaguely troublesome parody of coat-hook maleness to go with slender, goosepimpled thighs and, from the merest corner of my eye, purple-brown limpets at her chest. I swallowed. We ate. Father and boy charged up and down the beach while the mother combed the salt out of her hair and smiled.

'It's nice to escape for a while,' she remarked in an eased sort of way. 'I don't know why you're looking so glum.'

After which, back at my kneehole desk, there were days when reality and despondence had the same leaden hue, same beaten shape. With time, as with a finial, this weathered, acquired verdigris and crack black, something yellow as a primrose and a spot of rust, resisted thieves, sprouted fungi, got moss.

18

I cannot let it go. Have I been unfair? I have heard it said of a writer that he could not portray a convincing woman, had fudged up instead a cardboard shape with tacked-on hair and some delicate water-colours that have sunk into the surface. Well, here I am, Gruoch convinced me all right and yet I find her exasperatingly difficult to catch. Is my exasperation due to unease or guilt? He swarms through my mind at different ages, in different clothes, in different attitudes. She is an unreachable itch. I have covered that twittering canary again. I have scratched my face. And yet she is the love of *his* life.

Very well. My relations with Gruoch may be compared to a quite endless game of dumb crambo. It was she who first, in an aside – Lula likes it – mentioned this game to me. I did not, of course I did not, ask her what it was. I flick at my dictionary in private. Crambo is a game in which one player gives a word to which other players must find a rhyme; the dumb version complicates the matter by introducing mime. It probably comes from the Latin *crambe repetita* or cabbage served up again. Stale kale. And yet I found something astringent in the game which made me, when caught off guard, sway like a snail – a lovely image taken from memory; the creature contracted but expanded again with slender, slow-grained dignity. A kind name for stalked caution and a glistening if turgid desire to proceed. Lula and I watched a thrush as it waited by a thicket. It eyed us back. I shrugged. I know next to nothing about snails, think Roman snails are edible – snails being for me as unthinkably foreign as wild mushrooms – do not know what aspect of Rome a gasteropod-namer had in mind, though to mine that snail suggested a happy resemblance in its faceless pimpling to a helmeted Roman hero. I believe those snails are hermaphrodites and if I remember they come foot to foot, mouth to mouth and push calcareous arrows into each other's soles. I yawned. We had not long eaten; crayfish, salmon, lemon mousse.

73

'We are interlopers,' I said to the boy. 'The bird wants his meal.'

'The meal doesn't know.'

'What?'

'We could cheat, couldn't we?'

'How do you mean?'

'We could move the snail.'

'If you want to.'

'You,' he said. 'You move it.'

'You don't think your squeamishness is rather too thorough-going? And unimaginative? What would you do if I weren't here?'

'What *are* you talking about?' said Gruoch. 'Oh. How revolting!' She stooped, plucked and tossed the snail towards the midden. The thrush, a sardonically patient bird, loped after it.

'I wanted to save it,' said the boy.

Gruoch was still brushing her fingers. 'Don't be silly! They're a garden pest and they transmit liver fluke.'

'Is that a flummery?' said Lula to me.

'A what? Ah yes, well, I'm not a gardener and I know nothing of sheep diseases.'

'You should wash your hands in disinfectant,' said his mother. 'Now there! Just look at that. The whole cabbage head has been spoiled.'

'Could have been a caterpillar,' said the boy. 'Lots of cabbage whites around.'

And the woman looked very sharply at *me*.

'Don't be whimsical,' she said.

'The thrush is eating the snail now. Look how he's breaking the shell!'

The thrush was using a stone as an anvil. Gruoch frowned.

'That's a starling,' she said, 'surely.'

'The bird thinks it is all right to eat.'

'Oh come now,' I said, 'you didn't want to eat it before, now did you? You didn't even want to touch it.'

'I should think not,' said Gruoch. 'Now let's go and wash our hands.'

Her hands. On occasions like this in walled gardens I have often wondered at how a small degree of disjointedness can grow. Take the word 'whimsical', for instance, which she so often used in my presence and which she brought me to loathe, especially when politely pronounced. I pursed my lips. I watched my rival lead her child along the pathway. I had tried to turn Gruoch into something attractive, a fleshy slope at least, *something* I could concentrate on, a very close focus, dense little curls, a plump patch of bilberry and madder. Interposing myself. But I could not make her necessary, would, anyway, have been terrified of disappointing her. Did I even work out a way of breathing, like a swimmer in flesh? I admit it. I shut my eyes. I felt slightly faint. Jealousy. Another word I loathe. Perhaps my ear is faulty but in the language here *celos* is at least mixed up with the idea of being wretchedly on heat or in season. 'Jealousy' has none of the suppurating quality that passion really has – nor that sharp sloosh of surgical spirit. There is little to be done with the pronunciation, mere stagework. No, after due thought, I should prefer to see 'jealousy' unthroned. The usurper would be ignoble, gnawing, nauseous . . .

'Come on,' shouted Lula. 'You'll be late.'

Quite. I began walking. Another snail whom malign providence had set venturing onto the path tempted me powerfully to apply my foot. I resisted. I ran.

'What a splendid afternoon!' exclaimed a rather breathless Taha.

Gruoch blinked. She smiled minimally. She had an habitual gesture; tapping on my forearm, as if I might get ahead of her.

'Isn't it?' she said – and it occurred to me that she had touched me with her snail hand.

19

No, I am not going to apologize. Are my readers better than I am? The young man frightened and debt-ridden lying for a loan? The father impatient with his son? The cloacal bookthief in his capacious coat? The doctor rubbing uncertain hands? The disappointed wife who might like the way my hero sounds, the way whales sound in the deep? No, no. Do not wish for fleshier, better endowed statues. And do not love my MacBeth. This is a book. You appreciate the fellow, palpate him in your mind.

For you see – and this is not entirely a trick of speech – accounts like mine help one to know in secret another life. Oh, faithful spouses and unfaithful, glance up at those around you! Count your intimacies. Weigh them. Absurd task, defeatist talk, but for those who experienced sudden shrunkenness, why, here is my view of my friend. And for those of you who love in the particular – as he did, with an inexhaustible air of delighted discovery – let me embrace you, now, here, on this paper. Undoubtedly reading is the humblest and most imaginative of acts. I salute you. Do not worry at my generosity, but see the part of art, it is no more, that makes me unrepentant; blood surges and however much I value love I am unable to forget the rider.

Did I regret this? The spurs and spurt? Of course I did! But I could not sustain an exalted world. Or even one of spores. How brief, that is to say, how much time I have spent screwing up my courage to say it! How much time I have spent scraping my mind for some prime cause or explanation! When was the moment in which the ineradicable nature of my natterjack fate was settled? I do not know. Realization, in its coming, was by definition too late. The hot wax dripped, a brisk seal came down and as the stuff cooled – so quickly! – I looked up at the once and always uxorial man by the window.

A low view of life? Not at all. See my Uncle Hugh peel a pear. Come, let's sit. Here is Uncle dwarfing his fruit. He is furtive? Not really, a private hunch would be better for his position. A nice white plate. A silver knife. Now start. Clockwise, his blade eddying slowly over the swells and dips, he bares the ripeness, slicing from the white glistening flesh a curling corkscrew of pale freckled green. He blinks. I am a bachelor my dear, and rather lonely. Give me another pear and leave me my pleasures. You are *not* going to eat it? After all that care and trouble? You are going to let it go *brown*?

A cheap assault on dignity and morals? Then you are a poltroon, a pervert and a fool. Yes, you. No right of redress? How dare a book read like this? Shame on you. You will not be quick for ever. And what happened to toad? I did say I was singular – though look around, do. I never had much time for prim fylfots or grunting normans. My cosy glove is entirely at your disposal. Sword or pistol – it's the same end. Such as you may gnaw and chew the paper since you paid for it. (Bookthieves, see above.) Or try to find another creature. Natterjack is mine.

Justification by attack? Not that either. For I am conscious, reader, that neither of us has anything but centuries of death ahead. An ancient conceit but one still not moribund. It does not stop me wriggling now, as worms or flames will wriggle in us, in efforts to fix my unrequited love on this paper. And believe me, to be unrequited leaves all this, however frenetic or vulgar, unrequited – and I assure you I regret that much more than the germane but altogether lesser fact that the love of my life was embodied in another, marvellous, male.

How many times? How many times have I wished to cradle him in my arms, with cautious, crackling haste . . . but that is the mere swell of dream, Cicero's chicken skin cooked, a dull dog musing at a corner. The question is, how many times before I became conscious of what I was doing? I blushed. I blushed twice. Reader, I was a ridiculous twenty-five years old before I surprised myself. How extraordinary. How simple. I walked to the window he had just left and, aided by light and the reflection of a tree, examined the thing there, the ten years of friendship, the smiles and murmurs and, watching at least my reflected hands take on the energy of confident exposition, a previous disinterest not so much in males as in the workings of any kind of sex at all. This should have been difficult but was not. Subsequently I did not object. Once the notion was introduced, had ensconced itself in a snug corner of my mind, I found I enjoyed it, the prospect, the vein, everything. And once I had imagined it, I could not rid myself of the image. A surfeit of fantasy? A youthful habit of admiration tripping over its own growth? Possibly. But it was certain I never wished to spoil that new secret and uproarious enjoyment I felt when I spied him. It is possible my eyes bulged when I welcomed him. My lips may have parted slightly. But let me make this absolutely clear: this was an internal business. I never simpered outwardly. I would never ever have touched MacBeth nor made some ghastly approach. Indeed, even now I flinch from imagining it, the approach that is. And I certainly did not go about in a state of fantastic lust. Natterjack lust tires, fantasy droops and my pleasures were more servile and almost invariably gained via pen and paper. It is true I sometimes rewarded myself with a little daydream after a particularly hard stint but that soon became, as it were, after the honeymoon and rather traditional and wifely; wanting to tidy him up, comb his hair. Give him a fat kiss.

I appreciate it: intimate revelations of this kind can make for a stark mix. Your narrator still has some matters to discuss however. Do not skip.

My second reaction was to wonder if I were homosexual. And why not? I set to work to imagine further. But in the end I am not inclined to believe that capabilities of imagination say very much about physical capabilities. Some matters, I repeat, you cannot unimagine. Others vanish. No, my so-called sex life has in indifferent practice been unique and female and I have never felt attraction to any other member of my sex, and surely the word to describe me, which I took years to find, is mis-sexual.

Who will howl? The moon moons through the reeds, the slightest of shudders and then a cool riffle of breeze refreshes many varieties of amphibian.

Yes, yes, those with a declared or undeclared interest will smile. But the fact is I shy from the lumpen details of love and even have some sympathy for those gentle readers who may

78

ask why I cannot dwell on more pleasant matters, celebrating my love if I have to, but do it clearly, hating obfuscation, within a framework of unsaid things. But I think one confusion is enough.

And yes, it can be asked if my love was chosen for its very hopelessness. I will admit that what I glimpsed in a cave very likely began my adventure. It may be my jealousy was of a bizarrely inclusive sort. But what matters here is what I made of it. And given my discreet circumstances, my life, my work, what I soon wanted, courtesy of an ant-like size, was to wander through his bloodstream, examine the power of his heart, review his glossy, convoluted innards. How I should have loved to get hold of a good piece of his skin (not the peeled-off scrap after sunburn) and hold it up to the light! How I would have enjoyed tenderly tracing the run of each of the prominent veins on his arms, or down a leg or round the swell of a calf. I can perfectly understand the desire to bathe a loved one's beautiful feet. Bubbling soap, soft towelling. He was a young hairy statue, a nice preposterous image that nonetheless shows something of my mincing pleasure. Imagination is a loving butcher. Marble of course can give something of the delicacy and discretion of skin, the stretch, living parchment fed by capillaries, sustained by sinew, plumped by muscle. His eyes were green, his hair almost black, with a tendency to curl. His habitual expression was mildly sleepy, mildly amused. And my love, my desire to possess him, is the nearest to an absolute I have known. I loved his past, present – and future. That jaw that would acquire a pelican pouch, that thickening arm hair, the slight carelessness that would creep, was creeping into his appearance, letting the hair on his head get too long, not being quite scrupulous enough with razor and nail scissors. There, at the nose, in the ears – though I enjoyed the hairs on his neck. We love the reflection of ourselves says one of those tedious ancient essayists. Simpleton. How often have I looked at myself in the mirror, immaculately dressed and brushed fastidiously but wearily at my jacket shoulders? And why were there times that I was almost driven to melting, wanting to wipe away, very tenderly, a fleck of gummy spittle that collected at the left corner of his mouth? How I would

79

have loved him to be ill, get him his bedpan, wipe away pale pus.

And of course what I most wanted was to enter his mind, squat in his brain, look out of his eyes, luxuriate in his desires, fondle his conditionals, feel the tautness of his decisions, paddle in his daydreams, guard against any pain. Toad in a cranium. Now possible for realists. Accommodating myself to a bone bowl. I cannot help it. Do natterjacks eat worms? I think they do. This part, for readers who like skins and maps, is the yellow dorsal marking. Do natterjacks have a keen sense of smell? I think they may.

20

I think that, were I to write the consanguineous novel fraternal writers tell us we have in us, I should at least toy with examining the fantasies people live by. I don't so much mean the private phantoms that trot out dreamy routines for us as their effect on our part in the altogether stiffer and more public waxworks. Or to put it for those who appreciate this kind of thing: God found his material in clay, man digs in his own ear for wax and picks his eye for grit. I remember visiting someone who had suffered a heart attack. He told me that as he had lain on the floor he had thought – 'What is one supposed to do now?' Of course, a review of life. This has promptly vanished into the question – 'Have I been happy?' and that into – 'For how long?' The answer came to him with stunning and automatic precision – 'Two minutes and thirty-four seconds.'

Just for a moment there I thought I had met another toad in someone unexpected. Conditions make toads? But then I understood he was rehearsing a social sort of fantasy – Duff wished to be unassuming, conventional and dashing all at the same time. I muttered whatever it was he wanted to hear – not 'for goodness' sake, a soft-boiled egg gets more', but a 'do get better' – and gave him an appreciative smile.

On second thoughts, having, I presume, left him listening to me as a fantasy tuning-fork, I was intrigued by how little his relations with women had entered on his notional time of happiness. Or perhaps, I do not know, he was recalling and counting only prime orgasmic pangs, mere fractions of ecstasy. I doubt it. After a heart attack fantasies tend more to the social than the personal.

But let us see. Was it merely coincidence that I was promoted to be Duff's safety net? If he was a womanizer of pathological proportions, what was I? Less I think of an indistinct sexual identity and more of a doucie, conscientious complement. Perhaps at the very beginning I did consider the possibility that the pressures of his job made him require frequent outlets. But I soon tended to the opinion that the job was merely a convenient cover, to be shed with rapidity whenever his main purpose rose. Female buttocks swinging into view, the slightest evidence of bounce in a female breast and the poor man (who was fifty) would wizen up his face, his lids would droop, the corners of his mouth would twitch and creep upwards and he would convert into a suited satyr. He would be out from behind his desk and away from foreign currencies even in mid-sentence.

His trust in me was absolute and he took me completely for granted. Actually I do not think that is quite true. I do not think he gave it a thought. His risk-taking (with women and places, not currencies) was insane. In irritable mood I once estimated that each of his ejaculations entailed at least five lies from me. He hated going away on holiday and would, instead, come into the office for his and expect everyone to know. While nominally with his family he had utterly abandoned them. Seduction money came first and he had a taste for what he called 'little pendants' (a silver chain with something attached). I did once meet his wife, an impression of bleached plum fuzz and macerated skin, and his children, like extenuated seal pups in a slow, sullen swell, when they came in in an effort to obtain more consistent maintenance. They all lived in the same house. A cheerful Duff asked me to handle it, tried a few jokes on his eldest son – 'not much going on there', turning to me – and then recommended a new restaurant where the waitresses were 'encouragingly kitted out'. And yet everybody liked him! I was told he had once been good-looking, but I suspect, from a young woman presumably in a position to know, that the aspect I knew, all sleek-topped beef and eyes almost folded away, went well for him. She described his desire as 'touchingly uncomplicated' and his impatience as 'exhilarating'. So be it. I did once speak of him to MacBeth in a tone more amused than complaining, would have been interested to examine the element of humour in his seductions, but quickly gathered my friend thought I was being over-personal. Extraordinary chemistries!

Some are made for deference. What was I doing apart from covering up? What strikes me as I, without the benefit of a heart attack, look back on my life is how much time I managed to spend on fantasy. On the whole enjoyable times. They gave me a sense of much-needed balance. They gave me help in appreciating the fantasies round me. Help in separating mine out. Note please I am speaking in a discreet, functional way, from a practical point of view and only at a certain level, and in dealing with certain matters, usually contiguous, usually representative. Ask a portrait painter. Or even the legal profession.

Quine is a dialect word meaning girl I think and it probably comes from quean and queen. This is entirely by the way since I did not know of this when the word first came to me, possibly as private compensation for Duff's gonadal ways, as a convenient title and shorthand for my condition. And the fact that the word and sound may be familiar to some readers does not confuse that private meaning. A combination of whine and queen, queer and pine? I do not mind and it does not really matter, historically I mean. And I must also face the fact that Quine is a surname, of a philosopher amongst others, something of an indeterminist I gather. Well, well, I face it and nothing, I assure you, is reflected or intended outside my own world.

Quine then was a creature of containment, an entity, my love, its expression and, later like all this, the bloated sac that kept us apart. I nurtured the thing like a pot plant. Healthy or unhealthy (quite, of course), there are also aspects here of fat blisters caused by insistent rubbing, of umbilical cords and possibly even of placenta. I seem to remember that charlatans and others use sheep placenta in beauty and rejuvenation treatments. Perhaps Quine kept me young-looking? At any rate I had this emotional extrusion, a ghostly, secret hernia. And for a period, reader, of fifteen years, my sporadic Quine was an amusing companion and, in that balance I mentioned previously, had a role, a happy, disgusted one as an enemy of pretension and, despite his appearance, was a shrewd and earthy friend. I say appearance because I definitely saw Quine. Quine was a replete white, a gleaming, greasy lichee white and in shape varied from a stuffed intestine to a much larger, bladderish swelling with thin, puffy skin and the drunken movement of a maggot. Quine was not anthropomorphic, was well nigh featureless, but communicated well enough by the look of him, just before the limit of my eye where the slaughterhouse and seance begin, and by his shape and drift. Quine would float by if I began to ramble. He had a game of which he never tired, of interposing himself between MacBeth and me so that I had to peer through his distended membrane and sweetbreads – an early living pane. I indulged Quine. I thought fondly of Quine. I once even called my wife my Quine in an exceptionally absent-minded moment.

'You haven't been so tender for ages,' she said, 'but isn't that rather . . . strong?'

'Strong? No, no.' What could she have been thinking of?

No, Quine squeaked when rubbed but was quite happy to be my companion as a companion. After a time, when Duff was resting (not often), I began, very formally and cautiously, stepping out into a self-effacing ritual of polished toe-caps and fingernails, refined chatter and small portions of well-presented food. I am choosing these words with one eye on the service and a tongue as smooth as new leather soles. In effect I became ticket partner and chaperone to two career ladies quite a lot older than this toad. In justice of course they were very different but I wish to mention here my friend's (silent) thumbrule that my pair were at bottom megraine and vim or, for the difference, vain and megrim, but also to point out the almost literary luxury inherent in the relationships. With

Quine tagging along on a string, to open another door and allow them to pass, rustling, towards the sound of pre-theatre coughing or that of cellos warming up.

But amongst the things I learned was that there were certain aspects of women, particularly the soft ageing tissue about the eyes or the maturing set of the mouth or the movement of wrists and hands, that in the demurest of ways I enjoyed very much. Without comment, one of my ladies once slapped my fingers for following hers too closely. And I remember allowing the other one to paint my lips one Friday evening and her intentness and her firm, milkmaid's grip of my chin, her puzzlement (what had she expected?) and the cloying feel of the perfumed scarlet stuff before she wiped it off. And another thing was the organization of manners which, while not a small matter, is an exquisitely limited one. And then my youthful appearance and another promotion made me less obviously biddable, less charming as a continent, dapper companion.

Quine himself, of course, hung on, sometimes subsiding, sometimes swelling, sometimes, in a balloonish gesture, raising his eyes heavenward. There were times he looked bilious for me. And I remember he once had the stretched greenish colour of a fat, veined gooseberry. But finally I had to forsake Quine in Rome. I wished to be unencumbered. I buried Quine in a sardonic little ceremony; I imagined his desire to escape, a heap of earth, my respectful stance. Self-pity buried alive? You misread me. I was not sardonic enough. By that time – otherwise blinking and twitching – Quine had been transmogrified into something rubbery and rippling and too like the nasty club on playing cards here, an ulcerous-looking shellelagh. Unpleasant tic, breath bad from fear – I remember Quine with comparative innocence.

21

When I watched exchange rates jostle, my written numerals took on a runic dash, stick-like, but onto paper as fast as you can hear the click of beads on an abacus. Incidental? Of course. But I know that toads and natterjacks breathe, in part, through the pores. Skins thinks. And if my job with Duff glistened as a surface film, in stretches of quickly coloured nowness, my next was all slow, underwater ponder. It was, to furnish this pond a little more, to move from the level of the pond-skater to that of the diving-bell spider. The plan was for me to work under the legalist I have already mentioned but, in his finicky, melo-dramatic way, he only had time for his contracts. I do not mean he was happy to let me do as I liked; he was unhappy if I bothered him at all. Backstage with him.

Reader, I became by deflection and default and a large degree of willingness, the pragmatic administrator, the quiet, scrupulous fellow you see when something goes wrong with your pay, there are no pencils, your child is sick, you are unhappy, you are not sure how new legislation affects your taxes or, heaven forbid, your wife has run away, your wife has died. And not for the first time I found that chores others consider tedious and unwelcome were to me exhilarating. More or less wide-eyed, I paid closer attention as to why and how people work. In a firm there is self-deception, a little idleness, elephantine resentment, struggle, rather more interesting when silent than noisy and, occasionally, some grossly undervalued competence. I even shared personal prob-lems, being impressed I think by the amount of pain claimed rather than the often considerable pain itself. Information comes in strands. I gathered quite a nest of the stuff before I began tentatively calibrating what I had. Behind this were possible improvements to the enterprise. Discreetly, I talked over possible knots and likely links with MacBeth. I think, perhaps, he was at first amused by my particularity and my attention to detail. Some new door-handles, for example, were sleeve-catchers. But how much had they cost? Why was the same builder always used? He blinked. Well, did he know the state of the employee's pension fund? It did not take him long to encourage me, certainly in the less personal matters, and we would talk over my thoughts on walks, in his garden, going back and forward between sundial and pond, this last the usual undersized sort of thing with a few water-lilies and a couple of fish.

But to return to my point. Working with Duff and foreign monies had lent me a certain off-hand, cavalierly servant touch. As an increasing dealer in discretion and secrets, occasionally privy to the most startling confessions, I grew first self-conscious, then began to wake to a feeling that I myself was being uncovered. At four in the morning, bedclothes tossed aside, lamp still lit, work papers on the floor, chilled, tired, a considerable pressure in my bladder, I would come to on the floating seed of an anxiety with the implication of a gross root. I would shiver and yawn, and shiver again. Surely I have made it clear that I regretted the sexual turn to my love? I tried to be resolute, find something satisfyingly derisory in my guilt and an enchanting rigour in good sense. Notice my practicality! My sharp-pointed pencils! MacBeth secreted, Quine securely anchored, I was shortly and firmly opening doors on the most honourably intentioned meetings with a person exactly five years older than I, a shy, slender person who had passed very competently through a temporary substitution in my corridor.

I had thought of calling her Irene (the seeker after peace). Or perhaps Io (for injustice and hundred-eyed monsters). But I have settled on Iris (for the unavoidably aqueous humour in my eye). And I am going to draw this quite as fine as the tendrils of gold in the brooch I gave her a day or so after I had proposed marriage and been accepted, even after the brooch had transferred to her dam's left dug, because our marriage would have been an excellent and tender one and we had made years of plans. She would, I am convinced, have changed and saved my life. But she had already – one night of laboured breathing, with the soughing of the trees and a rattle of rain on the window panes – given her promise to and had it snapped up by her robust and repulsive old mother, coffin before wedlock.

Any number of schemes and promises failed to open the lid or break the lock – a phrase that I have decided to keep as apt expression of the bad-tempered stalemate that ensued. The old woman was utterly unmovable, enjoyed my gloomier sketches of her future poverty and my contortions as I sought to bind myself to some formula of nurses and lawyers that would satisfy her. Her sighs I read like tea-leaves. I only ever managed to startle her twice, as it happens both times within a minute.

'But you're too frightened to die,' certainly hit a nerve, on the upper right cheek, just below the eye.

'You can't shock me.'

I sat a while, listening to the beat of the blood in my ears, before giving in.

'And if I SHOUTED?' certainly made her start. This is a use of what I believe poets call sound-sense – but in those circumstances, as unworthy as a grunt.

The old witch is, not so incidentally, the only person I have ever wanted to kill – by popping one of her pillows over her face and then sitting on it. I admit, that was a quick sleepy harnessing a few moments before coming awake on disappointment and a fading memory of her grubby bed linen. I was not up to manhandling her. I was sweating and rather breathless. I was – oh, very mildly – disgusted by having slept restlessly and a perfectly normal physiological affair. Really no link, just sticky. I am not sure whether in the dream I was not squatting on the pillow, excitedly sucking a thumb.

But by then, of course, I was already beaten. One Saturday I pointed out to Iris that simply by opening the door, now, we could close it – I had arranged everything – an hour later as man and wife. Now, mind. I believe she saw the door opening. She certainly saw the ageing papers and the gold band I produced from my pocket. Her hand went to her throat. I told her we did not need the trappings of a wedding. We needed the papers. From my point of view a wedding night holding hands by mother's bed inhaling hard on pill dust and warm, milky vapours would have done quite splendidly. I reached for the doorknob and pulled. It was raining lightly and a soft breeze came in. I grabbed her coat and draped it over her shoulders. Now. But she could not get her biggish feet to move. And we stood, both of us looking at them as at torpid but independent life. I made one last effort, seizing her hand and pulling her forward. But I simply added momentum to her collapse, her coat flopped and I was shortly carrying her through to the sofa accompanied by reedy, querulous demands from above.

'What are you doing to her?'

A veritable splatter of replies came to me but she did not give me time to believe she was really interested.

'There's a draught,' she went on. 'Someone must have left a door open. Shut it. Go on.'

No need. In due if lengthy course the relationship ended, ostensibly on my reiterated offers of sorely needed money. The daughter accused me, understandably if not quite accurately, of trying to buy my way into that stink of stale old body, sugary linctus and maturing urine. I held out my hand to show there was nothing in it. Please go. It's for the best. Fact: I left quietly, saw myself out.

I have given nearly four years five shortish paragraphs. Count them as the dregs of the affair. But apart from habit, what made me continue with her for so long? The hope of timely death of course. But there was also Iris's refinement that kept me. We still, after all that time, shook hands, though the matter went from the conventional placing of her fingers in mine to a manoeuvre that began at the inner wrist and slid gently down the palm to linger at the fingertips, the trembling whole in five swings of the pendulum clock by the door. Oh, I could conjure up such pleasant pictures of us! Perhaps too there was an element of exasperated competition with the mother that served as love for the daughter. I would have fed her up. I would have continued to be solicitous and kind during her frequent headaches – though I suspected to the point of surety that these would vanish when her ruthless, selfish, quivering old mother was dead in her box. Amateur coffin designers! You will know how I felt! I would not have touched a coarse, sparse hair on that aged head but I would have lavished golden gargoyles on her coffin.

But finally and far more important was Iris's moral rectitude – of which her loyalty was such a part – that held and fascinated me. Was I cruel to persist? Very like, but the frustration was particularly galling because it was my brain and not my testes that commanded and I could see very clearly, as clear as an axonometric drawing – clear and clean as a spiral staircase – that she was the answer to more than one troublesome equation. From soulmate to checkmate.

Whatever happened to her? I do not know. When just about off to Rome and frantically busy she suddenly came to mind. It was easy to imagine that mother had finally died and that Iris had joined loneliness and rank laundry baskets as assistant matron in a genteel girls' school. That and an abrupt memory of her personal cleanliness made my eyes smart. But come, let's not overspread the thing. I had mountains of work and other loyalties. I have saved till last the circumstances of my first proposal of marriage, the only real one I ever made.

The place was a small zoo, a muddy enterprise that turned out to have its roots in a more squalid tradition than I had hoped. We saw an aged lion, its coat leaking sawdust, an immense tortoise claimed to be at least a hundred and fifty years old, some rattling porcupines, a moulting ostrich, and then approached a cluster of stone-based cages. In one of these was one of the dowdier members of the baboon tribe. I had a first impression of hunched hair and a plasticine striped muzzle but my attention was then distracted by an elderly, red-cheeked man in a white coat who contrived to tiptoe past us while carrying two milk buckets full of raw horse meat. The baboon turned out to be a masturbating male. Jism swung from the skinny gnarled stick – it resembled woody asparagus with a sea-anemone red tip. A few spurts. Well, well. I was about to ask Iris if the aquarium might be warmer and more interesting – a signpost in the form of a blue hand pointed the way – when I noticed that the animal gave no sign of satiety or even pause; instead, with the aplomb of a basic pianist, the other hand dipped into the simple rhythm and scooped up a taste. A flushed young man nearby was attempting, by means

89

of grimaces at the animal and fierce, pleading, sidelong glances at Iris, to get the baboon to consider propriety. I read the plaque – a perfunctory taxonomy with a coloured patch on a cut-out of Africa and quite a bit of the Indian ocean – and Iris smiled towards the big-eared fox. The balding young man grimaced himself almost blind and his left hand jerked clear of his body to spank hard at the air. The baboon screamed, did a cartwheel backwards over its puffed pink satin and blister bum, to turn again, pumping faster, hissing, performing a small proferring rush unmistakably towards the only female spectator.

Iris smiled graciously and moved on. I blinked. The baboon was still pistoning, the yellow teeth exposed in a rictus, the absurd young man had clutched at his thinning hair – and I moved on too, round the corner to some variety of squirrel, a lump of dozing, smelly fur.

'Let's leave,' she said.

'What?'

'Poor animal in that cage. Did you see it had been biting itself?'

I grunted.

'I'm sorry,' she said, 'it's expensive too, isn't it?'

'Of course it's not.' I was reminded – though why then? – in the name of malekind or apes, of ginger hairs, steam and mountainous folds of flesh. And my eyes, whether I liked it or not, were pointed at her fawn-coloured lap.

'Come now,' I said shakily, as my eyes dropped to her feet, 'it's not so bad.'

I shut my eyes, lifted my head and opened them again. I found – I blinked – that she was tenderly leaning forward to offer to my kiss the inside of her lower lip, a gesture at once delicate and, given the circumstances, rather splendid. I saw it, however, with a congested gloom, round which surprise sped and dissipated. And the subsequent supping of her bland saliva was jolted when her dangling hand touched mine, knuckle on knuckle, a shock which made my hand jump, then hasten to take hers. We turned and strolled on, I listening and feeling through her hand the decrease and steadying of her pulse. Suddenly, by the giraffe, it quickened. Lively, apparently happy, she raised her sensible shoes ballet style, one slipper, two slippers, in front of that marvellously long, maculate neck. I felt abruptly damp, as if my spine had gone tacky, were about to melt and trickle out, pin-in-egg fashion through my coccyx.

'Mmm?' she said.

I felt a tremendous fear, of losing her, reader, of breaking down, almost cricked my neck jerking my head at the converted bandstand.

'Yes, why not?' she said.

And it was there, on rickety chairs, by crates, in a sort of stacked summer, that I leant on the table and waited, for the scraping feet of an assumed waiter, once, twice, with steam warming my nose and my swallowing well nigh into gobbling, to ask her quickly, please, marry me and then watched her stopped tongue and throat and lips.

And I will not forget, ever, her smile and nod and the consequent leap of pleasure, heart and hope in me and her suppressed grin at my reaction and my still utterly unprescient disbelief, expounded half-stutter, half-croak, which did make her laugh out loud and slide her hand across the table. I took it and traced again and again the delicate run of her veins.

No, the past is not a zoo. Yes, there are certain stark links and inconveniences and juxtapositions in the circumstances of truth. She was the person to share with and cherish and please.

'We'll have to tell Mother,' she said.

'Of course we will,' I replied, smiling, coaxing her veins a little higher.

22

Protected by studies and rank, the fact of them worn like a fence, those houses of bones and the six pounds or so each of skin, the board members, much preferred a degree of dignity unmatched by any serious risk of responsibility. Unwonted?

Come now. Comfortable in theoretical discomfort, tailored to a pattern of consensus and imposition, they would wash their hands of business before lunch. I was privileged nonetheless, in addition to my other duties, to be given a task by these gentlemen and, at the same time, was also privileged to see them profoundly piqued. I had, of course, previously witnessed something of their virile world of politic chit-chat, the complacently gorged possibilities, the shifty royal we, the self-satisfied advice, the essentially egalitarian nature of non-egalitarian aspirations, and was now entranced by the verbal carnal-carnage, the furious blinks and open pores of these testicle-nesting nestors of the game. The game in this case resembled a spluttering sort of court tennis in which the wooden bats were unsprung, spiteful gargoyles spouted balls and live bats fell from the walls when struck to constitute crawling black banana skins on the floor. Rats and snakes were tossed in (though not at the toad in the corner), our side had too many players, the exact purpose of the game was unclear and grunting and thrashing noises came from alarmed elderly gentlemen. The language of an incendiary? Merely that of an observer watching and evaluating. This was the first time I ever saw Duncan frightened, possibly by all that tenebrous rage in his own board.

The matter here was incomplete but what was suspected was that the loss of two large accounts to a rival firm had *some* of its explanation in a number of damaging rumours too many and too sustained not to be organized. I admit, this natterjack was intrigued both as to the nature of the rumours themselves and by the tactic. It was entirely coincidence that attention was drawn to me when a message was delivered, informing me that my Uncle Hugh was dead. He had, just before graduation, summoned me to his house, a grey place on flat land by a little loch.

'My heir,' he said. 'You.'

'No need.'

'No one else,' he said and sat there, a bowl of fruit beside him, blinking unhappily.

The board gave me condolences and returned to business. The idea of delegation came up, some demented stratagems were offered but the only tedious difficulty was the legalist's desire to sue. Subsequently I saw MacBeth who had been placed in charge of acquiring new replacement business but I did not discuss the matter with him. We both did well.

At the board meeting I had heard some extraordinary suggestions, including physical violence, sabotage and an excitable scheme to put the guilty in compromising positions (calls, letters, prostitutes; delightful to *hear* such thoughts spoken), and these I passed on over lunch with someone from across the square. I sounded amused, he certainly laughed, and as he listened I watched to see whether or not mention of these schemes would be enough to quash the gossip. Rumour-mongers are rarely prepared to sacrifice themselves and toads are well schooled in the insinuating and the oblique. I certainly insinuated – though whether or not he accepted my points is another matter. He was happy to agree about old buffers and he really did not think there would be any more problems – or rumours of our financial difficulty. We shook hands. I then set about recovering as much business as I could. This was not as difficult as it may seem. Businessmen, particularly those in charge of pension funds, are unhappy with drastic, whole-funded decisions. I merely took advantage of the natural swing to caution, a natural dislike of rumour, and happily agreed a compromise; my only problem was with Duncan, for not only accepting but praising a policy of spreading their risks. All told we recovered funds that represented $117\frac{1}{2}$ of the original 200, had the revenge of seeing a further 25 taken away from our rivals (and given to another) and I easily managed to dish my lunch partner (by indiscreetly sounding out whether or not we could poach him, in particular, to one of *his* old buffers). MacBeth had considerable success in the south so that within weeks of the first rumours, 200 had become (forgive these figures) 340.

Pleased? Yes. But toads in general I think, natterjacks certainly, are unhappy at the idea of triumph. I do remember however an instance of domestic hubris, when standing by MacBeth shortly afterwards he correctly identified five out of six words that guests would choose for Lula's by now tedious insistence on dumb crambo before they played.

'I'm sorry. What were you saying? Ah, I know what it is! Poor woman can't spell!'

No, natterjacks dislike the exercise of pride but they do know what contempt is. And that starts thoughts that nag at them. I suppose one was how a glum old invert who had offered me no refreshment after my trip – indeed, had said nothing else – and who had never noticeably worked could leave such a sum. But thank you Uncle Hugh – I acquired a pretty mews house and very much enjoyed setting it up. It was the scene for my later plans with Iris, particularly that staircase.

And the other matter that nagged? Let us say biological arrangements of wealth. The family firm. Whose family? That is exactly the right question. Part of the information I had gathered in my office was an old-fashioned biographical account of shareholdings and family trusts, the which, carefully sifted, produced some incidentals (how cock-aloft Duff, for instance, sheltered behind his venerable grandmother's holding) as well as matters more germane to the conjunction I made out. The ramifications of a positive wood of gnarled, twisted, sometimes stunted and in some cases lightning-struck family trees would be tedious to trace. Likewise all the calculations I made. No, I am not going to suggest you look through branches at stars and possible configurations. My point is this. I do not believe it had ever occurred to MacBeth that he would not, at some time, occupy Duncan's chair; my gift was the feasibility of sharpening his traditionally limited and commanding notion of service into that of singular and personal control.

Was I overwrought? Had I been working too hard? Was the plan fragile because so complex? I must certainly report a degree of reluctance in me, a foot-dragging when I was up and formally awake. Somehow, especially after Iris, my tremendous desire to please MacBeth did not please me. It is absurd to blame a lover for the failure of a substitute. Even so. My plan had a gossamer gleam. I dulled it. And truculent Taha frowned and sighed a great deal and in costly self-inflicted scunner had the new decoration in one room of the mews house completely changed, from a pale silky grey to pale ochre and yolk, before imparting his idea to the only person he could. I was much too economical in the presentation. Or perhaps cantankerous pride made me less laconic than cryptic. Who can read the warts on a natterjack's back? MacBeth nodded all right but his eyes showed no understanding. Instead he put his hand round his stepson's neck, the gesture of an affectionate but very careful strangler. It was as if he measured the boy's physical progress in how much neck he could enclose. I had the slightly alarming sight of his fingers slowly waving as they sought a little more of that pale column. The boy's eyes hovered as if near sleep. Irritated, I expounded some more. MacBeth's eyebrows came up. How we want people we love to understand us without rigmaroles! At length, getting my passion down into a precise hiss, I got over to him what I had discovered, deduced and arranged into a pattern. As soon as I had I felt queasy. No, no, the shades were off his eyes – a confident, mildly unattractive cupidity in them – but there was also that mulling quality, as of slow, sensual musing, which meant he would never be rushed. He asked me precisely two questions: on the dire relations between two brothers and on costs. He raised his chin and narrowed his eyes. Could he think about it?

Do I sound premonitorily peevish? Well now, let's see what we can do, shall we? A respectable fortnight later, on a long lawn, on my fourth, perhaps fifth, flute of champagne, it was Gruoch who approached me and directly told me that MacBeth would not be pursuing my plan. Behind her the flower-bed became a rash of garish pinks. I transferred my attention to my glass and had my eyebrows rise with the slower bubbles.

'Disappointed?'

'No,' I replied. Correctly. I was offended.

At which she cocked her head at me and gave me a tender, lopsided smile. I particularly dislike womanly compassion when it is directed at some indifferent concept of male pride. Oh, you can communicate by the eyes. And here, reluctantly, I read that he so valued my friendship that he could not bear to tell me himself. The sensitivity that requires go-betweens!

'It is really quite all right,' I said.

'Are you sure?'

I blinked. Was that a touch of exultance there?

'Of course I am!'

She smiled. 'I'm not sure I haven't had far too much to drink. And you?'

'I have absolutely no doubts at all.'

At which my friend's wife smiled again, leant closer and bedded out a kiss on my thin lips. It had something of earth and dark pansies in it.

'Thank you,' she said.

'My pleasure.'

Yes, I was, later of course, to understand that they had translated my fiddle, hunch and careful calibrations. From their point of view what I had done was to declare and demonstrate an exhilarating degree of loyalty towards MacBeth. At a simple, adult level, egged him on. And the fact remains, all that information had many uses.

But as I stood there on that over-kempt lawn what first came to mind? After almost half my life then, nearly fifteen years, I remembered that chill water dripping from slimy grey earthenware. Oh reader, that was quite the last time in my life I was ever drunk. Alcohol disinhibits? In my case alcohol has miserable if somewhat pointless effects on my nervous system and emotions, too easily degenerates into a scheme of abject thought, slippery throat and a cess-pit beneath. The stuff also works on my tear ducts. It also prevented me from seeing the only real little cloud there. That pointed head, that louring look; surely Lula was too old to be capering in that flat-footed way?

'We've tried,' said Gruoch.

'What's that?'

'To have more.'

It was a frown and a wrench but I think I succeeded in looking sympathetically grave. Natterjacks are fascinated by juxtaposition. How much of this was drunken? Surely she wasn't subverting all my intricate calculations to some hereditary nonsense. How cruelly, if wistfully, matter of fact. In any case I have always found it hard to summon up any positive desire to propagate my flesh. I remember my father as the apologetic sort, who thought he had imposed on me. Against that, there did seem to be a lot of children, as it were, leaking through elsewhere. This is a pathetic observation, I know, however avuncularly put, but I still cannot understand the eagerness to take an interest in propagating another soul, an intimate half but, from observation, mostly a matter for patience and the acceptance of strange, lumpen reflections.

'Will you risk more champagne?' asked Gruoch.

'Oh, I really think not.'

Mind you, I had sometimes enjoyed playing the small boy to MacBeth. Discreetly though. And he bore his own childlessness quietly, though combined with Gruoch's attitude this added up to a garrulous stoicism.

'You've never thought of it?'

'What?'

'Marriage and children.'

'I am very bad at choosing the right kind of woman.'

Her eyes slid round. 'What? You've a taste for already married ladies?'

Really, the woman could be gross! 'No. The last one had an unfortunate mother.'

Her eyes widened. Yes, yes, she had drunk too. She let out a peal of laughter. But it was the *thoroughness* of it that showed me how much she took for granted that I would somehow see myself as ridiculous too.

23

Oh reader, when I think of the quantity of words that has poured out of me during my life, the pointless, thoughtless, inaccurate, presumptuous, unfair witter, I wince. How do other persons forget their cruelty to accuracy, their mistreatment of understanding or their pall on others? Am I alone in squirming at my fatuous mistakes? Does no one else groan in retrospect? I have two main reasons. I am haunted by shifting ghosts of unnecessariness. And never mind what others think, it is *my* opinion of my gaffes that hurts.

The law I think has certain time limits to do with offence, time and accountability. Though perhaps I am getting confused with the period required for a missing person to be declared dead for life assurance purposes and that business wherein human skin is supposed to take seven years to renew itself in entirety. In either case the policy and grave-marks are in a term. I could say then that my liking for quiet and neatness, my preference for the particular over the general and for the written over the spoken, is best indulged in solitude or with one other person. But my social reluctance is altogether less hale and riddled with memories of inglorious pauses and words as untoward lumps.

At any rate, when Duncan considered it a good idea for me to go out and eat with some of our clients, I demurred. I did not, I said, see why business should be overlaid with a varnish of chumminess. Besides, there were lots of others who liked that sort of thing. But in some distractedly huffy way Duncan seemed to want to cover up that first lunch of mine (in which my desire to quash the rumours of our insolvency was so intense it has displaced any memory of what was eaten) with a scattering of more casual, more expansive get-togethers.

'For heaven's sake, man,' he snapped, 'let the people we invest in get to know you!'

Circumspection is not practicality. I went along, I managed to avoid snorrels and inamicable muddles but I was obliged to the kind of dull experience I would have preferred to imagine. Take the word toast for example. Or hearty. I am immune to the kind of story offered. Though I did some humble learning, found out that indigestion could be much more than I had known and that behind the word heartburn lay a truly painful piercing sensation in the centre of my chest, impressive enough to stop any outward thought whatsoever. Duff had told me that his heart attack had felt like a flood tide, a shade warmer than lukewarm, that had rushed him into unconsciousness. But I also knew

MacBeth had come away with the impression that Duff's back had been on fire. The heat I felt was on my face and due to sheer alarm at the squeeze in the pain. I thought, did not dare think, that I was being struck down. The squeeze narrowed to a stiletto-shaped point and though I think I managed a social smirk or two, my fluttering efforts to sort out types of heart attack, angina for example, ceased; I assumed a passivity so complete even my meek pleading for the pain to stop hung back. I raised the linen napkin to my lips.

Did anyone notice? Let me put it another way. It is, over a period of eighteen months or so, three or four times a month, difficult to avoid sorely unsuitable food when food is most of the hospitality offered, others have carefully chosen the menu and conversation takes second place to chomping and swallowing. I had not previously given the gauge and twist of my intestines much thought. As at that lamb with mushroom, bilberry and port sauce. I did not believe that date and grape and fig could be stuffed with foie-gras. Here an incredulous natterjack scrapes congealing grease off a lump of goose, there uses a sharp, serrated knife to snick almost raw beef and watch blood and fat ooze. Firms really should pay employees for stomach abuse. I soon began taking antacids before meals. And those desserts! Gaudy, quivering. Or that over-ripe mango covered in bitter chocolate! And now a small belch soars up my throat, finds my mouth clamped shut but barely needs more than one nostril to clear away all that appalling chest pain. The sound is more shrill sigh than snort. There is a chill sweat on my forehead, some of it from indignation. Heartburn is the most Ciceronian of jokers. I take out a handkerchief and wipe. My host gives me an appreciative wink.

At all those meals I was affable I think, tried to be discreetly abstemious and frugal, but was always attentive, always ready to smile and nod. Toads know they are toads but may forget how others see them. Only partly true. Those meals were usually masculine affairs but when women were included I was always happy to be placed beside them and to some extent shelter behind their restraint. As for other women, those with whom I had no business, all I ever knew was that some loathe toads enough to be cruel and surely I had no need to have that regurgitated on me again.

Do you remember that man who found a toad by his pupae? Towards the very end of my professionally chummy time his abandoned wife – who? Ah yes, didn't she marry again? Yes, yes, of course – asked to see me. Perhaps I was remiss in not wondering what she might want. In any case my secretary arranged my appointment directly after one of those meals which turned out to have double cream in each course and lots of flaming brandy.

I think it fair to say that I had stomach cramps, not helped by having to scuttle back to be on time, nor by almost knocking over her two daughters in the outer office. They were, though not twins, identically dressed and had the same wide, flat, unyielding faces and very sturdy legs. I can't ever have known their names. But I gave each a kiss and asked my secretary, a nervous old man with a mother, to take them out for something. What kind of thing? Ice-cream. With syrup if they want!

I popped an antacid on my tongue, assumed a smile and went into my office.

'Sorry I'm a little late,' I said.

But I had to look around for the girls' mother. She was standing in the corner behind the door, her back to me, hunched up, with no sign of her arms and hands. She turned. I saw that her fists were clenched and crossed over her chest, her eyes wide open and that her mouth was stretching into something long and appalled. I almost looked behind me. Oh God, I thought, she is about to scream. Then that the poor woman was on the point of violently throwing up. Instead, like a person born deaf, she let out a loud 'You!' and then, on the second inhalation, 'Don't know!'

Sweat sprang at my hairline much faster than I could arrange any thoughts.

'Are you all right?' I said.

She took a step towards me. 'Criminal!'

'What?'

'Stupid!'

But despite the violence in her words I still had not understood she was not on the point of collapse.

'Can I get you a glass of water perhaps?'

'*You've* done all right!'

'I'm sorry?'

'He *said* you were a crawler.'

'But who?'

'*That* is why I have come,' she said. And then she walked over and sat down in the visitor's chair. I closed one eye on her. I felt fagged and feeble.

Now without a doubt I am externally prim and internally abject. But let me treat the reader as I wish she had treated me. I had to squint through a tempest of details, to do with a disastrous second marriage and a complex financial mess, all given over with irate relish and a bizarrely complacent bitterness but with very little in the way of coherence. It was not until she fixed on the word 'destitute' that I felt able to clear my throat. She and her daughters were 'utterly destitute'.

What she meant, of course, was that she was broke and had probably gone into legally actionable debt. She had a listener ready to provide prompt and sensible help on representation, rescheduling and assistance just as soon as he had the pertinent information. But it was then that I understood that this, while germane to me, was somehow immaterial to her.

I think that 'criminal' and 'stupid' outburst was wild self-description. She meant the words, however, to justify her behaviour and reinforce her complaint. And it was *all* coming out. The gnashing of untended children's teeth mixed with pressing mortgage arrears and the trousers of forgetful men. She spent minutes on a shopkeeper's slight. I know it is hateful to have to ask but apart from getting behind my desk to show a willingness to help there was little else I could do except skook and twitch in time to her distress. I recalled the plain silver bowl I had sent her for her second wedding. Somewhere about the rumours her second husband was spreading about her a saturnine Quine bobbled by and I had to stifle an unexpected giggle. Endlessly incensed, my visitor sat hieratically, her hair as stiff and as glossy as ladybird wings when the creature has landed but not completed folding them in. Stop a moment. Let me just flick there.

What most impressed me I think was the constant vibration of fury in her, the throbs and twitches in the veins and tendons of her neck rising up into her face and head and that lacquered hair of hers. I found my eyes snatching at the saliva meteorites springing from her lips. I coughed. I scratched an eyebrow. But as she went inexhaustibly on I found, and this is why I am susceptible to superstitious thoughts on coincidence and ugly, small deities, that red spots were appearing in front of my eyes. I began to feel decidedly queasy.

A piercing voice can make a wine glass protest. I can only think the rage in hers found the pitch to make me shudder. A question of ear and balance perhaps. Straightaway I pushed a finger into my ear and waggled. I swallowed several times. I am an awfully polite natterjack, dread hectoring and emotional sounds. I may even have, momentarily, dozed off or passed out. My stomach churned. One of my melodramatic little images came to me: I saw my visitor sitting slackly on a bed in a soiled shift picking dry white scabs from a sheet. I could not bear it any more. I leapt up and within a moment was on my knees beside her. I do not know if I said anything. All I know is that her voice stopped and that there were several blessedly thick heartbeats of silence.

Still, as it were, breathing out, I grew aware that her knees under my hands had begun to quiver. I looked up, saw shocked eyes and understood, hideously late, that my action, press and pity, might have been misinterpreted. She stood even before I had time to open my mouth. She jerked to her feet so abruptly and furiously straight that there was no space left for me to go other than backwards. To stop myself falling, I grabbed. Since my head was already back I am not sure but I think my fingers first clutched about her hip bones and then got more purchase about her thighs. My back creaking, my face swung briskly into her skirt and a smell of cleaning fluid and a small puff of talcum powder. Helplessly, I snorted. Her body shuddered. My nose was rasped by the roughness of the material though I was conscious of a certain swooning satin or silk slipperiness underneath.

Of course I let go! I wanted nothing more than to give a weak hup and scrabble to my feet. But I next felt astoundingly sharp hurt on my head. I thought at once of her long, enamelled nails, that she was tearing my hair up by the roots. But the sensation – a repeated stabbing – was too excruciating for further enquiry.

Joints of mine clicked and squeaked. I got one sole on the floor and a stab on my wrist and just on the forearm side of my left elbow. In this half-squat and suitor position I still managed a backward waddle and upward heave that was halted by the edge of my fixed, hardwood desk at my seventh vertebra up.

Bent, with one hand pressed to my back, hapless pain droning out of me, I doddered round and dropped into my chair. My visitor and assailant, a waxwork of ineffectual murder with the tooth part of an ivory comb acting as a handle and the pointed handle as a dagger, was still staring at my ghost kneeling in front of her. A trickle of something from my pain-spotted head zig-zagged down to and round my ear to form a warm, wet blob behind the lobe. I stroked, brought out a thick red smear. I licked; a slightly metallic taste. I was then taken by a redoubled scunner. I am not sure why, I have never done so before or since, but I uncapped my pen and jabbed rather than dabbed the tip of the gold nib on my tongue. I took a sheet of paper and wrote in my firmest and neatest hand. I would apply for (1) emergency help for her (2) an additional sum for her children's education and teeth and (3) would enquire as to the possibility of funds to assist her in acquiring any training she saw fit. In all of these I would be successful. I even blotted a small drop of blood that fell on the paper. I pressed my bell, used two fingers as tweezers to hold up my proposals and laid them on the forward edge of the desk. She snatched them up, turned and hunched over them. Neither of us said a word.

My secretary saw her – and her daughters – out.

'One of them spilled on her frills,' he said glumly when he came back. 'And the other kept waving her spoon.'

I collected another drop of blood. It was much less brilliant and fat than before. I licked again, partly to get rid of the stuff. It had never occurred to me to ask myself if there were female toads and if they were naturally aggressive. I waved the thought away. I had begun to tremble.

'There wouldn't be any antiseptic and cotton wool, would there? I've got some dabbing to do.'

24

I think it only justice to say that toads, however shaken or sore, can still be found useful. They are so anxious to apply themselves. Whether to deal with a cockroach or to gorge on a dragonfly. In consequence they can be fearfully unobservant and easily deceived. I do not mean that they may fail (they do) to see the stone-wielding boy or the approach of a lady's metal-tipped shooting stick. Swollen with dreams, troublesome memories and the task in hand they are easy to delude, if not to diddle, and to be fair are often grateful to be flattered. At the time I was surprised to see the grave little deputation, but blinked, was quite genuinely concerned, instantly forgot the seventeen scabs healing on my head and forearm and ran along to help.

I do remember pausing outside Duncan's door but cannot find anything prescient in the pause, only a brief check on self-composure and correct dress, tie and flies. I was then feeling my way forward into a brume and brown limbo. A few wary, peering steps later, I made out the old man sitting behind his desk, indulging his knuckles. Odd impression; he made them appear malleably soft. I cleared my throat. He looked up. One side of his face wore a twitching, sheep-lipped grin but the other looked utterly inactive, like an aestivating snail's foot.

'Oh, it's you,' he said. Two more matters. His voice had cracked. And despite his words, there was no sign at all of specific recognition.

I reminded him of my name.

'Yes,' he said indifferently and then, in a slurred, overly sly confidence, 'When they come in, they're not accustomed to the dark. I get the measure of them while they're still blinking.'

I nodded. How fusty the place smelt! But he had a sick and unwashed old man's ready conditional for that.

'You wouldn't want to open a window, would you?'

I shook my head. It was unpleasantly like listening to an unfortunate but feeble adolescent.

'Where are you going?'

'Just a moment.'

But my urgent and whispered questions received hopeless, if sympathetic, shrugs. Have you called a doctor? He refuses to see one.

'What are you talking about? Ranald. Come back.'

Now I had thought at first that he had suffered a stroke. I am no doctor but surely the vertical division into left and right sides of the body, the left all dull droop, the right ingratiating and compensatory twitch, suggested that? But then, when I glanced back at his call, something snagged. I went back and squinted but it still took me a little time to appreciate the old devil was switching sides. He was creeping that sluggishness across. There is here the charmingly named, I translate, toad-skinned melon. Taut warts and as round as an eyeball. Was he turning himself, resting in halves? I admit, I almost bundled him out of his chair, though I slowed as soon as I saw that he was unshaven and that his shirt cuffs were stained and grubby.

'You're not prying, are you?'

'No, no, I thought we'd walk as we thought.'

'Oh.'

He tried. As far as I could see he always dragged the same leg, the left. Was this a clumsy effort at disguise?

'No mirrors.'

'What?'

'I can't abide mirrors.'

'No.'

'If you want to . . . check on your appearance, just glance at your reflection in picture glass. It works just as well. In fact, you get a sort of favouring patina.'

'A what?'

'Now, now, we mustn't get despondent. It is easy with the immense loads we have to bear. I think I'll sit now.'

Despondent was not the right word. I was distressed and conscious of being possibly too agitatedly so. But as soon as I found out that he had exchanged his town house for a pied à terre and his barely country place for an even larger but quite remote pile which his wife was away fixing up, I contacted her. His wife, his pert wife, was delighted to hear from me.

'Ah, my dear, how *are* you? I heard you were doing terribly well. I always knew you would.'

I do not know. I tried hard to be exact but discreet and suspect the latter won. I heard a slack sigh as soon as I began. Ah, she had no difficulty saying that he had always, of course, been highly-strung and liable to depressions. Did I know that he had had a breakdown? He had found marriage a 'rather raw' business. He did have some pills 'to cheer him up'. I mentioned the state of his clothes.

'Oh God, men are so helpless. Well, some are. I leave him notes.'

'Sorry?'

'Notes. Have you changed your shirt? That kind of thing. Ah, and ask him if he wants some more electric shocks.'

I was going to say that this made me almost delirious with embarrassment but what it really did was stymie me. I even wondered if they had separated. But I decided that in their marriage – in common with others I had seen – age had brought about a self-centredness and the practical bands had worn down; a question of routine and diet and interests. One wakes at five, the other at seven; one eats eggs, the other prefers fish; one takes an afternoon walk, the other sleeps; one likes to read, the other to garden, tenderness and solitariness making their accommodation with old age and death. I blinked. But of what practical use was such an analysis? Was I squeamish with remembered respect? Was I over-dramatizing Duncan's desultory, incoherent bitterness? His pawing me if I got near enough to let me into another secret? The smell of his breath – a horrible, sharp fluting in something tepid and fecal? His abrupt naps? His head would drop. Or he would grunt and fight off drowsiness, swatting at an invisible fly. Or his weird, waking battle-cry – 'How are costs?'

Could no one else see how ill he was? Surely that was why I had been called in the first place. And had he been, say, a messenger, he would have been led kindly home or to hospital, had flowers sent to him, received cheerful and solicitous enquiries, all while the payment of his pension was being organized. But for some reason I still do not properly understand, such treatment, by default I think, would have been regarded as demeaning or humiliating for Duncan – with the result that he and I sat in the quietest of office ox-bows.

Enough. It was belated, I admit, but I called his doctor. Suitably prepared – 'Oh, I called him, did I?' – Duncan coyly collaborated, removed his shirt, stuck out his tongue when nobody had asked him to, and giggled.

'I don't want to tell him about the pain in my left arm,' he said to me in a slurred, stage-whisper.

I was so relieved! At last! Co-operation. With the floridly relieved indication of a flunkey (I had a filthy shirt in one hand, a clean one in the other) I offered him to the substitute doctor sent along. This irritatingly jerky young man took over an hour with his pumpings, probings and pokings. He then joined that group of apterous poets and the like (architects without a sense of texture, judges without doubts) who make for spiritual gallstones.

'How long has he been drinking this heavily?'

'If he does,' I hissed, 'he does it in secret.'

There was only a moment's discomposure in that fleshy face.

'Ah,' he said, 'it's like that, is it?'

'No,' I said. 'The man abstains. I have even seen him turn down parsnip wine!'

I am struck now, however – and yes, I was extremely

unpleasant to that young doctor, 'indifferent buffoon' comes, not too uncomfortably, to mind – that in more consultations with other, older medical men, I never did get a clear diagnosis; rather it was an exercise in medical sophistry and a soft, piebald notion of breakdown. Shortish, always grammatical sentences would be presented straight, but would then begin to undulate and disperse into patches of possible sense. Under that, beneath the skin as it were, they would murmur for a time about Duncan's liver, for example, but then, without ado, drop it and we would all traipse on to the right hemisphere of his brain. None of this stopped a mounting collection of pills, capsules and powders for him to take – including, as I believe is common in cases of phlebitis (left leg), common or garden rat poison to act as an anti-coagulant.

The doctors withdrew a way. For a short time there was the rigging up of a routine, making sure his leg was raised, scheduling his medicines, but that soon palled for both of us. I am no nurse or, rather, I am perhaps over-particular as to who should be nursed. It was not a question of a dislike of order, or a fear of infection or contagion. Not at all. It was a weariness, so thorough and so quick as to require a word not in my dictionary, the thoroughness and quickness being as remarkable as the weariness. Very soon it was a permanent night in that office, the patient fitful, the cantankerous nurse's blood tripping and skittering. My forehead acquired upward creases. Nobody moved, except down the corridor. Nobody helped. I began to feel I was shading into my shadow, a wrinkled arrangement, though this was sometimes leavened by exasperation. Simply by waiting outside after I had taken him to his pied à terre one very late evening, I was able to see Duncan, with a touching effort to his shuffle, trying to return directly to the office. I rebelled – oh, very briefly – but found the medical profession still resolutely vague.

'Hospital would not be a suitable environment for him.'

'What? The spirit of place is this?'

For which I was rewarded with a soft smile.

'Do you really mean hospital would kill him?' I insisted.

But this, for whatever reason, was regarded as bad taste, and the smile congealed.

At least I made sure Duncan washed and changed his clothes – with which he sometimes needed help. Luckily, his beard was sparse and I barely bothered with it. Have you ever shaved an old man? Had to negotiate wattles with a blade? A splendid definition of foreignness. Dear God, we were camping, had set up a cosmopolitan field tent, with his suits on hangers and his other clothes in piles. Noisily my patient dozed. Awake, he would pursue, circular fashion, some fiddling economy, his head bent to one side, a reproachful sheering, as if pushing against gravity to reach the relevant line. It was not there. I had his food sent in and cut it up. I made sure his napkin was well tucked into his collar. If he slowed too much I secured the food for him in an attractive way. He preferred to recall meals long past, his wedding breakfast for example. I really never thought my urgent note to his wife would be answered and she never mentioned it when I called afterwards. Children, I think, turn their mouths from the proffered fork. Duncan, his right hand trembling like an inverted violinist's, would try to capture a thought instead.

'Most people die at four a.m.'

'Do they?'

'Of course. It is when you are most defenceless. No, not just yet.' This last plaintively directed at the food.

I cannot, however, really say that he had the idea that if he were awake at that time he would not die. Only that he was always, noisily, up then. His most perverse habit, however, was of looking almost healthy in a laxly serene way whenever he had a visitor. I groaned. I looked into his economical mirror-substitute and saw the parody of a debauchee. Where had I got that bruise on my temple? I was definitely getting a bad throat. And my lids kept sticking and, when open, exposed bloodshot eyes. I was becoming, I became groggy. Tiredness had become fatigue, a mix of ache and scunner.

But had reluctance become resentment? Did I feel he was, in some way, feeding off me? That nurse and patient were in a slow tussle to survive? I am not at all sure. In a heavy-lidded way I fear it is possible. No, no, I am not afraid in that sense and let us dispatch at once the anxiously testicular phrase *man enough to do it*. I only mean it is possible, even plausible given

109

the chimes of the clock and my strong desire to rest and sleep, that somehow I shortened the circuit. Repeated his pills before time. I blinked. I yawned. He was talking, mumbling at length, about the need for more economies. Would the old man never have enough? Would he never be quiet? I do not know if you have noticed that four on a Roman clock is not marked as IV but as IIII. I winced and squinted. A question of subtraction. I-II-III. Time for more medicine? Yes. I administered it and he, having swallowed, at last fell silent. The final words I remember from Duncan were, 'I don't like the taste, Ranald.' I went to relieve my bladder and douse my face. How tired I was!

By and by I returned to lamplight and leather. I had, I remember, one eye closed, was picking from the other a bit of solidified gum from the difficult inner part of the folds where the lids meet, when I saw him slumped on the desk, the crown of his head touching the circumference of lamplight. In the light was the thick tumbler, the base and one side marked with white-grained dregs. My eyebrows felt wonderfully heavy and I believed I had gone cross-eyed. I blinked and grunted. Almost piqued I approached him, heard nothing and, very tentatively, touched his neck. Duncan did not stir. Now I pressed as hard as at a doorbell, kept my finger on the stop. My finger left an impression on the neck and a small mark which began, rather slowly, to fade. It was just then that I saw *another* tumbler. I shut my eyes then paused; increasingly anxious in the dark I put out my hand and felt the two tumblers side by side. I slid my finger round the two rims, then opened my eyes. Two sets of white dregs. I struck my forehead and turned away to appeal to my reflection in the window. Both of us girned and said 'oh'. I approached the image of myself to blot it out, to peer past it, at the elegant little square, at the night grass, the golden glows from one or two windows, the right angle of a path, an evergreen bush – and another gleaming tumbler. For a second I did not know which way to turn, a twisting combination of start and shudder. But who was doing this to me? I covered my face. Cautiously I parted index and middle finger and peeked out. Path, bush, huge, gleaming tumbler. I took my hands away, pointed outside the window, used the finger to come in along a line to find, almost beside me, a third receptacle with white dregs in it.

I thought I was going to wring my hands until they squeaked; the practical side of me however brought them together in a clap. I gathered up the three glasses, briskly rinsed them out and dried them. A natural reviser, I then considered Duncan again. At that time I was convinced I had killed him, was therefore doomed to shame and jail. Then I remembered my friend. I imagined him slightly pale, but quite cool and composed. I swallowed. I walked to the door, opened it, went down the little passage and opened the next. I leant out into the main corridor. It was quite empty and exiguously lit by two pale orbs. I fixed on the farther by the stairwell, licked my lips and bellowed thus – 'Po-TAH!'

There was an immediate, frantic noise of wooden chairlegs scraping on stone, then the sound of fat feet running up the steps. Gratified, I leant against the door-post. I was astounded by how calm and tired I was, a perverse, rich feeling of relief, as if I had reduced to a small puddle, but one reflecting scudding clouds in the sky. Oh yes, and I remember then a slight difficulty focussing, as if the veins on my eyes were a flickering gold net. I had the porter summon a doctor. I went to my own office to call my friend, MacBeth, myself.

Book Three

25

I should (in theory at any rate) be intrigued to know what images from this book remain in the brain after the reader has read. Which words. Which impressions. After five years? And after ten? The odds discourage. Though I suppose there are those unwarranted hagmires who perceive literary rape to be possible and might take me for a toadish perpetrator. Absurd. Toads cannot rape humans.

Please let us be more sensible. My own experience is that the majority of books, in a lifetime of inquisitive browsing, remain, at best, as vague wisps, a deal of indistinct murmuring in which there is sometimes an attractive phrase, an incisive line or a nicely caught physical gesture. Not more. I can also recall the reduction of a volume to a single word; I remember 'ano-esis' but have quite lost subject, author and title, possibly as a punishment inflicted by me. And, on the other side, there are those unintentionally hilarious or incompetent productions. Let me leave them in peace.

And go on to those splendid books that stay, as it were, instantly ready in a greyish mental sac; pierce the surface and they flood out and spread, assume colour and jostling characters – though, I admit, not always in the special patterns their authors gave them. That such a favourite paragraph or page should exist! That a delightful seasonal or periodical return to admired words and rhythms should be possible! And the other, your honour, let me proudly confess, can be counter-acted by laying my hand on the cover, not the dust-jacket but the textured stuff on the hard paste. And by closing my eyes, bring my memory and the secreted page together, a natter-jack's illusion of levitation.

I do not know if printers have a special print to indicate that the author's hand has begun to tremble.

Natterjacks are naturally if also helplessly nocturnal. The

night can be a gruesome extension. Full of foul scuffles, false calls and death. I remember my sweet nurse taking me to see a dead relative of hers. The old man had been laid out and, rather like a swaddled infant, only the face was visible. As I stared, various whispers and wails re-enacted his last moments to such effect that I realized that an impression of movement on his features was due entirely to my own pulse; worse, I had time to imagine his life going, doubtless incorrectly fancied the memories and experiences of many years leaking away out of his skull, trickling off the pillow, dropping into the air, settling onto floor and walls, hissing into nothing in contact with a light, till all of him had gone and he was left only as some small and insecure images in various erratic memories. Dear God. A few years later I had contrived the formula; life is a temporary discretion. But appreciate how I could transfer some of my fear of dispersion into a respect for books, as storable packets of brainwork, whose spines I could gently riffle. And touch.

I sometimes think that fear is the only vigour I have retained from youth. Please do not tell me that it is irrational, commonplace or can be treated. A toad must gamble horrendously that its appearance will disgust enough to repel but not enough to cause attack. I am quite aware of some troubling, loathsome, cruel books that have worried me for days as I tried to contain them; some of them sit reproachfully on my shelves as I write.

Reader, how must I envisage you? The best I can do is to turn round and look out. A natterjack, when spawning, needs water; two round, protuberant, gold-rimmed eyes break the surface to peer over the gleam and glisten and shadows. Small, swift, deep-shadowed shapes shift under the water while on the bank by moonlit reeds, drier, larger shapes prowl and sniff.

26

And now my canary has expired. You remember my bouncing yellow bird? It took me a while to appreciate the twitterless content in the silence this morning. But there it was, dead. I do not know why and let us not be sentimental; it was a reluctantly accepted present and was always, however full-throated, nameless. I did not, though, relish picking up that ounce-light body, feeling the slight, tensile ridges along its wings, risking contact with a tiny, transparent claw. So I lifted the cage and its contents and placed them outside in the shade of an old vine trained up and over the little pergola.

Only moments later, with barely time enough to get more than an impression of my notes for this section as a diminishing dribble on one page and a thickening clog on another, a storm cloud opened. I pushed back my chair. After months and months of drought the violence of the downpour made my skin crawl. I stood and it was only when I hastened to close the window and saw the height of the stuff careening off the sill and heard a click on a pane that toned into something like the sudden crack of glass that I realized the cloud had released not rain but chukkie-sized hailstones. I scurried to secure another window, saw frozen pebbles tear through vine leaves and reduce a nearly ripe bunch of grapes to a tattered, glistening lump – from plump, bloomed grapes to blistered stumps and juice-tinted hoar frost. Around me the house rattled and creaked. I gaped through glass. Within a minute the dust outside was a dun squitter. Within two, parts of it, bubbling, began to shift. Within three, patches of my garden curled up and started to slither downhill.

I think I was as much indignant as shocked. I snatched open the back door. For a moment, come, I had worked on that little garden, I was taken aback; my plants had been flailed, my climbers torn from the wall and a huge local terracotta pot had toppled and broken into pieces. A small fig tree was still upright but its branches hung and its leaves had been per-

117

forated. The walls echoed to gurgles and sodden sounds. And also a light clangour, like a leisurely idiot giving atonal flicks at a harp. Yes, hail on cage wire. I glanced up. Blue sky and the rear of a solitary cloud. I stepped out and peered inside the cage. A hail-covered bird. But no, there, a wing like a clumsy brush-stroke, a yellow streak. A stray hailstone stung my face like a pea-shooter shot. I brushed it away and squinted in again. But was that movement? Yes, a slight rocking. Reader, the bird was now floating in a chilled soup of water, droppings, grain and melting white beads. Then to the right a hump-backed shape rose like a miniature whale through granular ice. Nautilus the cuttlefish bone. This double-Dutch composition in a box with wire netting, dead canary and cuttlefish in hailstones and polluted shallows was then sunlit, acquired a greenish tinge. I do not know why this should irritate me but it did. Tutting, I lifted the cage and briskly drained it. Though at the end I had to shake it as with a rudimentary sieve to get rid of the last hailstones. The sodden canary dropped softly back. I put the cage on a stone and returned to my desk.

Now I doubt very much whether storm or bird has anything to do with what follows. A clearing of air and positions? That is possible. I crumpled my notes. There. Start afresh.

Oh reader, I love inconveniences, digressions and rancid old tales, loathe, for trite, those fabulous schemes whereby the stork gets the fox or the toad swallows the goat's cheese. Just let me open that window again. I am not writing an apologue. Who would I do it for? The horsefly in his heedless whirl-wind? And now a pair of storm-shocked ladybirds have tumbled onto my papers, righting themselves, winching in their wings to make small, bright-spotted semi-lunes. No, no, I am not here for a sublunar moral but for the gleaming, sensual, intertwined markings of a pairing. And yes, I know the word 'canopy', however gorgeously fretted and spangled, derives from the Gk for 'mosquito-net'. And I have indeed heard of that tribe in which the husband takes on the wife's birth pains, is surrounded by clucking family, screams and groans in the name of the swollen woman, silent and untended in a dark corner of the hut, and that this redistribution of labour allows the mother to return to the mealie fields almost at once. Mealie is right and I presume that the mother's milk is less amenable to transfer and that the newborn child accompanies her rather than the bed-ridden father. Let us then home in on human toads.

Is the reader even familiar with the natural sort? Ignorance of toads is remarkably widespread. Why? My gentle naturalist attributes this to their public image (lowly), size (small) and habits (largely carried on in darkness). In other words, disgusting, easy to overlook and hard to see – unless you are a night owl. But did you know that when threatened the natterjack puffs up and, presumably to present an even more misleading impression of dangerous bulk, contrives that its back feet stand on tiptoe? The name is commonly held to refer to the toad's persistent loud croak (natter as croaking chatter) and the jack either to John or to the jerky habit described above. By the way, I see the old expression 'Jack at warts' meant a conceited little fellow. More generally then, did you know that some toads have poison sacs under their eyes? That some have poison in the skin? That some have fantastic brows and horns? That some have spectacular warning colours – coral and mazarine for example? In the vivarium various insect meals crawl about unconcernedly. Do not worry. It is as it should be. Toads rely on camouflage, appearance and, in some surely belated, benightedly punctured cases, an unpleasant taste to discourage predators.

And the human variety? Oh come, you all know those young persons despised by their co-evals, seen as sensible and well-mannered by their elders. They lack analogous warning colours? Not in the soul, whose skin is thick and brilliant. And what do you say of all those who within twenty-four hours of my struggling into a pair of MacBeth's overlong pyjamas in that over-pretty guest room, exhaustedly unsure as to my role in Duncan's demise – 'No,' said my friend, 'that's over now' – wrote me such fulsome notes of congratulation on my new position? Come now, this natterjack has been toadied *to*. Those compliments that shimmered and went pop. My extraordinary talents. The support I never knew. My merest observation received smiles of winsome appreciation. You may consider all those exposed teeth merely the result of insecurity, but I, gleefully, am not so sure. And what's that? You have never seen an old toad? But you have! I am pretty sure old toads write ingratiating tales for children – at least that is my stalwart intention. Subversive magic with a pious platitude or two. There are so many varieties of toadery, so many varieties of toad. Perhaps you have come across one in your pocket? The naturally craven. The paralysed bully. The unreturned lover. My subject today is the natterjack matterwhack. Pay attention.

Who was it said prose was walking, poetry dancing? Meaning I think that prose goes to the shop, while poetry stays in the garden. I could as well say there is a wartishness in words, that some words act as warts. An example. 'Whimsical' is one of mine. We may then define a wart as an irritating but characteristic word we cause in opinionated others. In the same way that I loathe chess partly because I would appear to suggest it, it is a word you detest but one which is pressed on you. And yours? Against that, there are also those who themselves, when speaking, always rub up the same few wretched epithets. We could call these corns, though you may prefer mole for such annoying lumps, as you wait, Duncan still puzzling away, for 'immense' to surface once again. But this is merely by way of prosodic preamble. Let me remind you that my toadery was always singular. To help MacBeth I became an adroit wart seeker. I would search out in a person or group of persons an equivalent to my 'whimsical' and then, like some relentlessly purblind doctor, worry at it, prod it, anxiously try to burn it off. I recall an excellent 'pastiche' and a splendidly infuriating 'clever'. On a lesser level, of course, the verbal wart could be provided by an incautious speaker. I got good results from both 'convenient' and 'amusing'. I frowned, I dabbed, I repeated with a passion and so could burden someone with the onus of a word as wart, confound their good faith with all the appurtenances of concern and sincerity.

One of my subsequent pleasures was a common misunderstanding; someone who did not know my role would imagine that I had gone too far and that *now* MacBeth would silence me. But it was the passion that MacBeth respected, in my case at least, and the fact that it had to do with smooth-running, obvious honesty and the good name of our enterprise helped too. Oh, I do not want to dramatize. The sensation that pleasured me was akin to the whirr of a flywheel spinning unengaged. In a context, of course, of reasonable businesslike rapine. And if I suggested that someone's argument for a particular course of action 'might lend dignity to the grave-robber's trade' I was merely introducing a lick of emotion into the normal run of decisions, principles, greed and grudges. And insult. This was quite intolerable of course, but tolerated. Why? I was always, whether aggressively or extremely, representing his views, staking out calmer and more moderate ground for him.

I hope you have the drift and have not forgotten that I only ever had one passion, one person. I have few beliefs and probably fewer morals. This is merely observation. I am poltroonish enough to be anxious to obey most formal rules, regulations and conventions, but I should hardly call a poltroonish state of anxiety moral. No, I was representative. Of what? One, sometimes disagreeable, rarely subtle part of Mac-Beth's efforts to effect change. Surely you are not going to ask *why* my role was of use? Come, what I will call my interest in humans was of value to him. Of a personal, wartishly local and temporary nature? But of course! And remember, yes, I could be beastly, put iodine on a word like 'injustice' or verjuice on a 'fair', but I could also show sympathy, be kind, be concerned, know that porter's name, ask after a cleaner's children.

I really must apologize. We have to allow a gap there, say half an hour; I broke to bury my bird. The grave was already made as it were, the earth mud. I did not touch the corpse but got it to drop out of the cage door as in a crude ball and hole game and made final adjustments with a spoon. The cuttlefish dropped first, so I buried bird and bone together. I put a stone on top and stood. A prying neighbour asked what I was doing. I translate.

'My canary,' I said.

'Have one of mine.'

I was obliged to shake my head and to turn the mere act of

standing into a respectful stance. After carnival they bury a sardine.

'Ah,' he said, 'you're affected.'

I nodded.

'You get fond of them.'

'Yes. It's too soon for another.'

'Yes. I understand. But my offer stands.'

As I had for Quine, here with a dirty spoon in my hand. I nodded, he leant forward.

'Just tell me when you feel ready.'

'Thank you. I must (waggling the spoon) wash this off my hands.'

Please do not misunderstand. I cannot calculate the time I have spent struggling against misunderstandings. It is, when I consider it, easily more than the time spent on fantasy and terribly humble. How many hours in those years did I spend explaining, making sure, re-explaining, going over, finding the right words and formulas, words that would not frighten and mislead but encourage and enable, formulas that would ensure my underlings would do what they were asked! True, but surely you can taste something of the excitement available to us as we overhauled that decrepit and rachitic old enterprise. I am certain the reader too will, in some guise or other, have stumbled into some outmoded, creaking entity in which nothing much works, service is confused and derisory and knowledge of better complacently and dustily nil. Oh, it was all wonderfully well-mannered and homely in a self-serving sort of way. But forget talk of scalpels and dead flesh or violent shaking out. We added clarity and purpose to the manners, redefined aims, redefined tasks and targets. The partnership I formed with MacBeth (meaning the elect of life) after he assumed Duncan's chair, was ready. Someone described the relationship as a 'dialectic'. I am not sure this is human. But who was invariably charming and grave? Who had the task of terminating someone's employment in the firm? Who was strong? Who vindictive? Who would quickly earn the (gratifying) nickname of 'Queen Calamity', sonorously right, wrong in the root? Who was noble? Who was the stickler, all fuss and exigence? Who would have been far more accessible but for a possessive intermitter? Stop.

The most remarkable characteristic of this tandem was that we had almost no need to consult. I say it myself. Reader, in terms of human tussles and stratagems, I was akin to a dream lover, decidedly compliant, minutely observant. I was the most willing and eager of servants. Barely breathed in case I missed something. Not osmosis. I had the knowledge of long habit and urgent desire. Wise and gentle reader, understand this toad. It is not a question of taste, bad or disagreeable. Or if it is, ignore it. Let me ask you this – have you never wished to please the person you love? Never given in to an access of love? To assume him or her, reproduce the closest possible map of their desires? Never? Not to smother but to answer as another skin. The Braille in goosepimples. I am responsive, reader, not responsible. To anoint that body, slowly, generously, beautifully, with rich oils, seek to please each nerve and brain cell. Or are you too prim or dry to allow someone to try so hard to know your thoughts almost before you do? Oh, a natterjack has to be quick, a natterjack has to run. And by God, I did. At the slightest thing I clapped myself to him like a toadish poultice, taking the poison for myself. I was variously if inaccurately described by hot-mouthed buffoons – but 'hatchet-man' is as wrong as 'lightning conductor'. Toads, saucerish toads, do not take well to sharp blades and thunderbolts. You doubt that a human can be so? Please. My love was at careful, scrupulous remove, took its delight in service. The reason toads gulp and swell is that they remember so much, nurture their hurts, have gross blisters on their desires. A natterjack swells but does not go from saucer to globe. Look at that distended, maculate skin with its network of chocolate-coloured warts.

I think of those years as the happiest of my life. Our results were, even to the most jaundiced eye, impressive. Profits were reinvested, initially in necessary but long-postponed equipment and systems. I was in charge of that. From time to time MacBeth and I would meet and talk a little on the general run of things. His trust in me was absolutely delightful and his habit of referring to me as Taha to ignorant third parties was most gratifying. I never saw him fret. I worked, as a matter of routine, twelve- to fourteen-hour days, spent my evenings with draughts, minutes, details and difficulties. Within two years we were approached by two languishing, half-related enterprises. I was in charge of the consolidation and the entire movement from three old premises to the new one. We then decided on a restructuring and there was a great deal to do in the planning and function of the five new divisions we established.

I used to suspect, I am now clear, that I worked too hard. This is not a complaint. I refer to concentration and the occupation of time. I had very little for myself. I found, for example, that my dreams became intensely coloured, like painted glass with sun bursts often obscuring what was shown. I do not know if these were a warning. I also had a tedious problem with my gums; they were slackening their grip on my teeth and had a madder colour. My word-infected mouth? Don't be absurd. I was absorbed in my work; but I do remember a practical sort of hallucination. One morning before breakfast, after about two hours sleep, I saw a sidling old geezer of uncertain sexual past whose toothless mouth and mix of insinuating respect and hilarity made for a crude nightmare person enfeebled by the daylight. I made two notes. One to see a dentist. (I did.) The other was: salivating is not the same as lascivious.

27

It should come as no surprise if I say that my milder, meaner pleasures were incidental. One of my enjoyments was the rudimentary and banal relationship formed between Gruoch and Donada. As a matter of fact MacBeth's two ladies had birthdays a day apart in May. But they had no time at all for that and instead exchanged presents on the Sunday set aside for motherhood. I was privileged several times to see the two tall ladies advance on each other, their ribboned little parcels not so much proffered as awkwardly distanced, their discomfort touchingly translated into stiff movements, blinks and absolutely unfailing doubts about which side to peck. Neither quite leant forward but, with a jerky concave movement, addressed the air on either side of the other cheek.

Perhaps it was the idea of being another mother-in-law that confused his mother. Irritated for no good reason – it was some aged grudge against Gruoch's mother that led her to object to the marriage at first – Donada was too slow. By the time she began to grow fond of her son's wife and stepson, Gruoch had decided she had tried enough. Gruoch adopted a prim, patient face whenever she saw Donada and Donada in turn looked bemused and, after that, almost permanently anxious. With age she became fussy. I remember Gruoch with a tryingly persistent cold shaking out a handkerchief and Donada's anxious hands going like hirpling wings in sympathy. Or there was Gruoch, quite impassive, while Donada made fiddling little rushes to pick something off her dress or even her hair. Latterly Donada would scurry about *anyone*'s house, checking the level of water in vases of cut flowers, re-aligning curtain folds and picture-frames, making sure chairs did not touch the walls behind them, her anxiety to help, to my mind rather charmingly, leading her to ignore both other people and simple notions of privacy. A combination of nosiness, a desire to be useful and a notion, I think, that she had to pay for any hospitality.

'You've got an exciting little house here,' she once told me when I invited them for tea.

'Mother.' From her daughter-in-law.

'Thank you.'

'I've tidied your medicine cabinet.'

'Mother!'

'And the airing cupboard.'

'That's *very* kind. I don't usually have time.'

'I'll go and look for something else to do now, shall I?'

'No, no, Mother,' said MacBeth, 'it's not necessary. And his cleaning lady might be upset if she finds things moved.'

'Dear God,' said Gruoch. She had developed a habit of talking of Donada as if she were not there. 'The woman is mortifying.'

Ah yes, Gruoch reserved a rather quaint use of the verb 'mortify' just for Donada. 'I am mortified,' she'd say, but in the tone of someone saying nothing at all.

Donada collapsed and died one March Wednesday at the age of seventy-one after what I believe was only an hour of puzzled discomfort. The information was given to me in a breathy whisper too near my ear. Discreetly and briefly I passed the news on to MacBeth and adjourned the meeting. Back in his office I found him staring out of the window. I had never been allowed near my own mother's deathbed twenty-seven years before and was not at all sure what to say. I did remember my own father as plump, red and weeping.

'What happened?' asked MacBeth.

How was I supposed to know? I took a step or two closer to him and then I saw him wince. His face however immediately became grim again, he remained entirely silent and only his eye ducts opened to let out a meagre adult quantity of tear; two dampish lines, the right of which did not pass his cheekbone, the left stopping at his high beard line. He wiped. He sniffed. He muttered something I could not make out. And then a definite 'Mother'. And a while after, pressing hard against his breast-bone with a fist and thumb, another 'Mother'.

How his manner contrasted with his wife's at the funeral! Her face was wet enough to suggest she had been standing in the rain. From time to time her body shook and then a fresh fall of tears soaked her face. Her husband, dry and grim as a parched stone, supported her with his right arm and held her left hand. It is true Gruoch was easily affected and that there is nothing contemptible in that, but her sobs were loud enough to obscure parts of the burial service.

There was a rumble of distant thunder as we walked back, the patter of feet behind me. The undertaker tried to detach me, the organizer, from the mourners. What he wanted was my approval. This flapping headwaiter aspect against the clouds and the hills annoyed me. I prefer funerals to be for the buried rather than to seek references for the future. Some time after I received from what must have been a most detailed will a sample of needlework and an unfamiliar and exceptionally ugly flower vase. It was not Donada's taste and I wondered if she hadn't made a mistake, imagining I would give her something like that in the first place which she was now giving back. On the other hand, it may have been a present to her which she was now getting out of her family possessions. It was one of those garish and encrusted things in which the flower decoration on the porcelain clashes with any real flowers put in it.

28

I was deep in the middle of a sentence, paused over a comma, so that my automatic 'yes?' went out before my mind and eyes had cottoned on. *What* had he said?

'Well, you're a cool enough fellow.'

This was so out of character for my friend that I squinted up at him. But his expression, tremendously purposeful, I *had* seen before. Long before by the pond in his garden when a small Lula had toppled like a plump miniature Narcissus towards the smooth surface of the water. A couple of startled fish fled into a brackish corner. I could see quite clearly the boy's tight-shut eyes, his open mouth and outstretched hands against reflected clouds round real lilies. MacBeth lunged. He just managed to save the boy from the water. He caught Lula by the stomach and performed a heavy, spinning heel stutter across one end of the pond and through a clump of nasturtiums as he got his own balance back, the child hard against his chest. And it was here, as he turned again, that I saw the boy's shock-popped eyes and an odd gesture from my friend; his free hand swung out like that of a ham scout. I saw that the boy had wet the very tips of his fingers, to the half-moon of his nails. That a chain of ripples was reaching the rim of the pond while something in the water released small bubbles. And then Maelbaetha grasped that for the boy against his chest the suddenness of the rescue had been as shocking as a very chilly dousing, and he began waltzing and humming about the lawn until the business was safely into sleepy-sounding giggles. I strolled to the sundial. It was an over-complicated piece of ironmongery and stone grooves and all three of us then put a foot on the base as at some bar. MacBeth dislodged some moss, rubbed it judiciously between thumb and forefinger, and he then gave me that look which I have called purposeful but was also a mix of request and withdrawal – help me, let me deal with another worry. I cannot remember knowing what to say then – oh yes, I do. I talked to the boy of sand clocks and water clocks – but here, in my large office, despite a prompting glance at my comma, I still did not know what to say. MacBeth showed unmistakable embarrassment. He had a hot-lidded look and he cleared his throat not quite silently. Very reluctantly, I relinquished my pen.

'Well, it's not a secret, is it?'

His tone was joshing, reasonable – but strained.

'Her parents wouldn't come to me if it were, would they?'

This time I nodded. Then, just like a delayed reflex, the doctor with his little hammer, I jerked. I understood my surprise was escaping and snatched at it. His eyebrows went up.

'Ah. You didn't expect them to do that.' He sighed. He sat. 'It's probably natural,' he said, rubbing at an eye. 'Of course I assured them of your . . . probity and prospects. You look annoyed. Don't be. They were perfectly discreet. Just unexpected.'

Probity? Parents? He talked to me of unexpected?

'But what did they say?' I wailed.

'Who?' he asked – and gave me a surname.

This was quite, quite ridiculous; but MacBeth showed no signs at all of amusement. The name given meant nothing to me but by this time, like rain on cracked, lumpish ground, my mind had started to run.

'And you say her *parents* came here to talk to you?'

'I'm beginning to regret I told you! But why so secretive? It's unlike you.'

Really? My larder of women being decidedly bare I had fixed on a plump girl for whom I had fetched a while before. But what kind of love was it that parlayed an indifferently avuncular fruit cup into a proposal of marriage? I almost snorted – but did not.

'She's awfully young,' I murmured, mostly to myself.

'Yes, I gathered that. But what do you mean? You're not treating youth as a condition, are you?'

I blinked. I had been thinking of not hurting her.

'I have to go carefully.'

'But the proposal is made,' said MacBeth, 'isn't it?'

I have previously mentioned a delicious sense I sometimes indulged of being a little boy in front of his father. Not here. I took refuge.

'Not formally. Look, would you mind if I spoke to . . .'

'Gruoch?'

'Well. That would be . . .'

MacBeth nodded. 'Yes,' he said, 'I think that is probably a good idea.' For a moment he mused. Then he added a firm, 'When?'

I was altogether less relieved than I had imagined to be left alone and to let my face and body express something of the amazement and alarm in my brain. No doubt but that I had handled the interview badly. But what on earth was going on? Who had fixed up what? Could it be that MacBeth was pushing me into a safe berth? Was it some kind of warning? But I could not think of any indiscretion that might have exasperated his patience. There was none. Except that I was still single. No, I said to myself, aloud but rather hollow, you, a discreet natterjack, have been fished.

Of course I should have gone directly after MacBeth and told him the girl – or her parents – was a fantasist, that I had no desire at all to cause her pain but that the interview with him had been empty presumption. And I should have asked him what to do. That I did not was due to a glut of embarrassment, truculence and caution. Stop. I felt flummoxed by someone else's mirage. And I remember sitting there, frowning stupidly, a tingle beginning to crawl over my scalp and the tingle, as it were, settling into a patchwork of throbbing points.

Then Gruoch unnerved me by seeing me at home amongst a quantity of cut flowers and certain formalities I did not usually receive. She was smiling encouragingly and, apparently, 'dying to know'. Though it was unsettling to see something like concentration in her face, presumably as she tried to see what the girl saw in me. Her porcelain rattled in my hands. I mumbled something about nerves. She looked puzzled. This gave way to a sudden smile.

'Oh that's charming,' she said. 'I don't think my husband quite appreciated just how truly nervous you are.'

I blinked. My husband? What MacBeth loathed were messy couples and melodramatics. Gruoch was already onto practical hints on how to deal with such 'traditional parents'.

'I may say, when this gets out you'll be much envied.'

I cocked two quizzical eyebrows.

Gruoch smiled. 'No, no,' she said. 'That's very good. Strange how these things work out. We're so pleased. I hope you'll be very happy.'

I suppose I could count that as the second missed opportunity to explain myself. But I would never have risked it. I felt unpleasantly light-headed, had begun a weak-kneed flirting. With awful hope I think. My foot is jiggling. Stop. I mean I had begun flirting not with hope but with fate. I was shifty all right but I was also possessive and it was so easy to conjure up a life of modest companionship and domestic elegance. Love can grow. I was weary of being lonely and the idea of being sought out was attractive and gratifying. I sincerely meant to repay the seeking with consideration and respect. At this time too I was comparatively well off.

I spruced up and called. I was suddenly and very belatedly prepared to find the whole thing a cruel hoax but the future bride's father, a moustached old party with a colossal stomach, clasped my hand and my elbow, and called his wife. Both were impressed with my mother's ring and my asking them to safeguard it. The whole business took only ten minutes during which I learnt the date and place of the wedding and the relative who would conduct the service. We then repeated it (the business and the girl's name) with only one hiatus when my future mother-in-law wondered why I had not called before.

'Out of respect for your daughter's emotional well-being.'

Her husband went red with pleasure, rose from his chair to tuck one short leg under him.

'Now do you see? No *boy* has that kind of perception.'

A coy look passed between them across the rug. And at last, with heavy-handed discretion, the parental troupers left me alone. Domestic mice hurried and rustled. Feet sounded quickly overhead. I think a hairbrush was dropped. The door to the room creaked. I could hear young whispering. I scratched a sudden ferocious itch in the centre of my right palm. A curtain sighed and I hastily prepared myself to meet my future wife.

I had here one of the greatest shocks of my life. Morag is a common name. In an instant the plump fruit-punch one dropped away and I realized what Gruoch had meant. I had last seen *this* girl surrounded by a stamping, shuffling crowd of eager brawn. An unknown though I believe entirely natural elation filled me. I swept across the room and took her hand.

'Taah,' she said, 'Taah.'

I believe this all shows my well-meaning if witless intentions and my lack of knowledge of how people get married. The whole thing was ludicrously old-fashioned, I was a victim of my own protective colouring – but I was so struck with her looks I saw her in a perfect glaze. Her father had liked my quiet ways, my hardworking reputation and had considerable if inherently idle respect for my brain. For her part, the sheltered, lovely girl, easily in love but faced with a lusty herd, was glad of discriminate advice. Generosity and respect last longer than passion. A mature man knows what he wants. Even so, she had a question for me.

'Why did you not come before?'

'I had no hope.'

'Silly,' she replied, her tongue lizard in look and action, slipping out between her lips. I stared and suddenly understood the import. She shut her eyes. There was a double shock – first that of her lips and then the entry of a shrieking crowd of family, four younger sisters and a toothy little boy who had to be reproved for calling me uncle. And from then on I was wandering, often pleasantly, in the sugary rigmarole of a traditional wedding.

It was flattering and exhausting. I found most of it interesting, the unknown bits I mean, the tucks and pans and icing. I was working of course, quite a lot of it did not apparently concern me, but I enjoyed trotting along with my young intended. There was house-hunting and furnishing. Morag was delightfully impressed by my means and willing to be serious about expenditure; she bought a little marbled notebook which she filled with her round handwriting, 'i's like candles, 'o's with topknots, accounts at the front, lists and measurements at the back with dramatic underlinings and bunches of exclamation marks like triumphant stutters. I was, it was borne in on me, considerably better off than her shabby father. He took to calling me 'Ronnie'. Her mother had an expression I enjoyed very much, a moue from which the lips turned down while her eyes opened wide, her head nodded, and last, with a knuckle delicately to the right nostril, a little sniff, when impressed by a price tag. Morag slipped her hand into mine when we bought an elegant town house and, to tell the truth, her excitement was infectious. At supper, after work, she'd tell me I worked too hard. There was so much to learn! At choosing curtain material she suddenly leant over an oddly scented roll of cloth and bit my lower lip like a palm date, teeth to the stone. My young bride's eyelids drooped and slid into a wink. 'I think the wildest silk,' she said. Nodding, I tasted my own blood and turned, surprised to confirm the pain, to another roll. In a nearby mirror was a slight person, dressed handsomely and soberly with an evident preference for small knots and cleanliness, with a large head and fine, auburn hair worn back off a very regular face presently distorted ape-style by the tongue wadding out the lower lip. My hair used to be kept in place by a lotion that smelt, very faintly, of sandalwood. She had quickly found out who made it and given me two big bottles, supply enough for years of marriage, plus one smelling of pears and another of wild strawberries. I remember very well lifting out the stopper, that thick, syrupy waft and her expression of encouragement and pleasure. 'There's

lime in there too, I think. Now try the other one. Go on.'
Naturally, she disliked her young friends pecking my cheek
and would frown and tug at them. Those scents and perfumes!
She loved trying them, would dab, squeeze bulbs and present
her wrist to my nose. When choosing her some more clothes I
was ushered into the changing room. She revealed her
underwear.

'I'm not too thin?'

I shook my head.

'Kiss me,' she said and shut her eyes.

I do believe it was the first time we had been in such an
intimate situation. She was hot to touch and pleasantly
reflected rumpside in mirrors as green as egg glair. We were
surrounded by the smell of new clothes. She looked up, then
down at her plumped breasts, pink through the powder. The
skin had contracted, the fine hairs stood. I thought of fleshy
acorns, very gently ran a fingertip over a goosebump or two.
She murmured – an impression of a slow, twisting negative –
and then shuddered into the dress I had suggested: classical,
simple.

Morag had misunderstood my interest. I was thirty-six years
old and she twenty. I found her age and health – especially in
her limbs – shocking. Her youth rustled and crackled. Oh,
brain innocent she undoubtedly was but awesomely innocent
too in gesture and movement and flesh. And that louche cake-
shop colouring given to pre-matrimony, that aspect of diminished puppets and brandy-soaked raisins. I do not want to
sound like the bride. I knew my inner qualities were not
known to her, any of them. She seemed merely anxious that I
not be disappointed by the contents of her underwear. And
yet. She told me she liked my hands, from her point of view
elegantly chiselled by experience and maturity. Once, in an
appalling gesture of servitude to the idea of love, she made
knuckly homage, raising one of my hands and pressing it to
her forehead, cheek and lips. Reader, I, a natterjack, quivered
with shock. There was more. About two months before the
wedding she told me over some duckling that she had been
reading that love was 'largely based on smell'.

'At first,' she said, 'I thought of you as dry and ferny.' She

133

chewed and swallowed. 'Oh, that's heaven. But you know, you really smell like a blend of tea and I'd love to take pinches of different teas from boxes and put them in an old brass bowl until I got the right mix.'

I gulped. Ah, she was developing.

I looked into the mirror while shaving, at my lips sagging at the side, that stubborn hair in the fold between lip and nostril, the aged down above the beard line, the leaf skeletons by my eyes, the incipient fatigue in the pores of my nose. My future father-in-law gave me a drink, at first uncertain who I was or perhaps just surprised that I should crop up again, but indifferent now to his daughter's fate.

'I know exactly how you feel,' he claimed. 'I was exactly the same. Don't worry. It's her mother's day really. Don't disappoint her.'

The carpets rolled down, curtains went up, the tailor spoke through pins and I became if not quite depressed and not quite distracted, absent-mindedly anxious and inexorably more nervous. I sleeked down my hair, spoke smoothly, nodded sagely – but Morag did not help.

'What's sex like?'

'Tenderness.'

She took my hand. 'I *knew* you'd say that. You're so considerate. But I bet it's a little bit exciting too, isn't it?'

Oh reader, imagine me, a ridiculous thirty-six-year-old groom, virgin without vows, with the grotesque sensation of being waist-deep in deceit. Marriage is not all copulation but inexperience is a barrier. I could pray but I could not escape one fact: my ignorance of female physical detail was writ white as her pretty lawn nightgown and matters spied out by any prurient boy were unknown to me. I knew of course that I was looking for something that my dictionary, like a censorious blind man, had most unhelpfully defined just a day or two before, I knew roughly where it was sited but, as I set about the search, as I hoped with a gentleness that could be taken for experience, my bride set up a moan which badly rattled me. I also kept seeing the only picture I had of spreadeagled female anatomy. I had once as a very small boy woken to find my mother examining an intimately placed boil with the aid of a beautiful hand-mirror. Had I been more percipient doubtless I should have learnt enough to help me now, but I had been more intrigued by the boil, all purée and purple, than by its situation and much more intrigued by the delicate patterns on the glinting silver back which included the words, engraved in Arabic – *To you, my love, for our first son.*

I abandoned my position lying beside my bride. Perspective is also tactile. I crawled about, ridden by thoughts of duty, the knowledge that other men had desired her and a toadish desire of my own to please. What she did was pull me briskly on top of her. My elbow dug into her stomach, she grunted and I could feel the unseasonal sweat on my forehead chill. I gave up. A moment after her teeth shone in the dark and she muttered reassurance and what I took to be encouragement. I gave my attention to a breast which I found both softer and much lighter than I had expected. I enclosed a nipple with an eye-socket, a gesture I imagined surely to have been done somewhere before and which struck me then as hopelessly poignant. Our legs were entwined. Hers kept twitching. Under my lids flesh puckered and pricked and I grew conscious that she was lying rigidly still. A fraction after, she crooned an injunction. Her language was extraordinarily blunt, startling, like the touch on a nerve, a hapless forwardness in me. I had barely time to be horrified before her hands heaved hard at my buttocks. I was instantly conscious of a turgid, slimy heat, but then the whole fitment began to convulse with some discomfort to my part of it, while my bride's head went from side to side with an amazing vigour.

The matter stilled, grew cold and damp; a leaking of time, sperm and confidence went on and on. My bride lay dead slack. I began to wonder at what I had been party to and to fear it. The strain of that day, the sheer fatigue, the endless procession past the vivarium window – I think anoxia might have set in had it not been for the voice that whispered then – 'I knew we'd be all right.' I enclosed her in my arms and kissed, progressively, eyebrow, nose and her dry lips.

I have, it is fair to say, squirmed about including this haphurting episode. Was it not inherently tasteless? Did I really need that passage of turgid heat? Was it not, in the light of earlier and later events, miserably unfair? How I have blinked! But there are reasons that override these. Dismiss prying male youngsters. My main reason is that without a detailed account of that consummation, those events would have remained fey and etiolated. I should have disguised one sort of fear in another, made an aberration into an accommodation, smoothed too many lumps and warts. My lips are parched. I think what most troubles me here is that there is no sense of season following season.

29

I am undoubtedly now a prim, creaking old gent. However I cloak myself. I am fifty-four and somewhat withered. My skull is insistent. My hair, though unmarked by white, has thinned and faded from auburn to rust and old straw. It is very dry here and I have to anoint myself with expensive almond milk if I am not to flake away. My flesh confuses age and over-cooking, off the bone and shrunken. My fastidious sense of toilet is also old. My very first memories are hard pressed by my acute dislike of having my hair ruffled and my cheek pinched.

Ironic then and in its own way marvellous that the young woman I married should have proved to be such a slut. Some-how she had not shaken off the idea that someone told her to wash. But she had also picked up the notion that to be told, other presumably than by mother's time-honoured but imper-sonal routine with an eye on hot-water costs and too many daughters, was acridly insulting. She was one of those for whom to admit that sweat turns stale was somehow to negate her femininity. I think there was something else herein that she was blonde and consequently, by some very idle process of deduction, naturally cleaner than her darker sisters. I was never crude. Who'll bathe first, you or me? Or, shall I get in first? But her idea of dirty was unhappily, sometimes guffawingly, sexual. I sighed and washed alone. Sporadically she had great shaving sessions. The mess these caused with dollops of soap and blood, evil bristles and discarded skin does not bear description.

Respect begins with neatness. By that definition my young wife had none; the lack of privacy involved in our cohabitation spilled slow and thick over me – finding a hairbrush turned turtle and made creamy, learning to *begin* shaving at the chin rather than risk a softer part to a ragged razorblade, her wearing shirts of mine when her (many) nightdresses ran out – but let me stop this bedraggled stuff and try a suitable instance, I tidying up, my wife crumbling toast in bed. Dripping butter, she mumbled something.

'What?' I said, as I sorted some of her underwear into a pile.

'While we're waiting.'

I began putting pairs of her shoes together. 'For what?'

'We could adopt.'

I straightened up. 'But we're barely married!'

'Dear goose. Come here.'

Reluctantly I went. She gave, eyes shut, her open mouth to kiss – at least ten hours' sleep, a trace of old lipstick, a smear of grease, some wheatgerm. I got hold of her shoulders and leant carefully forward. I was in the act of reassuring myself that I was still dapper when a clumsy hand brushed my inner thigh. A moment after, with the comfortable senselessness of possession, her fingers squeezed my dangles (her name: two dangles, one dingle).

'I do love you,' she said and I, unaware that her fingers had been buttery, did not see the greasy fingerprints of evidence on my trousers until a privates detective spoke to me in a corridor.

'Keep off midwives,' he said, whipping a gnawed thumb in front of my nose.

Strange word midwife. Wife alone if it comes to that. In several languages woman and wife share the same word. Originally a neuter noun, etym. dub.

30

Today I saw a small boy sprinkle water on his lashes and turn his face, all blissful squint and sparkle, to the sun. But the fountains in this village are scarce and at least night rests the eyes. The fountain sounds, there is the scent and feel of watered leaves and the smell of dampened dust; the roof creaks, a moth flutters, a neighbour softly calls in a cat.

If I remember correctly, I do, I said earlier that I could not draw. Not even a wriggle. All true. And yet, I suppose just after my first wedding anniversary, I found one day in the office that my hand was affixed to paper with, on the plane above it, a skilful arrangement of highlights and shadows. I frowned. I remember looking up at the calendar. To my lower left my secretary's feet were showing genteel signs of excitement. The fire spat. I sniffed. I suspected some trick, some stupidity. But my secretary, stumbling in his eagerness, fetched and flicked open a thick folder of such productions. He had been saving them. It took only a few awkward moments and a fresh blotter – and you should think of the bald skin on the old fellow's head twitching, a kind of skullery he indulged in when very pleased and in the know – to discover that my deliberate abilities had stuck in dire perpetual youth. I sat quite still. How is it that I cannot, even with the greatest effort, tongue out, every tendon accounted for, take up pen and draw, say, a parrot as other than a crude stump, identifiable as a bird only because of its symbolic beak, wings and claws and yet, without conscious effort, while listening to a boring speaker, be able to produce a shaded shape, rather stark, certainly stylized but with a most convenient sense of volume, a bright eye and a broken tail feather?

I am not (please) suggesting anything at all to do with guiding hands and spirits. I am not, even for an instant, claiming that a tedious presence encourages some hapless branch of fine art. It is possible, though this is to brush my inner skull behind the crown, that I saw a grey parrot when I was perhaps nine years old (its owner had a wall eye), but is it really the case that it remained intact for nearly thirty years before, by some impressive combination of sinew and brain cell, nerve and acid, proceeding from brain to hand and off the end of a pen? Where would that leave the squid? Or the harvest mouse? No, it is merely a difference of approach. If I concentrate I wobble out lines, if I muse I shade. A doodle is something worked up and out, not drawn from, an acceptance and shaping of happenstance. In my case almost all my subjects seem to have been drawn from natural history. They provide gratifyingly cheap decoration and perhaps I see too much of them. I never drew a toad which, given the possibilities in warts and blotches, seems odd. So why have I included this gift to the superstitious and the ribald? Because at least this modest, secret passage of mine and its curio traffic make an interesting companion note to my earlier remarks on language – right channels, great delicacy and languidly unconscious skill – and some interesting aspects of intimate friendship and trust. Have you never run your tongue over the roof of your mouth and smiled? The only words I ever seem to have written in a doodle come below an owl – 'damned if I do'. I never knew MacBeth draw anything. So what? Some years later while we walked along a long western beach I came across a coin in the sand. I rubbed away fine grains – and years. It was obviously old but I did not know how old until I cleaned sand away from the image of an owl. Where had I last seen one? Of course. And I will now simply remind the reader of that dualism we all have when self plays tricks on self, serves, makes shift, makes inkling, rations the matter the other self must deal with, draws a blind, prods, leads off, an erratic quotidian magic but not one we have to look very far from our own persons to explain.

What strikes me most now is that I was quite unconscious of my sidelines on blotting paper – and that they ceased as soon as I had seen them. I had a few, the more convincing ones, privately framed. Listen to a mind not your own.

31

You all know those occasions when you are certain something happened but you cannot fit the events into your past. No matter how convinced you are the feeling is contradicted by stolid record. Fantasy? Probably not. A compensatory side to forgetfulness? Possible. But in the case, say, that you remember introducing someone at your wedding to a married woman who later left her husband for your guest, but then find he was not even in the country at the time – what has happened? The thing is so convincing you marvel at their acting and duplicity. You can see him there among the guests. And this is not a case of memory as a sophist with a fat, absorbent sponge. Rather it is like the cat in the Austrian adage, only there when boxlid and eyelid are up.

The special problem in recalling a marriage however is that marriage leads on, makes experience not so much redundant as endlessly, casually flexible, and memory joins imagination to make an indifferent but very supple kind of knowledge. Here is my wife. She appears effortlessly in this never-worn colour, visits with considerable realism a never-visited place. She got on well with Donada whom she never knew. Five years older than MacBeth's stepson, here she is giving the little boy a furry toy – a small fox it looks like. I have even, particularly when thinking of something or someone else, found her feeding my canary.

Now given that our cohabitation lasted no more than two years and three months, it is fair to ask why she has acquired such extensive talents. I am not sure I know. It may be the idle ways of my weary conscience – though that would make for a very mild sort of guilt. Let me try to do her justice – or at least let me take the blame.

As might be expected my marriage fared badly, though possibly only from my point of view. My young wife, thrust upon me in one of my weak-minded, plain, obedient phases, I found simply unnecessary – a much harder thing for me to admit than self-serving disgust or fear. I found her trying because I could find no emotional fathom-metre to help me react to her or to deal with her. My sense of guilt for mismarrying her was based on that absence, and while small irritations might flesh the thing out it was my lack of interest that made me feel most ashamed. I berated myself. But there are few sensations more alarming than finding none.

Her intellectual development was derisory but that is fact, not attack, and I am truly sorry for it. I think her weird language of diminutives can be traced back to her father, my impression of whom became a little more rancid with every revelation. She developed a habit of calling me 'T'. She thought drinking a little too much made her charming. I need not go on with this. Dismissively I snap my fingers: a spark flies up and performs an exhilarating arabesque. The spark revels. Flying with terrific elegance and speed it contrives a mocking and brilliant escape. But somewhere else tired feet scramble to get away, run down an alley between long-abandoned stables – to find that path closed by a wrought-iron gate. There are blacksmith's letters in it I cannot read. And the ironwork is so ornate I cannot even see a toe-hold. With a gasp I wake up. Then, with a groan and a glance at my wife's sleeping shape, I consider just what it is that has woken me. And I feel as annoyed by my dream self's twinning of my plight and desire as by some nincompoop of a relative. Of course I can do much better when I am up and dressed, can provide a fuller and more delicate portrait of my married case, all fluent ripple and fear. In bed, however, partnered but alone, what I remembered most hankeringly was the impression my friend always gave of *choosing* whether to accept or reject, agree or disagree. He had a lovely 'no', round and slow and as enjoyable as an unexpected smoke ring. I closed my eyes. I have sometimes considered where my fear comes from, more often what it is exactly that I have feared. It is not ridicule. It is certainly not failure. It may have something to do with being considered cruel and unjust. But I think it is more likely to have something to do with a dread of destructive clumsiness, with fragility, whether mine or not and with the appalling notion of causing grievous and intimate offence. Too late. As you cup a flame in the wind or cradle your infant's fontanelle, remember me. Imaginative reader, only you may care as you wish, with what measure of your own fears I leave to you, to provide the medium for a natterjack to spawn.

At last one morning while we were jostling in front of a mirror, I to shave and she to put red in her cheeks, an unseasonal guying of Christmas cheer, my reflected face showed me I had had enough of deceit. Still scraping, the words slipped from foam-surrounded lips, personal words I mean, the object of my love and admiration lay quietly tucked away, indeed it was the lack of love I mouthed. I love you, I love you – how many times had that been prised out of me? But to insert a 'don't' was harder than I expected. I stopped. I wondered whether or not she had heard me. My lips parted foam again; and I realized she had left the bathroom.

A door slammed. Drawers and other doors began to slide and huff. Carefully, taking magnified care at the upper lip, I finished shaving, patted my face, folded the towel and ventured into the bedroom. A chaos of bags and clothes lay scattered on, around and about our bed. Bear in mind that she had made no reply. It was then a heavy glass vase tore a chunk out of the wood door-post an inch or two above my head and shattered behind me. It took me a moment more – when I saw she was biting rhythmically on her own tongue – to understand how badly I had misjudged her reaction. Taha the Toad turned and fled back to the bathroom and got the door locked a fraction before she kicked it. There followed a wild tattoo in which my eyes and scalp dictated she was using her feet, knees, fists, elbows and head. I was alarmed that she would hurt herself, then that I might be accused of wife-bruising. Exactly what she said, the fantastic, foul-mouthed bitterness of it, is not important. Her words can be entirely attributed to her furious sense of humiliation. Besides, these, though shrieked, were not very clear. Screams joined her words, then sobs joined her screams.

When I lowered my head and saw the healthy-looking red of the blood oozing from the soles of my feet I sat and closed my eyes. Clear glass shards. After a while I clamped my hands over my ears and kept them there. I did this because I found her emotions uncomfortably sticky and, however ungallantly, I was afraid her tears would make her think of dangle, then dingle.

I waited. Sounds still come through the fingers, no matter how tightly jammed. When there had been spells of silence and when the tone had changed I took them off experimentally. Cautiously, examining the splinters of glass in one sole, I agreed I was still in there. I pulled out the biggest and watched more blood well. No, I thought it altogether too complicated to open the door. She snorted. She suggested I leave the house immediately. Her tone was brisk but calm. Next she suggested that *she* leave the house at once to spend two or three days with her parents. She would let me know what she had decided about her future during that time. She asked me if that was fair. Humbly I hid and nodded in the bathroom.

In fact she let me know by note the next afternoon that she was going to divorce me. The hotel writing-paper indicated that she had not returned to her family home. There being no children the business was straightforward. Hobbling and guilty as I felt, I let her have her own way, which included just about everything we had owned together. It was I who packed and left. There is not an iota of complaint in that.

Only a few weeks after the agreement and, I think it is fair to say, when she had seen I had not moved in with another woman, she sent me a letter mentioning my 'awkward honesty', saying she had never been so happy, offering her disinterested friendship and a 'civilized cast to the past', the simile of a decent ironmonger. I do not, I really do not, blame her. To be passed from a rancid onion of a father to a natterjack excuses a great deal. But I am anxious to have her part in this done. I heard from her once more, not counting her flower tokens at Christmas, when I received a letter, a kind of truculent fishing, after my return from Rome. It seemed I still had a little to do with her when rumour was roaming. I disagreed. At least I was too fagged to reply and the flowers at Christmas ceased but left, I had the impression, a watchful throb. Unfair I know, but I think of her now as a woman who gives dinner-parties where the floral pieces are more important than the food.

32

Now I shall sing of dismay as no other has sung. Let me hymn the stuff. Let me vouchsafe it. Let me restore dismay to its rightful rank. The delight to be had in dawning consternation. Dismay is the excessive fruition of the unexpected; a world of suddenly over-ripe faces. Note the stalk is now stiffer, curves a little, is almost brittle, that the top of the fruit is mushy and that the merest touch has the fragile, freckled skin slip off the flesh beneath; a touch, a few wafts of air and the flesh loses its glisten and softens towards brown. Bowels rumble in an anticipatory pang of acidity. The pear falls. A natterjack settles by it to watch. An autumnal snail comes along.

Watch dismay crawl about the face. As when it occurs to an aged gentleman that sluggish physical appetites might be coeval with sluggish mental attainments. That is, he forgets age has its perceptions and redirected rewards. Just for a moment. His face loses form and features, bloats. The observation of a sex-mad subversive, the brain as a heated gland? Mental impotents of the world arise? No, no. I have made it clear that my sex sleeps alone but does not discount verbal spawn. Here I speak of *dismay*, the antidote to an arrogant heart. As when, to be personal, I understood what that pansy kiss that Gruoch gave me meant. As when I realized my ingenuous young wife was privy to my nightmares but not to my dreams. Or when I understood that the delicately drawn bubbles I have called doodles were the poisonous products of guilt and insomnia, crippled feints at nature for nature, oozes shaded, shaped and blotted dry.

I have never prayed. There have been times when, before sleep, I may have given groaning expression to a desire to escape from this or that apparently intolerable set of circumstances. But these were met by morning, by breakfast and by plodding on, and as such hardly qualify as prayer. In spite of these remarks I consider myself a believer. There *is* a limit and I will recognize its cool, solid touch when I press my forehead

144

against it. I also have faith in death as stillness. I have heard that there are some men who believe death is a welcoming or possibly forgiving woman. In fact I am more sympathetic to this than might appear but, for myself, I can only hope to avoid a painful, long-drawn out or humiliating death and, having hoped, that's that. My faith is directed to the point after I have ceased to suffer. Death as utter stillness. I should like, of course, to feel, if only momentarily, that absolute rest but I would gladly give that up for an assurance that there is no other side. Why?

Because the faith that informs this little work, that I may die and rest in peace, is accompanied by a fear that I may be cast out of life defenceless, without even warts to protect me, into a ghastly weightlessness in which my innermost thoughts leak out to be read and seen and pawed. No, no, not in this life. In this life I have a queasy antidote in words. And in dismay.

Reader, it is dismay I have learnt to trust, dismay I furnish my pond with, dismay that gives the gold to my eyes. Dismay made me appreciate the doom in daydreams. The bulb and stalk of my wife's head and neck. Asleep in the bath! My flat hand laid on her crown. A sudden plunge downwards till the water rims my wrist. The swirl from the upsurge of her knees! And then, miraculously quickly, a huge bubble of air erupts through the scummy surface. Something as basic as mental amoeba divides into: I never did it! and: What have I desired! Let me reassure you. Dismay is the second.

As is the planing, tint and tabula that the enterprise you are embarked on now will *not* work out, is irredeemably flawed, that the elements will *not* come together, will crack and crumble. Or, more to our present doings, reader, imagine for a moment the novel dismay of finding that the book on your lap has, in the space of a blink, changed into a gulping creature, a fat, sorcerish saucer with cream skin and chocolate wattling; it wassles, settles, a sudden damp feel on *your* skin. Dismay can be a start but not too abrupt. Viscous colours, a touch of lemon curd, two reproachful eyes.

Dismay then is in no degree despair. Despair is the complete absence of hope. Let us say a collapsed lung. Despair can entail a certain gloomy satisfaction at knowing the worst. It is beyond the addictive attractions of self-loathing. Dismay is abrupt suspicion leaking through the absence of solid knowledge. The stuff can bob like a Hallowe'en apple. It can, like Quine, squeak and gurgle. But my main point is that, in among the puffy patterns and billowing movements, dismay always has something intrinsically and unavoidably risible. Whether spiritual, mental or emotional, dismay is a collapsing tent.

And that, possibly, is the main characteristic of my friendship with MacBeth. I *never* saw him as risible. Too longwinded. Yes. Exasperating. Yes. Mistaken. Yes. And come now, I am not as fatuous as to have sustained an unadulterated adoration past youth. I swallowed Maelbaetha whole. I loved him for his mistakes. And if I sometimes wondered if *he* would ever take a holiday from loving her, show even the merest trace of boredom, then the notion of intelligence subsumed to love applies to me – or to anybody. And it does not. Love? My love was always secret, its expression of the most toadish and oblique, and the dismay there would be in my miserable hygiene and my incapacity to love anyone else at all.

So why do I hymn dismay? Its ability to surprise is quite a good reason. And not just with me. Look, over there is Cicero. But you know him! He is the fat boy who contrives to ignore the severing of the chicken's head. When the blood-spouting remains start running about he nods and intones 'it will fall'. Seven minutes later, the headless chicken now scratching for food, the dog clears his throat and looks away, a glaze of alarm illuminating his sense of self-dignity. I may be natterjack but I was never a dog. Nor a chicken. Admit dismay. Do it promptly and you have the second good reason. Dismay is a trapdoor. To? Nothing grand but quite often commonsensical. Take something quite unexceptional, the sensible notion that there should be a time limit on the exercise of power. I should say certainly no longer than ten years in the very best of cases. MacBeth and Maelbaetha were to do *seventeen*. An exceptionally successful first ten years. Undoubtedly. Do compare. But the next four? And the last three? No matter what – it is too long. No matter who – it is too long. This surprises? But I loved him, not the appurtenances of his job, and I could see, rents and remnants of my matrimony notwithstanding, that he had

146

begun, in the yearning way of middle age, to think beyond the limitations of the practical. I disagreed. The fylfots with their 'ah-ha, ha-ha' – surely the fantasy antonym to dismay – were delighted with our first polite, public disagreement. They knew nothing. Quiet, contemplative, divorced toads speak up. And as I wondered aloud as to why he should want to commit our firm, from a small, hard-wintered country to an international association, based in Rome, with high initial costs, clanking impositions and nebulous future benefits, I pointed out simple differences between kind and degree. He gave me an excellent mark, indeed, seemed delighted with my objections. Was he tired? Bored with limited successes? I stared at him. He gave me a nod and a leer of complicity. Faithful and reliable Taha! Doubtless I should never have married. He should certainly have had more than a natterjack to disagree with. His idea was that there was little choice. I do not want to be pedantic. But *is* that an idea? What are the assumptions and presumptions that so contrive to limit choice? Surely choice, however hectored, remains choice? Did someone snigger there? I looked around. I was the toad? The untoads murmured, pouted and assented to everything he said. Perhaps I should not have begged to differ. Perhaps I should have insisted even more. But I am better equipped for private than public confidence. I thought he was running to meet a future, that he was premature and, accordingly, vulnerable. It does not matter. I was outvoted. Eight gamblers to one reluctant conservative. I insisted my disagreement go on record. It did me only honour when I should have preferred uncertainty. Dismay is always uncertain, always doubtful.

I once had a scholar enthuse to me about a tenth- or eleventh-century Japanese poem about an old pond and a drizzly day which contrives to conjure up the pang left after an amphibian has jumped in and disappeared. Perhaps I was in the wrong mood or he was too enthusiastic in presenting the poem as a brief time capsule of laconic subtlety, but it seemed to me the usual stuff on transience, mortality and memory. But then, if I understood him correctly, those few characters, a calligraphic skeleton fleshed out by the movement of the reader's eyes and mouth, did not mirror a traditional pang of nostalgia and resignation but rather the pang caused by recapturing from a ripple at the rim what had caused it, going back through the zest of a water echo, droplets and fat tongue, rewinding as it were the parts and movements of the creature's spring. At the time I nodded. Now I clear my throat first. Well, well.

33

I now have the most footling, most unfortunate, most grievous incident to record. There are numerous ways of negotiating a formal agreement, the most time-consuming and enervating of which for me is what we found in Rome; we were, that is, presented with an exhaustively detailed, often contradictory document of extraordinary length which nonetheless ignored three of our five main concerns. Now my Arabic is infantile to fair, my French simply reasonable, my Spanish quick rather than sonorous, but my Italian is a parody of school Latin with small forays into, most literally and literarily, Dantesque byways. Of course there were translators. Of course we had employed professional help. But I trust the reader can grasp how distracting it was to suspect the translation or to have words go off like little puffs in French or Latin and Spanish. The other monolinguists around me, however, decided that my languages, the mere fact that I could conduct a half-witted conversation in Italian, and my insistent lack of enthusiasm for the plan, made me the ideal negotiator MacBeth already considered me. No, I am not coy. I can still remember the delight in the eyes across the table from me when I objected, in part by waving those one hundred and forty-eight pages between thumb and forefinger, to the form of the negotiations. The man across the polished wood was tiny, pale, plump and bald and had a lust for detail, compartments and other words.

I think we disagreed about almost everything. For over a day we talked of procedures. I learnt, incidentally, that *isbigott-*

ite was translated as 'dismayed'. I mean I took little rests, small dips in my linguistic pond as someone droned. The Spanish *desmayado* means 'fainted' or 'swooned', from shock – or pleasure. I had and have no idea of the origin of the attractive Italian word but thought of narrow-mindedness, its similarity to misbegotten and the Spanish *bigotito*, 'little moustache' in honour of those facing us. Have you ever had to stretch words and sentences, make them like latex? My jaw began to ache. At least I got us all separated out into five work groups along that very long table and as I waggled a clause or prodded in a suggestion I knew that others were doing the same with the same resolute patience and almost grim good-humour. When, on the third day, my opponent rubbed an eye and suggested we were like rowers in a boat trying to make our strokes strike in time, I commented that the process struck me as more like two fat caterpillars clambering about a cluttered chess board. Please, I know what makes me laugh – I was so tense I worried immediately that I had sounded tired. When not sit, sit, sitting, we were standing in corners preparing drafts and tactics and checking sub-negotiations. For a week we barely moved from a run of three elegant, cube-shaped rooms with faded pink and flesh frescoes, except to walk, consult and sleep. Please do not misunderstand. We were well looked after, well fed. Relations with the Italians were excellent. Indeed, the only frictions were from some of my side who considered I was moving too slowly or who had not understood why I had failed to bring up this point or that at a particular time. With these people MacBeth had much more patience than I and would cheerfully explain where the point would best go. By the time a half-day recess was called I was beginning to resent the figure painted on the wall facing me, a venerable but muscular old man with a blanket arrangement over one shoulder and a small hound in the crook of one arm. His expression appeared to change, but whether alarmed or protective was never very friendly; when he began to droop and look put upon I knew it was time for a brief but complete break. MacBeth, by contrast, was thriving. For *his* afternoon he had two activities, one cultural, one phil-anthropic; in other words an exhibition of Celtic jewellery and a visit to a small church, then being restored with funds from us. I decided to take a stroll alone.

I do not really blame Ricci. An amiable, anxious, cultivated man a little older than I, he was always rather persistently wishing to talk of what he called 'the larger issues' or '*the* matter' with someone he imagined suitable. It is because he considered that caterpillar and chess-piece business 'delicious and astute' that I have remembered it. I am not at all sure I agree with him. We had a light lunch together. But then I insisted. The afternoon was overcast and I went off to get an umbrella. When I came back Ricci pressed a small book into my hand.

'In a foreign place,' he advised, hoarse with seriousness, 'always look to your own great countrymen.'

The name of the philosopher on the spine had enjoyed centuries of fame.

'Thank you,' I said. 'Is it yours?'

Ricci had a habit of placing his hands like brackets or protective buffers on either side of me. He dropped them.

'Oh, it's not mine,' he pouted. 'I found it down there,' he said, pointing along a very long corridor. I nodded and took the book. I was thinking of unruffled, clear water, fresh air, of getting away.

In my effort to keep off the main tourist routes, I first had a drink with a dispiritingly infantile and arachnophobe priest, then spent some time trudging along narrow and rather dismal streets, full of dank smells and dilapidated façades, before I came upon an opening as much an abandoned excavation as a square. A shabby coronet of columns was surrounded by a dry moat of shallow scrub and round this were strewn numerous blocks of stone. At least the place was lighter and the weeds were green. Was that limestone? I brushed the top of a block and sat. I laid my umbrella beside me. Then, breathing in, trusting to luck, I opened my book at random. Yes, the prose, elegantly aged, was just at the point when the laconic becomes limpid.

I remember, I had just raised my head to reflect favourably on the quietness of the site and a certain admirable, if touching, confidence in the philosopher's words – 'A man of mild manners can form no idea of inveterate revenge or cruelty; nor can a selfish heart easily conceive the heights of friendship and generosity' – when there was a loud clatter of plates from a nearby house and I noticed a cloud of small black flies, the kind that smear if you brush them off. Irritated, I jumped up. Just pause a moment. In doing so I lost my place in the book. I could definitely smell a drain. Thus it was that I combined strolling and reading, turning slowly round those untidy classical ruins. I frowned. The book had flopped open on a page that had been thickly underlined. It is a habit I loathe. Worse, I saw it was for an annotation not even by the philosopher but by some garrulous and eagerly personal editor. His clogged prose footnoted almost all the page with a particularly inane anecdote. Without any sense of premonition I noted here how warm it was, that some greasy sweat was on my brow, and wiped.

Our long-suffering philosopher, though often plagued by fools and worse, was invariably affable and patient. Accosted by a 'Christian gentleman' (an interesting phrase in itself), he was offered 'a Devil's proof of God'. To wit, something his informant had seen in his modest manse pond, a toad clasped to a goldfish 'in an amatory embrace'.

'I think you will find that a curiosity rather than a proof,' said the gentle atheist.

'What? Is there to be no proof because a conjunction is disgusting? Is not such a coupling against nature?'

'That I do not know. But I am certain that the copulatory organs of toads and fishes do not match. Accordingly, for the embrace to be amatory, either toad or witness is mistaken.'

'I do not follow you.'

Evidently the philosopher's companions were neither as affable nor as patient as he. One of them, an unnamed 'gentleman of fashion', interrupted the conversation.

'He means, sir, that there exist other possibilities aside from a Roman puddock and a Sabine fish.'

'But how could that be?'

'Simply experiment with other motives, sir. Imagine a raft

rather than an object of lust. The toad may have been fatigued and called on the fish to keep it from sinking.'

'What?' exclaimed the aghast pond-owner. 'You suggest the fish was *willing*?'

That a great man should be involved in such sniggering rubbish! That such would-be robust and seedy facetiousness should be tacked onto a treatise on human nature! That someone else should have taken the trouble to underline this apocryphal gibberish! Trivial sir! Gentleman of fashion! I paused – and wiped more sweat from my brow with my book-hand. Possibly from turning round the square and reading so furiously I felt a little queasy.

Come, this is absurd. That repulsive anecdote had put me out of temper. But a while considering round columns, unyielding grey sky and even sniffing for that drain did not clear my uncertainty. I did not know which way to go back.

I could have asked for directions, but I was irritated and decided to try one of the three roads then facing me. It was dark, and difficult to gauge the progress of the paving – but surely the first street had not been so steep. I looked towards a corner shop. How many similar had I seen already? And then, my eye already casting about for a likely-looking person to ask for help, my mind already rehearsing the necessary phrases, I saw along a narrow street a particularly ornate portico which I recognized. Evidently I had been going parallel to my original route. I ploughed straightway in that direction and turned.

All of you will recognize that feeling of self-congratulation at finding your bearings in a foreign place. Perhaps you will also recognize the exasperation I felt on coming to a previously unknown square, this, in its wretched way, much larger and more grandiose than columns and drain. I shut my eyes. On opening them I saw a grey-green bush in a stone pot and beside it a curly-headed youth. I could see no one else.

I made directly towards him, registered but somehow ignored his fondling his own genitals with dreamy self-regard, and got to within two steps of asking him directions. It was then that two short but very muscular arms came round my chest. I looked down at grubby, wriggling fingers trying to seize at each other, finally realized someone was attacking me. I opened my mouth. A clammy, dirt-caked hand clapped over it. The other hand in this then sped about my pockets. But there was no lightness; it was all dunt and yerk. Something between a shove and a wrestling throw finished the attack; I fell hard onto my umbrella which made sounds, flapping and cracking, like a duck at slaughter. My head struck the ground and my eyes opened wide at the sight of a flying shoe. It stopped just short of my face and kicked up dust in my mouth and eyes. A moment later I could feel through the ground six feet escaping.

The worldly reader will already have smirked. Spitting, trembling and rubbing at my eyes I stumbled to my feet. The indifferent rattle of normal sounds had already resumed. I blinked. The umbrella was comically misshapen and ruined, the borrowed book adrift from its binding. My sense of shock (mostly physical) was stubbornly matched by the guard I finally found; he was to insist I did not abandon that wretched umbrella until back with the other members of the delegation. I mean, he was thinking of litter rather than proof. The graze on my temple buzzed with pain. I felt chilled and very sleepy. I had to repeat the story far too often and it became shorter and starker.

'Ah, my friend,' said Ricci, 'how aggravating for you.'

He was, I noted, the only person who squatted down to my seated level, there to look into my face and at my hurt. He squinted.

'Hush,' he said. And putting out his hand, he carefully picked something off my forehead and held out his index finger in triumph.

'Aha!'

A slight silver and husk gleam. A dry fish scale.

'Fish,' he said over his shoulder at the guard. 'Fresh water.' And he looked at me.

'*You* understand,' he said.

I very near gagged – at the idea of the dried scales and guts on the hand that had closed my mouth.

'Do I?' I said. But it was not until then that I even remembered the grotesque anecdote in that now ruined book. I am not, God knows I have tried not to be, superstitious. Is that even the right word for gruesome and susceptible coincidence? All I knew, as Ricci nodded encouragingly at me, was that something awful and definitive had happened. But I could not identify it. Something in me had parted, had allowed something insidious to invade me, but I could not get enough light or air to work it out. My thoughts went from – *who* is doing this to me? near the surface, to a sort of mental breathlessness, as if I were being stunned through water.

'If the boy washed more he would be caught less,' pronounced Ricci, with that pride foreigners feel when they are pleased by the sentence they have prepared. 'Leave it to me.'

At least Ricci smiled. My standing colleagues looked grim or shiftless. I blinked. I muttered unfelt thanks. And decided to examine my hurt in a mirror. Surely it was clear from my turning away that I wished them to leave me alone. Very well. I do not see why a mirror should not have a handle on it. How else is a hand-mirror to come equipped? And why on earth should it not be beautiful, with a barleytwist grip and the back delicately engraved? It is silver. It was my mother's and my father gave it to her on my birth. But are we not to use mementos? Whyever not? Beauty, memory and economy are compatible and even the hairiest fellow is half his mother.

'I'd put that away for a start.'

Just for a moment I considered the eggish shape on my head and the darn-like look of the graze. Then I turned on the manly mutterer.

'Never!'

But then, seeing the faces start as if I had roared, I repeated the word rather more quietly, as in a whispered croak. 'Never.'

MacBeth winced. 'Not so much vehemence, old friend. Not so much . . . vehemence.'

It is a feature of such situations, when far too many people are in your room and the business is grim and disquieting, for speakers to repeat themselves. I had begun it. Gently I turned the mirror face down.

'I was not – I think I remember this correctly – carrying this inoffensive item when attacked, but that umbrella. Should I have put that away too?'

Another aspect of such affairs; your haggard enough irony comes out as sarcastic contempt.

I peered directly back at those faces. I should not – some of them began shuffling away – have been attacked. I should not – other faces had closed up – have reported it. I kept thinking I was near collapse when I had probably already collapsed. So be it. If they could not help they could at least leave me alone. It was my turn to start muttering now, amongst bits of doggerel in a pond. Oh reader, I have never been a man's man, never gripped a bicep, slapped a muscled back. If I remember – and I regret I do – I began to swear. A double scunner, at me, at them, into which there became mixed a ribald ballad or possibly shanty which I did not even remember knowing, a shameful, rollicking chant which involved a princess at hunt and an owl's insistently beaky interest in one part of her. Wince with me if you wish. The song of the furious natterjack.

At least – a minimum – this foul-mouthed natter worked; it drove them away. When I saw that only MacBeth was left I stopped at once. He sighed and patted my shoulder.

'You're in shock,' he said mildly. 'Rest. Recover your calm.'

This was kindly meant but I remember blinking and, when he had left, letting out a prayerful groan.

I have no choice but to leave indignation out of what followed. The three boys were quickly picked up but we, I, chose not to prefer charges. My companions were doubtless correct. We were informed the square was 'notorious'. I did not know it. The boys claimed that I had made 'an unnatural suggestion' and that revulsion and abhorrence had done the rest. Of course I had heard of this time-honoured and utterly banal defence before, but was not, I think, quite prepared to see how much leeway this tosh was given by the grave, bearded legal official in charge of the matter. Enough. We sat in that foreign place, all hush and hunch, speedily trading in my foreigner's innocence. My papers and a derisory quantity of money, an irrational token, were returned.

'It hasn't occurred to you the thing was put up?' asked my frowning friend.

'Eh?'

'A deliberate attempt to cause us embarrassment.'

'Why?'

He shrugged. 'To remove you as a negotiator?'

I shook my head. Taha the hopeless stoic. 'Altogether too complicated,' I said.

MacBeth cocked a swift eyebrow at me and nodded without much conviction. I should not have been so quick to turn down this sop but the sheer shame of what had happened made me dreadfully stupid and unconvincing and depressed, too much so to think there might be someone who had planned my discomfiture. My case and appearance were not helped by a woebegone metastasis, a boil on my upper lip which pressed hard against a nostril. I have never, ever, suffered from the pimple tribe, not even in sebaceous adolescence, not even with pork fat to clog my pores. But here, in Rome, my neck aching, my features slipping off a hand-mirror, I trembled. A sudden surge of almost unbearable pity for my mother surprised and alarmed me; I had to writhe not to weep. None of these sickly reflections lasted. How painful the damned thing was! A rind of bitter itch, a hard crystalline core in that mountain of pus.

An apprentice fishmonger's hand? A different diet? A warm place? I do not know the cause. And yet, surely the reader will understand how my boil made those who saw me avert their eyes. It made me for those chanceless normans irredeemably old, an irresolute bore. They thought, and I do not guess at all, that bad health and vicious fortune are self-inflicted. My body humiliated me further, a pure, diabolical coincidence. Diarrhoea poured out of me. My skin turned sallow. I groaned a great deal. And, of course, I was sure the story was improving with the telling, was taking on baroque flourishes.

Only one person behaved as before. Ricci, with his easy preference for intimacy over privacy, would call in and tell me how the negotiations progressed. His English was good but with tics. As he spoke he would make brisk shifting movements with his hands to match his short sentences, using a tongue click for punctuation, and he would often repeat a sentence as if looking for a better place for it; after a while it grew as irritating as watching someone at dominoes so intent on the game they are unaware they are scratching the table.

'Your friend does well.'

'Yes.'

'Quick mind.'

'Mm.'

'He misses you.'

'Ah.'

'You are like me.'

'In what sense?'

'No illusions.'

'I think I have altogether too many.'

'The first condition.' Pause. 'You are like me.'

I dare say I could have done without such pious eluci-dations, but again he was, apart from MacBeth, about the only person who called in on me. And was I like him? He seemed to me much more worldly-wise than this toad. For his part Mac-Beth was solicitous but brief. Did I have everything I needed?

I think I then made a terrible mistake in burying Quine. I suppose at some abject level it was something to do. An unhappy kind of self-attack. Rancid irony. Curdled disgrace. And while I could and did explain away and even ridicule my reaction, which complied with neither my beliefs, my perceptions nor my decisions, I could not stop the recurrence of three evil shames: that as in a nightmare I had exposed myself, that I had somehow betrayed MacBeth and that I had been hoisted on my own respect for written matter. But what hurt me most was that MacBeth should have worked his mouth as a stupid fish – o, o, o.

Book Four

34

Curtains twitched, someone tugged. Rome revealed me marooned in myself. In the poverty of my amphibian emotions and accident. Oh reader! Bruised to the soul by a footnote. With the quack of an umbrella still crackling in my ears. Plunged by a stink-fish incident involving narcissistic young genitals and my wallet into an ignominious game of bait and forfeit. Don't tell me of coins and two sides. Don't tell me to fight back. Don't tell me of humility. Circumnavigated by so-called colleagues and infamized by justice during the day, beset by bowels and boil at all times, I had also to contend with a Roman nightmare while I slept.

The dream will enter no annals of subtlety – but I have need of that foul water. The stuff is almost milky, clouded with the debris and release of decomposition, clogged with specks and starry fibres and misted flakes of flesh. Some way down in this muck a natterjack wrestles a fish. It is a dream fish. It has the carp's pout and cedilla, the bream's hump, but is otherwise more like a sea fish, the red mullet, about a foot long, its scales as clearly marked as chainmail.

There is a moment when the fish looks just alive. The natterjack clutches and grapples. The fish mouth gapes. And from then on there is no doubt but that the fish is quite dead. It swings belly up leaving the natterjack upside down. The toad lets go. The fish rises slowly towards the surface but stops short. The natterjack rights itself and cautiously lands on the muddy filth of the pond bed. Now none of this should trouble those eager dream mediums who translate from the subconscious to the world – or even their apprentices. Nor that the natterjack should then hear not watery plops but a delirious stutter, like unstrung pearls bouncing on a marble floor. Or marbellized insect eggs. Or even idiot cake decorations. Above me, through the paler, lighter grey of the surface, dropped a myriad loosety of small white roundnesses. They descended as irregularly as snow flakes through air. But what's this? As they sink they take on a gleam, an oily yellow spark, a refulgent halo. The natterjack scrabbles. But there is nowhere to hide, not enough silt to burrow into. I writhe. I squirm. But those hot pearls touch and sink into my soft, wart-skinned back – until I constitute an over-encrusted, broochlike, horror.

This stuff was exceptionally tedious and aggravating, but after five nights, first gagging as I woke, then exasperatedly sitting up, and lastly waking already bitter and irritable, I was a very weary toad, could feel myself, my boneless, saucerish, blinking self, crawl out of bed and flop down over by the door as the rest of me struggled on in dream. Diminished? Yes. Benefit? Nil. Rest? None. That boil did not burst, it leaked pasty pus.

35

At least, when the agreements were signed, the wax had dripped and the formal ceremony was over, I was bundled up with the tail end of the party and shipped home. 'Remember me,' said Ricci. I said I would but was frantic to escape him. But to what? A previously unfelt degree of chill, a thicker tone of grey and gloom in the northern light. With an almost constant nausea, only broken by a dispiritedness as flat and brackish as a sodden, awfully isolated moor, I lay up in my bachelor apartments. Despondent and home. Two doctors, one with fingers like chill elongated pebbles, one with soft raw sausages for digits, came to prod and palpate me, hold down my tongue, hold up my eyelids. The complacent, stay-at-home one suspected some enervating foreign bug. The more cosmopolitan fellow, with the purple and pink underflush to his fingernails, wondered whether or not it might be viral. Hepatitis and various initial letters of the alphabet were mentioned. Blood was extracted. Urine collected. And results awaited. Time passed with the consistency of gruel. No virus, no bug. 'Run-down' was their homely diagnosis, with a 'quite interesting' tacked on from a very idly imagined notion of my self-esteem. They suggested vitamins, sleeping pills and a holiday. Peeved, I declined.

And then, getting up to release untested urine, I found myself staggering. I thought at once of being drunk on the vapours of MacBeth's absence. Had he – here I took hold of my bedroom mantelpiece – shown even the slightest interest in my condition since our return? No. The bones of my feet felt spectacularly soft and insecure. Had he even sent an enquiry? No. And yet I knew then that I was not drunk because of *him* and that I was about to have revealed, if not the cause of my intoxication, at least the wretched symptom. A horridly pain-ful mix of squeeze and leak. And I realized that since my return to my own home and my own bed I had ceased to dream. I stared. I had ceased even to have nightmares. But how could I know such a thing?

No pearls. An impression of levels, of my own shrinking cowardice, that my feet were chilled not on warm wood but unyielding granite. And as I blinked dishevelled bits of dream began to flit by like distraught fireflies. How desperate I was to rest!

My bladder is about to be attended to, though I thought it better to sit. Shakily enthroned, urine run, my mind, a small sluggard, considered the subject: had my subconscious been usurped by what had happened to me in Rome? Had events there been so appallingly dreamlike that I had ceased to dream? A mind can slur sometimes rather like a tongue.

Now I think I have previously mentioned that, childless myself, I have never found people talking fondly of their own children of any interest. Children are like others' dreams. And such parents as boring as those who, presumably in some compensatory way for dull days, are proud of and loquacious on their rich nocturnal transmissions. I mean by this that I did not respect dreams, wanted to kick them rather than trade in them. But I needed to dream. Needed not the stuff of dreams but dreams as stuff. Not as a dream epicure. Not particular symbols and syllabubs. I needed nourishment, dreams as food to survival. Without them you wither and grow mad. This was no ethereal stratagem. I wanted to *rest*.

What then was the point of dreams that concerned me? That *you* are not the director but some torpid, mothy hyperbolist. You fight for your life as a ship goes down, faces around you bobble like Hallowe'en apples, the feel of a child's head, used to gain purchase and safety, clings to the sole of your foot, begins to crawl up your leg – but the cause is, again, a full bladder. You claw at a cliff but it is a weird translation of your fingers *about* to touch the floor. Oh, remember Iris and that turnpike stair but forget Argus and peacock tails; we have our very own little night watchmen with pore-sized eyes ever ready to tingle, blink and race sensational lies to the brain.

Of course that is only one type of dream, and physically caused. There are also gross heavens, neuronal highways, in which desire and wistful appetites join the physical. And there are anxiety dreams (on stage, lines unlearnt) and reassuring dreams (the prompter speaks). There are dreams when a tricky diurnal problem is solved through weak by-play (you go to a cupboard for linctus and a bent old lady hands you a slip of paper with the solution). And there are, surely related, dreams I think of, not quite accurately, as Malaprops, both verbal (I remember 'simian crumbs' for 'simulacrums') and visual (your friend and his wife swap heads), or, just a fraction more subtle, your father unscrews an eye (he is busy on something else; is that the sole of a young woman's foot protruding from behind a gauze curtain?) and offers it to you. 'Could you look for me?' means, 'You do the looking.' You hold the eye up in front of yours. But what are you looking for? The eye tugs, your fingers slip. The eye drops and breaks like an egg, white around, green iris and pupil as black-centred yolk. And the worry is – what on earth will you say? 'Father, I have broken your eye.'

I believe that what I have said is commonplace enough. If not quite the same, the reader has experienced similar, will recognize that, however bizarre, footling or bathetic, dreams mend, dreams enable. The reader will also know that *I* could not be the dream director. Taha the toehold could not behave as a slack fictionist and throw in a couple of surreal details. I could not indulge daydreams and wish-fulfilment. It could not be that flirting with sleep, when drowsiness traces a sensuous line between pillow and cheek. Ah, my relation with sleep! And marshmallows. And fat pillows.

Rather shakily I got up. Reader, do you know what a nictating membrane is? There are some animals that have two eyelids, the normal external things and also a transparent lens cover. Some have even more. Taha the dream plumber caught the tail end of cycles – when you yawn and close down for a while – and, with legs crossed, hands on stomach, had the memory of his subconscious minister to him. Yes, I should still have seen you had you come in, but you would have walked through a dusky horizon between water and sky and then a very pale curtain or screen which would have made the outline of your head double. I'd wait, through a slowing pulse, for the sun to go and shapes to flicker and move. What is a limner? An illuminator of manuscripts. What is a limnologist? A student of pond life.

36

Are you there, my friends, my maculate, nugget-eyed companions? How I had wanted these pages to be a shelter from harsh light and worse cruelty, Taha the caveman gently pottering in pigment, warm lamplight and aurora borealis transplendencies. But there are three reasons that urge me to hop directly on. The first is that my dream director is a positive medicine man. He plagues me, insists that the improbable and the impossible clap hands as in an arrogant call for service. Are my readers as implacable?

And the second is that if my dreams will never forgive me, let me at least try to forgive them. In other words I believe dreams to be inherently confused. Dream images are bright shorthand, a partial, misleading translation of emotions and thoughts. They can unreel fears but they do so in a reductive, tantric, finally nonsensical way.

And the third is surely that a brief life is no place for the machinations of a biographer's dream. No, let me place the dreaming over the dream, the process over the anecdote, the effect over a particular run of little ghosts. Perhaps I also have a rather tired notion of a clumsy spirit level endeavouring to mediate between health and image. Have I said something on dream as antidote before? It does not matter. After fourteen weeks at writing this memoir, at rather after two in the morning, taking the hush of the Mediterranean below me entirely for granted, I am sure that any attentive reader will need no reminder of the twists and the minimum of time needed to render a grim, implosive shock bearable.

37

Forgive me, reader. But I am unable to swallow and go on. Natterjacks gravitate helplessly to double negatives. I cannot not. I must spell, whether words or dreams. Nor, to be a little more positive, are there many things I loathe more when reading than to find an effect claimed (witty conversation, a moving elegy, a magic word) but then no evidence or direct instance of it (the conversation is not recorded, a grown man sobs, the word is not given). Oh, I understand *why*, all right. I claim a cure and have only a few paltry images to show for it. So be it.

Yes. To pause. To rest. Those first tentative returning twitches of dream! I could feel fatigue begin to unravel, rest begin to seep and trickle down into my bone marrow. The marrow of dreams! At once I gulped down two glasses of water and hastened back. To what? To rest. And nothing, I insist, either spectacular or of interest. Unless images are particles given off from the unravelling, specks that settle into sediment.

My dreams themselves – and you should think of them as trickling and dribbling through a succession of days, nine if I remember correctly – usually concerned some simple visual puzzle of the sort a cautious and self-concerned dreamer might find comfortably intriguing. On a dream midnight, sky as taut as a nearly ripe plum, uphill lending a bend to my waist, a tilt to my trunk and a pecking motion to the climb, my breath contrives to reach down and fog the shine on my alternate toe-caps. Shine and fog, my reflected face and mist. I think we could safely describe this as my dream faculty gently testing its medium, me, with bipedalism, ingenuous light effects and a cobbled hill. May we progress? We may.

I have climbed such a slope to come to a shady private viewing. Let us pass over the usual louche touches, that aspect of insinuating riddles and bits of sawdust sticking to the soles of my shoes. It is a painting I have come to see. Though here a crowd of people and wretchedly coy lighting make it difficult to discern more than glazed patches of varnished black and a bobble of flesh and rose tints. A vowel-trawling voice beside me murmurs and I hear four words: suffer, supper, suppose and pose. I blink. I am instantly able to have the private viewing made singularly private. True, the room provided is small and close and that tedious shady business is now handled by a flickering fire below the painting on the chimney breast, but at least there is a brass plaque to help me:

R. D. – Dancer & Mistress to the Count A.

Does this formula mean that she danced just for him? Or is the word 'dancer' there as someone's idea of decorum, to show she did something else? Or does it merely mean he was first captivated by her on stage? I leave these questions for another. The painting is dated as for an enormous novel, took ten years from start to finish. Meaning? Surely no one works that slowly. I peer up at paint. And of course! There is the answer. Brief dates, long gap. The top half, head to navel, was done ten years before navel to feet. It is the same woman but described at two different ages and very different girths. A pert young trunk, nipples like red jujubes, has had grafted onto it adipose lower quarters more exacerbated than disguised by strips of gauzy scarfing swirling round her hunkers in a purely visual if mannerist breeze. Those slender, impudent young hands are paired with swollen, bunioned feet.

Let me repeat that this is a dream; I did not pause to ponder tritely on the novelty of the painter's treatment of time or the possible loyalty or disloyalty of the woman's lover. The triteness of my dreams tends to the lexical and the subject of the portrait was resolutely determined to show me what *she* understood by the word 'dancer'. By means of a device like a cylindrical commode at the thighs, simply pulling off flesh as soft as wet blotting paper above them, she revealed what she had been long before oils and canvas – a muscular, acrobatic adolescent.

And she really was most muscled. As she cleared away first the commode and then the plinth her fattest self had been sitting on, I saw that the muscles on her thighs looked as hard as my knuckles, that those on her shoulders and back resembled those mouse-shaped pumice stones I used to see in old-fashioned bathrooms, and that her stomach had the tuck of a Greek pot.

Now I did not expect, not in a dream, the minuteness of the next process, of what I think is called 'limbering up', nor, let us abbreviate, the charming if long-winded aspect of her stolidly imitating a large number of animalistic courtship displays. Rather late but with a deal of incompetent haste my dream director tried to cobble together a slightly more convincing backdrop and background. While I waited for her to run out of muscles to exercise, I suddenly found I had been placed in a wing chair, my foot raised, and that I had damaged my right knee; it had an overdone bruise of burgundy and black ink. I had also been given a cup of what looked like camomile tea and two blobs of strawberry jam or at least something gelatinous and red in it. And was that a game of solitaire on a side table in which the pieces were crumbling mothballs?

Enough distraction. At first I thought my little acrobat was divesting herself of her features; the colours on her face slid like a bright jigsaw off a small round tray. Then I saw that she was smearing on greasepaint. And creams and lotions and powders. And not just to her face. Thin oil went on her shoulders, thick, fluffy-looking grey stuff onto her joints and what I found animating was the graceful ease with which she covered her entire body and her slow crouch and swivel as she covered it and the matter of fact way she would blow away excess powder and then have oil or cream obscure the mark of a muscle.

The music off-stage was suspiciously like the sounds from a rhythmic butcher's shop; a slow cleaver, the bounce of a large bone, the flop of liver on a wooden chopping board, the thud of steak. This thud fattened and settled. Let me ignore that bath folded down from the wall to one side of the fireplace, though I could draw you a sketch of the simple but ingenious way it worked. Your toad is feeling excitement, enjoyable gulps, a stretching satisfaction that sinews, flesh and especially skeleton should be so supple. The little acrobat, now on the chequered floor, reduces. Limb by shape, she closes up. There was a moment she reminded me of a mass of dough or, given the colour and the cracks, of marzipan. But then, with the lightest of liquid clicks, akin to a politely doubting tongue coming away from the back of the front teeth, she became round and within this roundness contrived to make her fingers shift and stroke cream and oils so that finally there was nothing to identify her as human, no extremities, joints or partings. I shuddered. An amorphous globe of flesh and several colours; a pale madder, yolk beaten in milk, lemon-grey, a lightly purpled violet and reflections of a charcoal glow. But imagine my shock and delight! On either side of the orb an eye opened and began, rather stickily, to peer about.

Hush! Do you remember that delicious childhood sensation when you *wanted* to be caught by the adult playing the slow ape with you? I woke, a long, thrilling sensation of rising, my consciousness eager to join dream, through two levels of sleep and two dizzying conceits: that those were wide-spaced, round-tipped fingers and toes appearing at the base of the orb; that the rocking motion meant she was about to leap out of the painting at me onto my lap.

No, I do not apologize here either. The reader may know those occasions when considerable thoughts at night turn to a puddle of pollutive doggerel in the morning. Bleary, dishevelled, mopping up, I felt little different from that. And there is no need at all to pick out for me the derisory and vulgar elements with which my dream was riddled. That dubious art work, the pear-shaped navel, that golden-hearted trick for non-touching gentlemen, those twists and links with other parts and clauses of my life. It was undoubtedly a mediocre and tawdry little show.

And yet it was as if I had glimpsed another state of being, full of light and lightness. I felt in such good health that I was almost guilty. I could recognize myself. I felt re-housed again, at home once more. Absurd? I am sure of it. Had events been changed? No. But how I would have protested if you had suggested that dreams be arrested, led off, banished!

38

Then enter MacBeth in banker's blue and vanilla silk! He cocked an eye at me, loomed closer and I, uncombed, unshaven, pyjamas rumpled, heart scudding, flinched.

He nodded. 'Yes,' he said, 'you've got your old colour back.'

What? Now I might have expected vigour in his voice, or encouragement, but not that stolid contentment. Not after his banging so insistently and imperatively on my door. I peered back at him. But my brain felt flat and dry as an old pancake – and all that occurred to me was that I was not perhaps as well as my floating bedtime spirits had previously indicated.

Have you ever seen a natterjack or other toad react to an unpleasant taste? It spits out once, goes through a series of contraried but somehow resigned twitches, its lids first closing and then dividing one by one, till the eyes are revealed again bulging in reproach. My ornaments shuddered and tinkled as he walked in.

'Can I . . . can I get you anything?' I said.

'Oh. Yes. That's very kind of you.'

I was, of course I was, enormously pleased that MacBeth had called, however belatedly and unexpectedly and early in the morning; but what snagged was the lilt I had heard in his tone, a combination of the glum and the bright and the formal.

I stopped arranging saucers and cups and, for what I think was the first time in my life – though not for want of temptation – spied on my friend through the vertical gap between door-hinges. MacBeth had slumped onto a self-striped grey silk sofa and was considering without any sign of interest at all a shelf full of my favourite books. It was then, in something akin to an elegant and slow version of that gesture some make when startled by their own stupidity, he brought the heel of his hand against his forehead.

I retreated at once. I wriggled into some clothes but forgot, I was to see later, to shoe my feet, splashed water on my face, dabbed at but almost instantly gave up on a cowlick of hair and hurried back. I finished preparing the tray and carried it through.

'So,' he said when I had filled his cup. Except that nothing followed. He sat up, tugged at his trousers and kept his eyes resolutely on the stirred contents of the cup. Both of us watched the liquid spin a while. I have often enjoyed people behaving as if food or drink were alive and mobile, as if it might escape or someone else grab it while it was defenceless. But MacBeth seemed more deliberate than covetous, as if waiting for the spin to reach a certain slowness. He grunted, lifted, drank.

'Yes,' he said, 'I'd forgotten. Excellent.'

Surely this too contradicted the intimate tone of our past? I was not at my best but I presumed that meddling fylfots had stood up against unfamiliar ponds and possible pederasts and that he had called in dressed for a board meeting on his way to one. Well, well. I would cause him no more problems. Two of his fingers stroked round one of his eyes, moved down and turned across his lips, swung back over his chin. A brief, irritable shake of his head. Abruptly he stood, turned, walked to a window and, with his broad back to me, jammed his hands into his jacket pockets.

'Old friend,' he sighed, 'I don't really know how to say this.'

He turned his head and growled at me in profile over his shoulder.

'I'm afraid it is cancer.'

Stop. One day, reader, someone may feel called upon to be as

171

honest with you. I blinked, then let out my previous willingness to pay for a footling pond in a rapid riff of lid and lash. I have never been one of those who behave as if cancer should be pronounced with cogs and ratchets. But my eyes drifted to the marble mantelpiece and the unlit hearth. I felt traditional, creeping cold, but stifled a shiver. Then my frown, squint and blink shaped into a wave of outrage at my miserable medical poltroons. 'Run-down!' 'Quite interesting!' Dear God, was that the best the idiots could do by way of preparation? Couldn't they at least have had the grace to come and tell me themselves? Here, however, it occurred to me that it might have been MacBeth who had volunteered, first to rouse, then to tell me. I sighed. I sagged. Yes. And so much for dream cures! It was hopelessly late to feel foolish or gullible or the self-deluded alchemist. I had understood I was recovering dream, not that the dreams were a part of dying. As completely as general cases can be, I gave in. I saw an image; like liquid from a pot, a run of speckled ashes and pearls from an urn. Is it strange to say I felt alleviated?

'Ah.'

MacBeth turned to face me in a pale aura of northern light.

'I have come directly from the hospital.'

I had already started to nod before he finished speaking – but pulled up. Just what was he saying? Hot with the news? He could not mean that he, not *my* Maelbaetha . . . I looked down, saw my naked, splayed feet and jerked them together.

'What kind?'

'Eh? Oh, the breast.'

Wait! I watched him, kneading my shoulder, holding my breath. Despite the thick, curly hairs on their paps, it is still possible for men to have cancer of the breast.

'They took out the lump this morning.'

Oh reader! MacBeth and I were together in my steel-blue and grey study. My hands came up. Palms towards him, they hovered on either side of my jaw. Not me, not he, but *she*! I could not help it. After a grimace on the very brink of tears, after a swallow that well nigh choked me, I breathed out to the accompaniment of little spurts of relief that felt extremely like joy; the spout of bright fountains under a dull sky, gold-

172

flooded courtyards, a bubble of richly inlaid cupolas. Ah yes, that poor little rotten mammary (the left). Strange that this ancillary attribute in which I have never had much interest (though I do not discount a point of bland curiosity) should be her betrayer. I mean we all have bowels, stomachs, throats and lungs and that the breast was not strange at all, and that my dreams and fears were jostling like madmen.

'I have a favour to ask you.'

'Of course!'

'She needs time to get better. I want to spend . . .'

'Shhh.'

He started, stared, set off on a gloomy nodding.

'Yes. Thank you,' said MacBeth. 'You're right, you're right, of course you are.'

Was I? This exchange seemed dizzyingly quick. I had three thoughts. That Gruoch was probably still under sedation. That I really should put on some shoes. And that MacBeth wanted and had come to get Taha the caretaker, to allow him to be staunchly and entirely optimistic. And so it proved. Gruoch's cancer was a matter for determination and treatment. The subsequent radical mastectomy – I admit, I am squeamish, for some reason dislike the idea of a scalpel slicing into soft flesh even more than into muscle – he presented as something almost cheery, a resolute saving. I had already crept discreetly back to work between excised lump and no breast, some days before the start of the next gruesome treatment.

39

Everything depends on the telling. Good cases can be lost, a tragedy made derisory, a liar believed. Had MacBeth really chosen the best man for the task he wanted done? He had certainly forgotten – no shame at all on him – my murky immediate past. Very well, there was no question as to my loyalty to him, but before I could start I had to find out how much Rome had depreciated me for others. I was prepared for a great deal but was not, I think, quite as ready to find how a month away (including my dreamy convalescence) had affected those chanceless normans' manner towards me. Most were just, if sniffily, polite enough. But two did not even bother to be polite and two more actually chose to be snide.

Do not misunderstand. It is not that Ricci was right. I am not sure I do take the wider view. But, in reasonable health, I am a very mild-mannered but also very cold-skinned and observant toad. I wrote to Ricci, received an ecstatic reply and it was not difficult to come to a private and exclusive arrangement to exchange opinions and information. I sat down quietly, got entirely up to date on the day to day running of the enterprise and carefully worked out what was likely to happen, what difficulties and pressures would arise, what structural changes would be necessary – and thought on how to implement them. If before Rome I had felt inelegantly pessimistic, I was, when I had studied the agreement signed, almost satisfied with my restraint. Again, please do not misunderstand. A natterjack prefers to serve than to be right and loves to make out ways of being of use. In the eight weeks Maelbaetha was first and entirely preoccupied by Gruoch's health and treatment, I conceived of my job as a cool report to him.

More enjoyably, there was something leisurely about it too, to do with musing and an unfamiliar but luxurious sense of freedom. I was more than discreet. I was exceptionally thorough. And I think the freedom came from a sense of anticipation. Gruoch's treatment was to last a specific time and the decisions would be made after that had ended and my friend had returned. I took some enjoyment too in familiarity softening disapproval, that a scandalous month away is counteracted by a quiet month at home, that people fall into old patterns and that a colleague who had not bothered to be polite will come to see you, agitated, even upset, having completely forgotten his behaviour to you days before. Such a person speaks and not even very obliquely identifies his problem. He even sometimes gave me the impression of begging me to understand that he was mooning over a girl his daughter's age and not complaining about the quality of her work.

Yet he had no cognisance of what he was doing and I understood he would be insulted and further upset if I mentioned it. Yes, yes, all this is very routine and run of the mill but I think I needed a re-introduction to other people's worries, other emotions.

40

For Gruoch there was a tremulous little homecoming party within a much larger affair, all as early as for a child's birthday, an uncomfortable mix of bright colours, easy digestion, fading daylight, tea and malt whisky. Cloaking her with a rug, glum, virile, fussy MacBeth placed her in a wing chair and held her hand and kneaded her knuckles. In singularly slow motion, she turned her head to smile at him. She used the downward loll of her head to help one side of her mouth into a smile.

For a time I watched her in other faces, most of them resolutely fixed open, especially after shocked little rests from her appearance. Some did not appear to know why they were there and MacBeth may have chosen this way of informing acquaintances of Gruoch's illness. But how ill is she? I heard. Some murmurs too on the treatment being worse than the illness and, unnecessarily, of her being tremendously tired. She had rigged up an almost Moorish arrangement of white cloth around her head and neck and was voluminously dressed. She still looked emaciated. She had applied far too much make-up; it resembled wood stain and rouge and, of course, her eyebrows had been painted on. In a corner a tall, tweedy skulker hunched over something. Her plump son had hot cheeks and indignant, tear-sticky eyelashes and indulged a heavy-footed rocking motion, like a tantrum made slothful by distress. In all fairness I do not think that Gruoch was particularly vain. But I doubt that I would have exposed her to such a trivially social ordeal. A criticism? No, an observation. I followed the poor woman's forearm, reduced to two bones, skin and veins, above

175

the hand MacBeth clutched and worked, saw her wince and reclaim her fingers – whereupon he held onto her sleeve.

So. Taha became mother. I called Lula and had him fetch more hot water and ice. I distributed plates and food. MacBeth sat beside his wife on a footstool and she saw her visitors little by little. Gruoch ate nothing but from time to time behaved as if she had bitten her tongue, clapping her fingers over her mouth, squeezing her nose with her thumb. After an hour of bearing recurrent varieties of encouragement, a bilious gruel spurted through her fingers. I gave her a napkin – she even smiled – and indicated to MacBeth that it was high time for privacy and rest.

I had expected him to get her firmly and briskly out of the room. But no, in a startlingly shaky parody of gracious leave-taking, they strolled, stopped, exchanged words with this little group, nodded to that one, to end by turning round at the double door for her to utter hoarsely whispered thanks and a hope that she would be well on her feet the next time she saw everyone. Skull and skilled smile in a wooden frame. An extraneous element, as of a ghoulish bridal bedding, when he clumsily scooped her up and had the bald bride's head-dress slip. In that formal drawing room, however, came the doucie equivalent of a ragged cheer.

I had Lula see out those visitors who wanted to tip-toe directly away and myself played the elegantly dressed waiter whose shift ends in half an hour. My irritation was not feigned. How messily so-called civilized people leave plates! In what places the coy and furtive balance or secrete them! I had just bent and retrieved one that had been slid under a sofa when I grew conscious of spindly, heavily tweeded legs beside me. As I straightened, he spoke.

'I was so sorry to hear about your marriage, old man.'

The remark seemed to me on a par with the plate and I replied accordingly.

'Best over, I assure you.'

It was not until I saw the manner of his start, matched the thin legs and the hairy tweed, that I realized this was Malcolm. His spectacles were larger and thicker than ever and the effect – his skin was pallid, his eyes a bleary blue – was of something multiple and swollen. Had my hands been free I might have caught hold of his spectacle frames and peered in. How he had aged! That bang of hair over his forehead had gone to reveal a brow like swelling bread dough. Yet surely he was some years younger than me. Reflected in his glasses a determinedly small shape stirred. I looked down at a tiny black-haired woman with powdered freckles and an extravagantly loose dress.

'The baby is due in February,' she said.

'Ah. Congratulations.'

'My wife Margaret,' said Malcolm. 'She's Hungarian. Originally.'

So that was the marriage business. The last time I had seen him I had talked to Ingeborg, his first, also foreign wife, rather charmingly blonde and large. I nodded and offered my hand to his second. Her firm little paw tugged downwards on my three central fingers.

'Is Taha a nickname?' she enquired. I had made a mistake. Her accent was perfectly good. What she had done was banish any hint of irony and add a slight lisp.

'No, it's my middle one.'

'Have you found it an advantage?'

'How do you mean?'

'To be called something special.'

'Well, if someone calls out Taha I am usually the only one to turn round.'

'This is a boy,' she said. 'We've decided to call him David.'

'I'm so pleased. How's your mother?'

'Eats cakes and plays bridge all the time. Here!' He summoned a tall, bare-kneed, blond child. 'Duncan,' he said, 'say hello to an old friend of your grandfather's and mine.'

I shook hands with the fragile boy. I am no gossip but I did wonder as to how Malcolm rather than Ingeborg had got custody. Briefly. I had merely preferred her to him and I had in one hand a tiered arrangement of messy plates; someone had used a border as a scraping edge.

'Ah,' said MacBeth, laying a hand on our respective shoulders, 'seeing you together reminds me of those delightful parties your parents had.'

I thought Malcolm looked as embarrassed as at his father's memorial service – but without the dispatch.

'Yes,' he mumbled, 'delightful.'

MacBeth squeezed my shoulder and I watched Margaret carefully consider at least double her weight re-arranged into a large, bizarrely sentimental male. But what nostalgic rubbish was this? I had made my judgement of those 'parties' years before. Gruoch was seriously ill but why prettify tedious patches of the past? Nor could I believe that she would have agreed with her heavy-handed husband. I called Lula and gave him the plates.

'Here,' I said, 'I think you'd better take these. Your father has something he wishes to tell me.'

I was aware; perhaps I sounded as tetchy as I was. But MacBeth smiled, even his sentimentality resolutely capacious, and told me he wanted to strengthen the 'numbers side'. And research. Accordingly he thought Malcolm should join us. There was a great deal to reorganize after the Rome agreement. Didn't I think so? I did.

'He is presently a Senior Lecturer and doing work on non-linear mathematics,' said Margaret.

MacBeth smiled again. 'You're agreeable then?'

I had neither the disposition nor the power to object, so why did he insist?

'Of course. When will you start?'

'Oh,' said Malcolm, scratching the back of his hand, 'spring I think.'

'What are we talking about – March, April time?'

'May,' said Margaret.

On the other side of winter, seven months away. MacBeth grinned. I was not even sure he was listening.

'Very well,' I said. 'I'll look forward to a meeting to sort out details, contract, staff and so on.'

Malcolm patted at his breast pockets while his wife opened her bag and handed me a stuffed, sealed envelope. Evidently that was quite enough for MacBeth; he gave me a light knuckleworth on the shoulder, shook hands with the couple and left to see Gruoch again.

That bulky envelope I opened next day to find what was described in the covering note as 'a proposal for a contract'. The thing was thirty-seven pages long, a veritable permutation of options, and conditions to meet any case from cosmic accident to Margaret's finding a similar dress at a 'business function'. I do not know if Malcolm thereby meant to demonstrate the thoroughness of his approach or was simply revealing an obsession with security. Detail, which I honour, can be comically thorough. I admit, however, I found the pernickety prose of his demands more irritating than amusing and it was out of irritation rather than for his information that I sent a copy to MacBeth, the only time I bothered him in all this. I have always disliked professional special cases but knew, of course, that my friend never found variety a problem. The proposal came back a few days later and I think those were pencil ticks on pages 1, 2 and 3. There was nothing else until the last page where he had written, very faintly, the unheard of, 'Well.' Gruoch was about to go back into hospital after a bare week at home.

41

Any reader with experience of working in an organization will now recognize my concerns. I give Malcolm as a token. My mind churned with churlish questions. They included asking myself whether Malcolm was to be a superior addition to or would displace the heads of two departments. Should I tell the two competent people involved? Now? Or nearer the time, when working out any notice would overlap with Malcolm's arrival? Add in many pressing non-Malcolm matters. But I was most dispirited by MacBeth's method of telling me I now had to act alone. I am a scrupulous follower. And somehow that little piece of social theatre, even more infestive than my dream, made me feel not so much alone as gratuitously adrift. It was demeaning. I felt as if I had been given a perfunctorily wrapped present; on opening it you find a dried-out pomander and on looking up robust amusement from the giver. You would like to be flattered by the confidence but the pomander itself depresses. What will you do with it? You pick out a strand or two of desiccated herb with one hand; your pomander palm begins to itch.

I used two matters to help me. I resisted another verbal wart. In this case the pompous 'parenthesis'. As in a parenthesis has opened. I liked the lack of agent. Do you remember that legalist? We had long since parked and limited him, his retirement was at last, in his own self-important expression, 'at hand' and he may have had some complacent idea of an extension to his employment to go with the relish with which he pronounced his parenthesis.

'Do you mean a bracket?'

He had the gall and whinny to look put upon. 'Wah. A period of considerable uncertainty.'

'In what?'

'In MacBeth's return of course!'

'The only doubt there is as to when, surely?'

'But that's what I am saying! The duration of his absence is uncertain.'

'Considerably?'

'What's that?'

I sighed. 'He is,' I said, 'preoccupied. But after all, he is not the one who is ill. He could be contacted now. Except that there is no need. His instructions are perfectly clear. The firm functions, we have aims, we have a timetable. I know, for example, that you are retiring at the end of the year. I have your farewell dinner in my diary. I know what your present is. I see here I even have some notes for a presentation speech.'

'Ah.'

'So why not close those brackets of yours?'

'What?'

I know his hearing was poor but I have a certain appetite for scunner. I drew him a (

'Yes?'

And I closed it thus: ()

'Oh,' he said, 'I am not sure you *can* do that. I think they have to be ( ).'

I laughed. How long it had been since I had laughed out loud! I enjoyed it from the sound to the rhythm of throat and lungs and barely bothered whether or not the old fellow might be offended. But he started nodding away.

'Ahhh, I *see*!' he said. 'What you're going to be is a sort of pipeline!'

I grinned. A what? For some reason I thought of pipe-cleaners, those things left over from their original function that children have to twist into animalistic shapes.

The second matter was entirely mine. I cannot explain it but I had to see Gruoch. Within a very short time it was a craving. I needed reassurance. Of what? That she was really ill? That is as absurd as saying I had to smell surgical spirit. But I had to go.

In the event I was rather taken aback by how healthy she looked tucked up in her hospital bed. We chatted briefly and cheerfully while I ponderously noted that she spoke of future dates and plans. Later, as I wiped sweat from my face in the corridor, a terminal gossip of a nurse told me something of the newly acquired cosmetic skill and effort in Gruoch's cheerfulness. She rewarded my stare at her greasy, open-pored complexion.

'It's in the lymph nodes.'

'Meaning?'

'Are you family?'

'Friend.'

'Then pray it's quick. Doctors pass by, we have to sit with them.'

Stupidly, I suspected the nurse's motives but accepted the venal tidbit. Enough that is to make some discreet enquiries and notes as to funerals and to situate myself most carefully within a calendar. Behind that was a desire to dispatch Gruoch's pain quickly. And his. But in practical terms I considered that I had nerved myself not to let him down in his absence.

42

All that business! It shrinks to a dot and even that shifts. Though there was purpose and point and, above all, effect to it. A natterjack takes sixteen weeks from spawn to toad. But I recall first the brain-deadening hours in which I ceased to exist and became something gelatinous held in by sockets and a dreary indication of edges. It is not, I assure you, what men do but what they resist. Discuss, but only in part. Incidentals are just that. I look up through the window pane at the sky and insist that the trappings, the papers, notes, drafts, assistants and messengers do not usurp the poor individual. Poor is always relative but remove that poverty and you will, I trust and believe, have carnivores browse on your arrogant members and extremities.

Forgive me. If outwardly prim and calm, internally I jiggled between the distraught and the overwrought. Have I ever believed decisions can be quite rational? I can't think so. And the more I considered the matter the more stubborn I became and the less I wanted to cause any hurt to the persons Malcolm might or might not want to replace. Neither of them was in the political or emotional parts of the business and neither was aggressively ambitious. Reader, I had no desire whatsoever for shrill spats and squabbles. I hankered for the triumph of quietness. Or, to put it another way, since I had to fight, I wanted quiet on my side and noise to fight against. Accordingly I arranged my proposals for the changes required after the Rome agreement with numeracy on my side and flair on the other. I could dress this up in a degree of decorous rationality but I am not convinced that would be a necessary or a more accurate reflection of how I worked. Publicly I waged slow wart on flair.

Privately I toyed with heliography, hand-mirrors, water and sun. I made my suggestions very cautiously, bit by bit, encouraged implications to stiffen into possible solutions, had those solutions take their place in a possible scheme of action and was always prepared to listen. To these more or less legitimate elements I added the legalist's fraudulent pipe-dream; I behaved as one sent to consult the oracle, when there was no oracle to consult, only a husband suffering from a very sick wife. Shabby as a medium, doleful as an ectoplasm, I talked in meetings of figures that would not forgive, of staff reductions that could not be avoided – and after an objection would return, re-vindicated, from the hospital.

I began to think it was impossible to persuade anybody to anything unpleasant unless it was disguised. And please, I have few doubts that, from the thin, practical point of view, my methods were probably justified and my proposals, in business terms, about as right as they could be. I was not really surprised by how little people who had worked on the agreement had thought about it. What struck me then was how many people indulged personal or departmental dramas but ignored answers for others, of how many were led by the self-defeating notion that it was their right to object but not their responsibility to suggest a solution. I had hoped that after the first loud objections someone might contribute other possible courses of action. Not one did. The result was that I spent weeks listening to indignation and passion, gradually working my way down through levels of patience. To what?

It must be obvious that none of this was in the slightest enjoyable. Let us leave for a moment the grounds by which one individual keeps a job and another does not or considerations of how early someone's retirement should be. I am not, by nature, combative. I need help. Exasperation, boredom and anger in myself – stupidity in others. I could not pretend. I was waiting for trespass. Let me pat and stroke the back of my mother's hand-mirror. Now. In an excited state, with an under-bubble of guffaw, the buffoon asked me if I thought I was behaving as the surgeons with Gruoch, treating the firm as a diseased body. I have always loathed similes and metaphors to do with desperate health. But his question was a suitably gross and inaccurate insult and I was, in a pottering, private way, awfully relieved.

'You have a tremendous gift for the inapposite,' I said. 'Anybody else wish to pursue a surgical companion?'

In point of fact I found not one but two private huddles. I do not know why so-called conspiracies always attract those who have no talent for plotting and no clear aims. I tried in my amphibious way to warn those involved. Fair is fair. Though I see that, by chance, I started well down the firm. I sacked the porter. Porters should not report old gossip. Vindictive? Mean? So be it. That wasn't my point. I merely looked at him, shrugged and asked him to pick up his cards. And if my quiet, numerical friends blinked at my action, and if my enemies found my action ignoble but obscure, well. It is clear that I have only ever felt willingly answerable to one person.

43

So many visits to the hospital, with its patchwork hygiene, the scrubbed wrists and hands of an occasional doctor and the rank armpits of a shifting legion of nurses, confuse my memory; I cannot now quite remember the order of all the incidents in Gruoch's illness. Like coming to the top of another ramp and looking left and right, seeing exhortatory notices rather than directions so that I learnt the markers of the route to Gruoch's room first as imperfections, a huge crack in a wall or a stain on a ceiling. And then my feet learnt. I traipsed along, all squeak and echo, to bring her bright flowers and to watch, appalled at what was being done to her, the tilt of her grotesque wig and the effort of her eyes – they appeared to stick – as I tweaked the blooms into an arrangement.

'I'm sorry about these irises again. I only know a few kinds.'

I am not sure what this lie was meant to be. Jaunty? To fit the male? As she stared at me it occurred to me that she did not recognize who I was.

I blinked. I saw her right hand begin to crawl across the top sheet. Horrified I watched it until, with a start, I realized I should put out mine. Gruoch made to grip it. Moist, nap-worn skin, very little pressure and that mostly due to a fumbling, as if she were not sure what she had. I saw that she was weeping; no tears, no sound, but a hopeless girn and grimace.

'Taah,' she whispered. 'Taah. Help him!'

Oh reader, to be borne along on that broken voice! I nodded. I pressed my lips hard together and shook my head against my own susceptibility to tears.

'You,' I said, 'you recover.'

She blinked. She frowned. I mean it took her some seconds to decide I had failed her; at which she winced, closed her eyes and withdrew her hand.

'Understand!' I blurted. 'I will always help him.'

Her lids opened again. Her eyes were discolouring. Under the glaze of pain and sedation, tiny pus-coloured and rust cracks. I leant closer and urged on my voice.

'All that I can. In every way that I can.'

Gruoch gave the slightest and driest of nods, as of a now relatively unimportant item on a long list checked and ticked and, after a gesture that troubled me, a very slow, lascivious-looking lick of her lips, turned her head to sleep. It did not look like disbelief. Could it have been a smile – or a try at remembering the taste of one? I watched her a while, pre-posterously agitated, dreadfully miserable because she would never know how much I had loved, loved and would love her husband – when would I ever have told her – and much in the same way left the room on erratic tiptoe, a distraught hirple.

MacBeth was outside, at yet another window. He turned on me a face bellowing with grief and hate, which slumped when he saw who it was. I let my heels come down. How worn he looked! There was a separation in his face; compact bones and facial muscles and on top of them a slack float of skin, soft macerated walnuts under his eyes, over-ripe patches of shadow at his temples and lower cheeks. Oh, and with what pity I saw the gleam of his scalp at the crown! Instinctively my right hand came up. A private cupping of his pain. To my surprise he reached out, caught my fingers and squeezed hard.

'Thank you for coming, old friend.'

'Don't be silly.'

'How much longer will they make her suffer?' he said, letting go of my hand.

I shook my head, touched his elbow. He shuddered.

'Yes,' he said. 'I'll go in. Be with her.'

44

Is revenge a furious sort of self-regard? Perhaps. I was never that self-confident. My eyes always tend to lower in the face of a mirror. And my revenge was, if thorough enough, secondary. I mean that I did not instigate but took quick, tight-jawed advantage of circumstance, and I think it is probably true that Gruoch's pain stiffened my resolve. Yes, revenge has to be final, cannot be undone, has to be paid for, but for those of you who will never have the opportunity to repay gross arrogance or the nerve to castigate ignorant abuse, let me share my vengeance with you now.

Rather pathetically when I come to think of it, financial details of currencies and markets had filtered through my months as MacBeth's mammet. Now, if I in a sideline could see what was coming, why could not the hand-mirror man? Too busy plotting. Beautifully written, culturally wrapped letters from Ricci confirmed my reading. What was so special or difficult? A group of interrelated currencies; much the strongest was becoming even stronger. The relationship required change, and as power is power the weaker currencies (of which ours was one) devalued. This meant that the real costs of the Rome agreement rose considerably. If real costs rose, other plans were jeopardized. Earlier on, I hymned dismay. This was one of the richest dismays I was ever privileged to see. Those faces round the table! No, no, I offered no delicate mirrors. I merely observed those woeful eyes, the shocked, beefy cheeks, that stunned look after the first hurried calculations. 'You wart,' I whispered. And while quiet is common, even in emergency meetings, such strong epithets are unusual.

There was the slightest of stirrings, as in secondary shock, to my right. I smiled briefly at it and went on to describe the hand-mirror man as arrogant in the general, disloyal to Mac-Beth in the particular and incompetent in his given duties. Accordingly I could see no reason whatsoever not to ask for his resignation – immediately.

Oh, the best man is never the groom, the elegist is never the corpse, but this action gave me the intensest of short pleasures. Naturally I had a list of considerations and queries to follow up on. Wait, there was, just a trifle, an effort to reply.

'I'm sorry,' I cut in. 'We don't have the time. That gentleman is no longer with us.'

For those who like tastes in the mouth, this was strawberries and cream with, for the sweet-toothed, a sprinkling of sugar crystals. Easy? Long awaited. A few days later I even made a gap in a very busy schedule to receive the hand-mirror's handmaiden. I was I think considerate to the point of compassion. It is true I told her I was disappointed that he should send her (loganberries) and that I also enjoyed using such expressions as 'dreadful misjudgement' and 'complete mis-reading of his position' (gooseberry fool) and that I could see her beginning to doubt his old boasts and his new injustices, but I also suggested that I was partly responsible for allowing him to be promoted beyond his abilities. Was this despicable? I daresay it was. Was it ignoble? Without a doubt. But if you have ever wondered as to the intentions in certain behaviour, if polite, quiet persecution is possible, then this is my example. Besides, I had no qualms at all in getting rid of him – or his followers. And I certainly was not above rudimentary mean-ness. I ignored all the customary stuff among gentlemen of fat settlements and fulsome references, though I have reason to believe that this was not taken as spite but as cost-cutting indication of how serious the situation was. It was. And while at confession let me also say I took time, a few minutes but decidedly savoured, to cut off all help to the woman who had tattooed my scalp with an ivory comb. I was tired of persons who think they deserve and that wrong decisions have no costs, but there was another element too, doomed and fatuous, of trying through practice to acquire a taste for simple, ruthless actions.

By the time Malcolm joined us I had dismissed over a hundred other people, almost all of whom were simply and innocently unnecessary to the new scheme of things. I had saved up a little bile to enable me to stomach what I had to do, I used a few like the comb woman to offset the nausea, but even so I felt wretchedly as if I were, dismissal on dismissal, poisoning myself. I ignored all the congratulations, commendations and praise. Oh, I know some of those people were able to find other jobs quite quickly, that others professed themselves delighted to retire early, but somehow I was never convinced I had not harmed them. Did I blame MacBeth? Yes. But it made no difference. And thought made me no happier. Self-knowledge can be no reward. I encountered my position between helpless self-importance and an abject desire not to act alone.

45

In my demure and servicial youth, when I was popular as an escort to the theatre, I was fortunate enough to witness a famous actor near the end of his career, a very old man playing an old man. In Act V he lost his way and place. There were several moments of an almost delicious uncertainty; some stutters and barks from the other actors sputtered out to be replaced by a buzz of embarrassment and sympathy in the stalls. I concentrated on the actor. He looked soaked and saturated in greasepaint and fatigue but at the buzz he gave a ham's twitch of annoyance and incredulity. He shrugged his padded shoulders. Turning away he muttered something indistinct – and instantly received an eruption of serried palms, applause so rapid and dense it was difficult to hear the claps. The poor man looked back over his shoulder as if he were being ruthlessly and inexplicably hunted down, then shook his head as if too weary to care. A hasty confabulation backstage, a bow from him – and the play went on. The voices took a little time to make their way through the pleasant tingling in my ears.

My companion told me two things. First that she had thought the actor was about to collapse and die on stage. Then, how sad it was that a great career should end in that theatre in that way.

'That might be an attraction for that kind of man,' I said. 'Besides, he may simply have been out of sorts.'

She blinked at me. 'I hadn't thought of that.' And after a pause, 'You hate drama, don't you?'

That miserable latch has rattled again. And to make sure I heard his interruption, my neighbour pounded on the door. He has been kind. He has given me both a small cage and its gross dowdy occupant. He thinks it may be a fledgling chough and has found it likes maggots, grasshoppers and centipedes. All I know is that the creature is reproachfully ugly and can emit a monotonous single peep at three-second intervals. I have taken it outside and hung the cage from a hook. Now where was I?

Yes, Taha was at doing and making do in the dreariest of presents. I can hardly complain, not when cancer had moved into Gruoch's spine, but I was working without hope, a literally dark condition. Yes, I was serving MacBeth but the action was joyless, at such remove that the notion of being definitively isolated but not run out of time sat on me like a wet stone. How I missed him and what he had been! His sly, ironic smiles. That characteristic gesture when he used his index finger as a kind of covering sketch for a smile which turned into a scratch by his eye – and then he would laugh. I felt my tongue drying up, becoming stiff, stumpish, sore. I noted that I sometimes had difficulty recalling a word; it might appear, like the flattened v for bird in wrongly taught children's drawings, but would vanish in a blink, lost against the cliffs or shelves of books behind.

Likewise with Ricci's letters, often almost a review of a book he had lately read (essays mostly, geopolitical, ethical or economic grapplings); I found myself finding that if I held up his writing at arm's length it took on the appearance of rows of extraordinarily regular blue waves. I mean that the quality of my observation, thought and language – surely you have noticed! – had shortened, become distractedly blunt. I barely cared. I continued, drearily, to suffer. At last I had certain if unwelcome knowledge: I had absolutely no possibility of competing with a dying wife.

Nor could I, with any self-respect, even as the roundest of solipsistic toads, look outside the confines of my own hand-mirror. Several times I turned it face down and decided that I should forsake him. But I could not do it. As in a parody of the most hopeless of marriages, a dragging sensation of loyalty, habit, fear of being out of his remotest shadow, even sometimes pride in the utter thanklessness of my position, kept me listlessly and wearily there. I am not sure I even thought that clearly. Like him, I was dragged hopelessly along. I recall someone – with more than a trace of pleasured spite – describing MacBeth as having, like a mannikin, 'had the stuffing knocked out of him'. A guying, not that hard to manage and, if not accurate, at least insinuating enough for me to remember the phrase and not the dog who said it.

46

Malcolm arrived in time for the second round of cuts and I suppose I was blearily surprised to find in him a stoutly insipid ally. I mean that at board meetings he positioned himself (physically) beside me, never (even in private) disagreed with anything I said and was extraordinarily prompt (if brief) to disapprove of the slightest show of disagreement in others. I can hardly think this had very much to do with me. It may have combined an element of his mother's nostalgia or his astute wife's perception of my position but mostly it had to do with his own concept of loyalty. It was plain as to whose future this was directed. Please do not misunderstand. I was doubly grateful, for the bland support and for the self-centred clarity of his ambition.

Over the next year or so I found him to be gloomily optimistic in the general and the particular. Malcolm was an enthusiastic definer, with an imposing belief in systems, rules and regulations. He let me get on with the cuts, proved adept at winning over the numbers people and we would discuss, tentatively, future expansion. The contrast with MacBeth, a sceptic when it came to detailed plans, a man who had relished personal contact and conversation and persuasion, was considerable. But why on earth not? There is certainly a case for both, though for reasons that may appear clearer than they really are I preferred MacBeth's old approach (with safeguards) to Malcolm's (in which the system tends to take on a despotic life of its own). I think I probably found his little wife more interesting; she treated her stepson with an air of holy apology and their own child, from the earliest age, with blissful exigence. But to my point. It was gradually borne in on me that there were energetic persons waiting to take over the firm and I could not see – their ideas were as valid, they were a deal younger – why they should not be allowed to do so.

47

Twice I think, yes, twice, I have – how leerily! – considered calendars, touched the edges of Gruoch's pain, riffled a thick whirr of days and not been able to stomach it and let the fat last *year* drop down in a block.

What had she done for such a punishment? I am neither flippant nor credulous. The devout can look forgivingly confident, the atheist can look cynically askance and the artist may very well look elsewhere for his art; I do not really expect to find an element of human justice in a process far, far slower than a snail's oververtebral pebbles. No, Taha the Toad, self-described natterjack, a very humble historian, does not look for reasons and motives in such pain; I merely showed irritation at the human agents, the doctors with their shifts, duties and resolutely contrite manners.

But why did they keep her alive for such a time? What was the precise point of their holding off death in that way? At the patient's cost? I remember going to see Gruoch a few days after Malcolm had completed his first year with us. I thought at first they had moved her, that a child was now occupying her bed. Then that Gruoch had died and they had, almost as quickly, found another occupant for her room. But dear God, it was her, reduced to a hunchbacked, jut-jawed, leg-trailing dwarfishness. I saw that her hands and feet had retained something of their old size but the rest had collapsed. Her head rocked on her ribcage. The sight of her made me dizzyingly distempered. As I left I was seized by a sharp pain in the prostrate, as if someone had jabbed a needle deep into my lower belly. I doubled up. In front of me dangled some scrubbed hands.

'Are you all right down there?'

I looked up. 'Why shouldn't I be?'

'Do you need attention?'

'No.'

He watched me straighten up.

'Ah,' I said, 'why do you do that?'

'What?'

I indicated Gruoch's door. 'Keep her alive in that way.'

'Are you family?'

'Answer a question for once.'

He twitched. He gave me a good-humouredly condescending look.

'Now that lady – she *is* a fighter.'

'She's going to recover then? Good. I am so pleased.'

He sighed. 'We do the best we can you know. I really have to . . . get on.'

'In which case I hope you get the same. Illness and treatment.'

'What?'

'I've never seen the need to express curses grossly. Or loudly. But quiet manners do not mean the curse is not deep.'

'I beg your pardon?'

'Like a collapsed, bony, agonic accordion. Didn't you say you had something to do?'

It was here that MacBeth appeared.

'What's all this?' he asked.

'I asked him why they were keeping Gruoch alive.'

'Ah. I've done that too,' said MacBeth. 'But his moral sense is superior to any mortal pain.'

For the first time in months I felt a leap of hope . . . *My* MacBeth!

But then I saw him slowly offer his hand.

'How are you, Doctor? Good. And your patient?'

And I realized his incisiveness had been an accident or the product of flat despair. I shut my eyes. I left.

48

My distemper may have had some of its thinner roots in the physiological, an unusual awareness that skin has layers and, about a handspan below my armpit, a shuttling between ripe itch and petulant prickle. When I got home I took off my shirt and at once recognized shingles. Some eight years before MacBeth had had a tremendous cascade down his back. Lula, then a plump, downy adolescent, stretched out his hand and gave his stepfather, just between the shoulderblades, a compassionate pat. My friend behaved as if abruptly arrested, hands shooting up, back curving, a look of shock at the pain coming through a wide-eyed, round-mouthed grimace, the nearest a face comes to a ripple expanding into a pond. A while later, his mouth now clamped and his lips invisible, breath eased out of his nostrils. I think MacBeth could have spoken then but chose not to. Lula had raised his patting hand to his face; it waggled there like someone blowing on dice.

MacBeth tried to give him a comforting smile, shook his head, had a finger work like a metronome.

I refer, priests aside, to the adult version of chickenpox. The difference in terms of discomfort is astonishing. But there is also the look of the affliction. My own case was a humble enough band confining itself for once to what my dictionary defined, a strip some six inches wide which ran from my spine round the right side of my body to end at my sternum. There was a sharp-lined geometrical neatness in that – I was grateful the line ran just under a vulnerable-looking nipple – and in the quilted rhomboid shape of the pustules or blisters. I notice that, locally, shingles comes as *'culebrina'* though I do not know if the allusion to vipers refers to the pattern and lustrous look of the affected skin or to the feel of sharp fangs releasing poison or to both.

From time to time I could feel my brain whimper. With faith then in the powers of just description I compared the sensation to a sharp, slightly ragged pin pressing a point of hot mustard deeper into an open cut. There. Now I would say it was like having my nerve ends munched by pincer-like small jaws. In any case I had chosen the wrong day and time – a Friday evening – to find I had shingles. For a number of reasons, one being economies in distribution, certainly for non-medical people, I could obtain neither the drug that would have reversed the shingles (if caught early enough) nor the anaesthetic foam I would later be prescribed. Another reason was an almost luxurious indifference on my part. For a few days, during which I went to work, told no one and wore a small, fixed smile, I relied on an old-fashioned bottle of calamine lotion. There were a few moments, when the chill pink stuff provided a fresh coating of relief; then the solution warmed, dried and the colour faded to white. The powder would crumble and I would watch, courtesy of my engraved hand-mirror, the rise of sheen, warts and pearls. I do not know if this was compensation of some sort but it was definitely a small, if perversely possessive, pleasure.

49

As is usual I think, my shingles lasted a little over a fortnight. I woke one Sunday to find, instead of glistening blisters on my chest, a set of raw pits and a mess of ragged grey and black skin. The pits were impressively deep and smoothly scooped, there was an equally impressive lack of sensation and I considered, not uncheerfully, that I would be marked for the rest of my life. The scars have indeed faded, resemble pale brine stains, and the sensation over those ribs remains, in a comfortable, distant way, deficient. I managed to clean and wrap myself up just in time for an unexpected visitor.

'Uncle Taha!' said Lula.

Surely he was rather old to be still uncling me. What was he? Twenty-four? But of course I smiled. Whereupon he embraced me and I patted him. Naturally I thought of Gruoch.

'Is everything all right?'

'Yes. But, you see, I want your advice.'

'Whatever I can do. Come in, come in.'

'And I want to introduce you to someone very special.'

From the shadows a girl appeared whose navel had advanced so far that it had become convex rather than concave and showed through the material over her belly like the soft teet at the end of a not quite fully inflated balloon.

Later that day I went to the hospital and accosted MacBeth.

'But I don't understand,' he said. 'If they want to get married, why don't they?'

'They want permission.'

'Is she under-age?'

'Monetary permission. An allowance.'

'Yes, yes, I'll keep them.' MacBeth glanced at Gruoch's door. 'Why didn't they come to see me themselves?'

'Some sort of delicacy I think – but don't ask me to explain it.'

'It's *his* mother.'

'I don't know if that's the delicacy.'

There followed an inconclusive chat about jobs and education, with a vague handwave from him towards the latter.

'Are you sure that's wise?'

MacBeth scratched his cheek. 'How do you mean?'

'Correct me if I am wrong. He has not so far finished any course.'

'So far.'

Had I offended him? MacBeth said nothing and did so gloomily for some time. Then he gave up and announced it with a small groan.

'Thank you,' he said. 'I don't know why you should get . . . You couldn't . . .'

'Yes.'

Oddly enough it was Malcolm who did something about getting Lula a job with the firm. I was not sure I understood his reason; but he too used the word 'delicacy' when he referred to step-relationships, presumably thinking of his own first son and Margaret. Lula lasted for about four years in some odd job capacity to do with the preparation of prospectuses and reports, specializing, if I have this right in graphics, coloured pies and so on.

The wedding was a small affair with the groom tearful and the bride triumphant. I did my best to make the reception elegant. MacBeth and I were by far the oldest of the guests, the bride's parents, out of some economical and vulgar sense of morality, not attending. I gave the young couple an extravagant sum of money and after a huddle between them was rewarded with the secret site of their honeymoon. MacBeth downed a glass of champagne.

'I sometimes wonder if he is all there,' he grunted.

I think that was the last time we were together in that way, two middle-aged men standing by a wall and looking on. We considered his stepson together. Lula began with splayed feet, had short stout legs and buttocks that made him tilt forward. But then he reduced to a narrow trunk, a soft little belly and thin sloping shoulders before swelling out again at his neck which was thick enough to form a straight line with his cheeks and head. Pale blue eyes set in a puzzled frown. The puzzlement could quickly become damp and emotional.

'Happy?'

'Gloriously, Uncle, gloriously.'

'I wonder,' I said to MacBeth, 'if it will be a boy or a girl.'

My friend turned his head to look at me, then shrugged. He and the newly married couple left immediately after the meal to visit the groom's mother. I had to stay on to look after the young guests.

50

I have never been sharp-witted. Nor very resilient. Routine joins with me to make a dull talent for surprise. I never knew how I would find Gruoch, whether moribund or cheerful, whether incoherent or precise. A week after her son's wedding, two months before life really did depart her, I went once again to the hospital and found her propped up, smiling and feeling, she said, 'almost euphoric with pain-killers'.

It had been many months since anyone had suggested she would not die and I was happy to think of her as dignified and brave.

'I hear you've been doing awfully well in bloody circumstances,' she said.

'I wouldn't bet on that at all.'

'And my son.'

'Oh, that was a pleasure.'

She patted my hand. 'Dear Taha,' she said, 'what would we do without you?'

Do you remember that long-ago session on a lawn when she kissed me against a background of pansies? Of course drugs make drunk. I do not believe things repeat, here found myself uncomfortably hoping my belief would not be tested.

'I've been spending my time remembering,' she said. 'Small, pleasant things mostly. Common in one way, not in another.'

'Good.'

'Do you remember, a long time ago, when Lula was barely

197

more than a fat-legged toddler, we once went to a beach? We went swimming.'

'Why yes. I think I do.'

'And a mist rolled in. We thought we had lost you. And when the mist rolled out, there you were sitting morose and stark naked on a rock with a gull, or maybe that was a cormorant, for company?'

I stared at her. I managed a slight laugh. 'You're not very good at birds, are you?'

She smiled. 'It was quite lovely. Rather pathetic and funny at the same time. You were facing Norway. And you came out of the water muttering in Arabic! Yes, but the main thing was you hadn't noticed the *mist* had gone!'

No, no, none of this was in any way correct! 'Are you talking about a little bay with one head like an old molar? It was hollow and had bats in it.'

She frowned. 'I don't remember any bats.'

'But it was as high as a cathedral inside!'

'Oh yes,' she said. 'I remember – all those fantastic stories you told of your childhood!'

'What? Ah,' I said, 'when I was young people used to ask me what the matter was. Was I all right?'

Gruoch smiled. 'I can believe that.'

Now if she wished me to live up to her fanciful image of me, I supposed it was well and good. But are dying people allowed to ask anything at all that they want? She shook her head at me.

'What was it,' she said, 'that went wrong with your marriage?'

'Oh, I was too discreet and she was too pretty.'

'What?'

I tried again. 'Age difference.' I tapped my head. 'A lack of shared interests I think.'

'Yes?' she said doubtfully. 'I remember her telling me she thought she loved you almost too much. I told her you were a vulnerable, sweet person. But I don't think she knew what I meant.'

Dear God. Gruoch smiled, replete with the satisfaction of solution. It was like seeing myself in an old mirror, a cloudy thing in a dark storeroom, with patches of silvering gone, a spatter of black spots and an unfriendly crack.

A moment after she began chortling over me.

'Oh, and your father!'

But this was too much! Why had I presumed that bad health was a defenceless state, that dying people were if not wise at least circumspect?

'There was that business – wasn't there? – at school when a master who didn't want to say anything told you about "a little chit". And you thought your poor father had taken his own life. And it had to be explained to you that he had run off with a young woman.'

'She was only young if . . .'

'. . . you were a bachelor master of sixty. Yes. And you kept saying, "But a chit is a note, isn't it? Isn't it?" '

Have you ever seen someone mortally ill almost choke with laughter? There are humiliations so deep, so absurd, you feel in some sort of abeyance. At the time I ignored the wrongness. I was struck that this other woman, my friend's wife, was casually, if with appetite, dismembering my memories and my past. It may be innocence, even of a desperate kind, but I still do not think that her action was in any way spiteful; no, her laugh was too boisterous and genuine for that. Yes, my father did run off but he was a widower by then and, rather more important to me than a woman, he ran because he had (I knew him only as an excellent mimic) made certain signatures his own. That he was subsequently accompanied across the Straits by someone else's wife, a lady bored by Marrakesh, remains secondary. In any case I was much more practical than Gruoch gave me credit for. The 'chit' that exercised me was the one that kept me at school, a list of hastily unearthed scholarships, the most charitable of which, absolutely necessary to make up the sum required, was for, of all things, woodwork – something I never had more than an incompetent pipe-rack to show for.

I do not see why I should have mentioned these wretched circumstances directly. I am biographer and narrator. We were both fatherless. But MacBeth's was dead and mine abandoned me. I suppose I did try, never very successfully, to make my father an amusing anecdote, but only ever privately in front of a mirror and what made it difficult for me to join in with Gruoch's laughter was that the subject of this study, my closest friend, had, in circumstances I could never know and only hazard, told his wife and allowed her to garble it. There is nothing quite so chill as intimacy shared out. But I was not about to tell Gruoch that.

'Well,' I said, 'you are remembering as you will, aren't you?'

She smiled with what looked like affection. 'It's been lovely,' she said. 'They say laughter is good for one. I really have enjoyed it.'

A few moments later she quietly, even cheerfully, announced that she had had enough conversation and that the pain had started again. At first I did not think I could get up but I considered how jealous I had been of her, of my efforts to slide between them when she had not been reduced to a dwarf, and that acted as a lubricant on my knees and lips and also, though I got out first, made my eyes smart. A hand patted my shoulder.

'It's all right,' said MacBeth, 'it's all right.'

51

Gruoch was buried in the country in mid-winter. There might have been some cheer from the relief of her death, the end of her long suffering – but that soon shrivelled in the rawness of the day and the looming presence of the widower. Raucous ravens made wing to the clump of bare trees beyond the cemetery wall; under their mist-borne caws the faint creak and buffet of feathers working in cold air and something, as they occupied their tar and clump nests, like the muffled rustle of stiff silk. The priest was nursing a sore throat with a knotted scarf and a reek of peppermints. The cords on the descending coffin creaked. Coughs and sobs joined caws. Weathered grave stones and brushed, black-dyed wool, pinched grey faces here tinged with mauve and pink and there by broken capillaries on cheeks as fat as peaches. The earth landed on the coffin lid, thud and very short scrabble. MacBeth did not weep but as a huge, long-coated contrariety found it horribly difficult to breathe.

To mourn a wife, to mourn love gone; yes, yes, that is pain. But I was to find him next day going at it with a wilful lumbering. Dressed in a dowdy motley of clothes he was engaged in scraping frosted moss from between the flagstones in his formal garden with a tiny hooked knife. Saliva seethed on my tongue. Distress, fear but some anger as well that he had lost his intelligence, talents and competence along with his wife. How wrinkled and swollen his eyes were! He cleared his throat and sulkily tucked away the knife. I took him inside. He sat and didn't say a word, his jaw moved sometimes in a ruminant way. How thick and excessive his skin seemed! I do not think he was aware of the dirt and thin green moss stains on his hands. He looked in some astonished, slothful way to be savouring what he had lost.

The next morning however I found that he had at least shaved. He was sitting like an invalid at another of his windows watching small birds swoop and feed. He turned his head and looked up at me.

'I have been away too long.'

My friend had understood. Had he given me time I should have dropped to my knees and very likely wept with relief. But I saw it happen. The unravelling of perception into resolve, from unwrinkling forehead to lifted chin; he had confused sensible admission with a sense of duty.

I moved quickly. 'You are quite right,' I said. 'No one at all is irreplaceable.'

But I don't think he heard, despite his, 'No, no, of course not.'

I had one, awful, last try.

'Everything has moved on. It has been years. But there are people there. They are willing. Very likely competent.' I could not bear it any longer. 'Oh, forget this fiddle! What does it matter?'

He blinked, and then a very small eye squinted at me and my outburst.

'Ah,' he said. 'I appreciate your concern, I really do. But I am . . . sure this will help me.'

And sniffily clearing his throat, he plunged in somewhere about his old job. It was then, of course, that I should have resigned, but my exasperating and craven sense of love and loyalty and hopelessness took precedence over the simplest common sense.

Malcolm came to see me very promptly, sat, put his flat thumbs together and briefly sifted me. In effect, I think he was making me an offer – but I stepped in. I was not interested in serving under him – or anybody else not Maelbaetha. That was not really a squint Malcolm had. A lower lid pulled towards his nose and twittered and twitched while his glasses magnified the effect. It was only then I realized that his lip tug was a substitute for calming his eyes. And let me be clear; Malcolm was patient to the point of inertia, whatever small signs of nerves he showed. He considered. Next, of course, he wanted to know, to reassure himself, that I did not mean that I was personally ambitious, that I would oppose him. Not at all. Who did he take me for? There was a certain gloomy – and self-righteous – satisfaction in this. Malcolm sat for quite a while before mumbling something about pity and if ever I should reconsider. I shook my head and he offered his hand. I wish I had not taken it. I wish that I had not left my country a few months later. But I had mistaken my role and I did both.

52

A pair of English words that some foreigners find insuperably difficult to separate when they speak, with which they are forever forging a link between sea-going creak and live bleat, are ship and sheep. A number of these timid, woolly creatures were stolidly consuming kelp, stuff like monstrous shredded cabbage left over from the tidal wrack. I sighed into the huzz of small surf. We were past the ogee hill, were what? – five hundred yards? – from the headland and I was waiting for my friend who had disappeared into the dunes to relieve himself, when I saw a humanoid log on the shore line. I looked back. Still no sign of my friend, though some peewits were pattering about in their own rhythm and, to one side of them over the sea, there was a rosy, salt-laden flush in the air. Inland a curlew called. I drifted on.

That log was undoubtedly a remarkably convincing happenstance of flotsam. It lacked rigor for a broken branch but was long for a seal, burly for an eel. I cocked my head, then craned my neck. The change of angle did not help. And since my friend remained stubbornly out of sight I began, cautiously, to approach it. In amateur beachcomber fashion I was widely prepared to distinguish the elements of the composition. I believe that dead people bloat after much time in the water. That was not the case here. I was some seven or eight yards past the little flock of sheep when the composition took on sodden navy blue. Very little later I saw an impressive imitation of a clay-grey hand. I pulled up. I jammed my own hands into my pockets, found soft cloth in one, a still sandy silver pebble in the other. Some of the sand I gently brushed off. Then, still pocketed, still with my thumb circling that Athenian coin, I moved forward staring out at the green and foam sea. Imagine for a moment that it was a corpse. In that case the legs would face the sea but were slightly askew because the trunk was turned towards the headland. I marched directly ahead, past the shape – was that a pale flipper or a foot? – and then turned.

I had two glum flegs. First, that I was looking at a misshapen, blubbery merman. Then the rearrangement of that into a youth of some fifteen or sixteen with black fuzz on his upper lip and, responsible for an earlier image of the wintry quality of drowned men's bruises, dark, sodden patches that had first blotted and obscured his snub features. I shivered. I noted the thick wrinkles in a foot but somehow could not shiver again. I heard a loud shout. My name, Taha, echoing in salt and sound. I looked up. My friend, elbow raised, quizzically shading the westerly sun.

MacBeth ran forward. It took me a blink or two to appreciate how hard he was going at it. I remembered him years earlier bounding down a muddy field. Face grimacing, muscles straining, thirty yards, twenty, ten and then throwing himself over not so much a white line as a shaved parting in the coarse grass. For what? No one was pursuing him and the purpose seemed absurdly unmatched to the effort. On the beach I do not think I was alone in giving a startled skook and I do not count that sudden barge and huddle of skittish sheep. Pounding towards a corpse? Oh, and I remember a twitch of incredulous embarrassment, that he was going to use me as a finishing post. But no, the widower arrived in a shower of sand, all bustle, middle-aged bulk and frown. He flipped the body over. Various squelching noises, a trickle of sea-water. I stepped closer. The eyes, blue-irised, were open and touched with grains of sand. Despite this MacBeth pressed his fingers to the slimy neck just behind the jaw. Had he seen something I had not? Now, face up, those bruises resembled purple and black fruit, less berry than plum, with the parody of bloom and finger marks due to a thin coating of sand. I think there is some business whereby apparently dead people are merely comatose, that instead of drowning in water life shrinks to wait for air. MacBeth dunted hard on the dead man's chest and got up some brackish-looking stuff, some slimy weed and a dribble of bilious foam. A clump of the corpse's hair fluttered in a small surf breeze. I should have thought that was enough but MacBeth got up directly and started scanning the horizon. There was a moment when I squinted out with him. But for what? Traces of a shipwreck? A waiting vessel?

'But he is *dead*!' I protested.

MacBeth caught hold of my arm. 'There may be others.'

Other what? Corpses? But no, he was thinking of survivors.

'Caught by a wave,' I said.

'What? How can you tell that?' he demanded in a tone as if I might have that information.

'Ta-ta-ta,' I tutted. I don't think we had ever squabbled, at the seaside or anywhere else.

He nodded. He sighed. 'Yes,' he said. He sniffed. He pushed his tongue up into his top lip over a dogtooth and sucked something.

'Who'll stay?'

Did someone have to stay?

'I will,' I said.

Now I might have objected, seen him stay put, but I was, in an indifferently fatalistic way, too fagged to care. So I squatted and kept sporadic watch on the diminishing spot of my friend towards the headland, his attempt to go round it by the sea, his return from that and then his progress as a climber. He vanished. Small cross breezes. The tide had turned or was about to. The sun was the height of my head above the horizon. I scratched my neck and looked round at my companion.

I do not think a yokel can be a fisherman and I could not come up with a word for rusticity on the coast. I had been reasonably sure before, after an hour was quite so, that he had been a seaside bumpkin. The few corpses I had previously seen had their vacancy plugged up and tidied and combed. This one looked innocent and stupid as well as vacant. Oh, the bruises changed in the setting sun, became lusher, and the grey skin flushed a little and a dead pimple or two gleamed, but he lacked that prim, arrested look undertakers give, looked more of a natural abstracting into nature. Josh MacBride I called him and I was to find I was generally right. He was the junior member of a salmon cobble crew sent to check the nets for seals. Armed with a gaff he had scrambled over rocks to find the meshwork threatened, he thought, not by a mammal but by an exceptionally large eel. I do not think it is interesting that those are the two creatures I thought he might be. I was to see the eel later, an impressive stretch of power more than six feet long with its greasy blue back and at its thickest as round as an athlete's thigh. It had received a number of gashes and cuts but the wound made by the excitable boy was clear. It was, I was told, a toss up between his losing his balance himself or the eel making him lose it. I blinked. It was explained that the eel was probably moribund and the boy was wearing over-large thigh-length boots. The boots may have filled with water. He may have knocked himself unconscious. In any case he could not swim.

I sighed. The tide had turned. The sheep trickled away inland. The moon rose before the sun set. I have always enjoyed that effect when the sun, having hung, swiftly sinks below the horizon. I was left with moon-licked surf creeping closer and a lump of flesh and cloth on the sand beside me. It grew a little chilly. I straightened up and strolled, but always, as it were, eye-moored to the dark corpse. Was I nervous? Did I feel eerie? No. I did wonder if gulls, loathsome scavengers, scavenged and pecked at night. It did cross my mind that if my friend took a very long time the tide might oblige me to drag Josh further up the beach. It was surely unlikely that his clothes would have rotted. I mean I would be able to pull him by his collar and not have it part. I underwent a spell of salty aphasia, got involved in the number of tides since Josh had fallen, could not remember the opposite of ebb tide. Flow? Flux? Flood? I did not recognize any of them. Tired, stiffening up, I caught myself at a moonlit game of noughts and crosses – and that was probably the eeriest occurrence in my vigil. It made me look up and round at the headland, whereupon a light appeared at its crest and, seconds later, another glimmer appeared at sea. Progress towards me was slow and I remember repeatedly checking back on the corpse – but to see what? That he was still there? Was ready? Both lights danced a little and I cleared my throat.

As in some dreary old ballad, walkers and boat converged on me and pudgy, dead MacBride. It occurred to me, presumably in some left-over of childhood reading, that I should have made a small signal fire, but I had neither dry tinder nor kindling nor anything to make a spark. All I had to hand was a handkerchief and an ancient coin; dull coin, pale maculate moon and something insidious about the two lights approaching us, but I could not think what it was. I was on the point of clearing my throat when my friend pre-empted me, swinging his torch, letting out a long fog-warning of a 'Here!' The boat slackened, bobbled and turned in, just short of the wide moon-beam on the sea. And then MacBeth loomed up, arms raised in a mix I think of breathlessness, cursory apology for the time elapsed and a heavy gesture of at last. He cocked an eye at me and then, resting his hands on his thighs, at MacBride.

'His mother . . . a widow . . . is beside herself.'

I squinted at him and his panting. What else would the poor woman be? Or did he mean he had had to spend time comforting her?

To my left the boat came in. Booted feet in shallow surf, the rasp of wood on sand and the craft quickly turned about. The men MacBeth had brought were only three in toto and all old. Moonlight and torch; there was no pity in them, more a silent exasperation, though perhaps that was shadow work and aged discomfort at young death.

'Daft beggar!'

You can still learn a little something in the oddest of circumstances. I had never noticed before that beggar is merely a genteel vowel shift away from bugger. Half-amused I turned round to MacBeth. But he had not heard. I blinked. Some vigorous prophylactic spitting started up and an unhappy noise that I traced through sea hush and huzz to saliva, few teeth and wrinkled cheeks.

'Not *all* night,' said the beggar man. 'Give us a hand there.'

The body was lifted – I touched, sporadically on the trundle seawards, a chill heel, a toe with an overgrown toenail and a swollen ankle – and tumbled into the boat. There was a sound like a dog peeing against a stone wall – more water from the corpse's clothes probably – and the old spitter who had accompanied my friend over land looked back at the denser darkness obscuring the way he had walked and stepped in.

'I'll take the tiller,' he said. 'A push, sirs?'

There was something laconic and shifty-eyed about all this that I did not fathom, something dislocated and stagey, like an incompetent nightmare enacted by shy, pointlessly cunning greybeards and a dead dummy; to leave us, the discoverers of the corpse, alone with one torch on a long night beach. I pushed, warily and perfunctorily, but I pushed. When the oars creaked and dipped MacBeth lifted his hand to run his fingers through his hair and I saw that his knuckles were spectacularly scraped and bloody. He told me he had fallen. He watched the boat settle down into less bobble and more sea for the oars to pull. He muttered something about strong stuff. What? But it turned out he was flattering me. Sooner me than he to sit by a corpse. My thanks old friend. This struck me – remember I had salt water in my shoes – as eldritch comment on my social abilities. And what was that about strength? And then, as I drained my footwear, he could not help it, he cleared his throat, and I knew, oh not specifically but certainly unstoppably, in the way a sunset turns into night, in the way a light will gleam in a boat, that in some excruciatingly unjust and crude way that extraneous young corpse being rowed off had done for me and that my forbearance and anxious service had been hopelessly generous, the unwanted gift of a pauper.

I did not understand but I knew. Even then I could ask how that was possible, how I could know for certain without understanding. But then in an effort to dry my hands in my pockets I found the tetradrachm. I brought it out and stretched out my palm towards him. The Tahalismanic talisman.

'Here, you take it.'

'No, no, no. I couldn't.'

My friend!

'If you don't want it,' I said, 'I'll see if I can skip it on the water.'

He lowered his head. He murmured something about the distance we still had to cover on the remains of our walk.

The urge had already deflated. I nodded, looked at the moonish part of the sea, imagined the old coin skipping once and then feebly disappearing, a silver spot in sea and moon glow, nodded again, eyes pricking, my lips feeling fat, and simply let the thing drop onto the sand. I had no idea of marking MacBride's spot, rather the reverse. I wished to return the coin to its unfound state.

Strange; as soon as I had dropped it I felt lighter, as if I had been in a bubble that had popped and could now move freely.

'Over the headland?' I said, gently swinging my arms, and it was his turn to look amazed at me.

Better daft than humiliated. No. I felt a sudden enormous desire to sing. But I stifled it. Wait!

'Do you remember your voice lessons?' I said.

'What?'

' "Widow, window, winnow," ' I pronounced.

He shook his head before he spoke. 'That's too much for me,' he said. I nodded. It occurred to me in a sort of fierce fatuity that what I should have done was write Gruoch a wonderful love poem, subject myself to his love for her, felt my way in words and conjunctions and images, gone through his love for her to show my love for him. I blinked.

'That hand looks nasty,' I said. 'Better look after it.'

53

I used to think that great books stay stiller than we do. It was the reader who provided a moving, necessarily partial mirror. Let me just, very gently, touch and trace the engraved lines on the back of mine. I have also thought not of silvering but of watery refractions and a multitude of natural colours, of the shift and shimmer of splendidly perceived states of being, of the illusion of containment, of beautiful markings, of bliss. I had so wanted to produce a book for dull days, provide pages to dip in, to refresh, not this exigent beating of a soul alone.

Is it possible for an ignoble narrator to enchant? I am blinking too much. I think this southern light is destroying my eyes. I am becoming myopic and have to peer and blear foolishly. This irritates, of course, but that is only residual pride. And however much a norman (who likes yarns) or a fylfot (who runs with modern issues) twists or ignores the stuff, I have endeavoured to make pride's place here piddling, have endeavoured to show myself even stupid, even lame, even cheap, even fey, have recorded that is, as scrupulously as I can, the natterjack nature of the narrator, have clustered together the intimate manners and details of my soul and impressions of how I was seen by others for one reason.

Is it too obvious to say that, even describing limpets and bilberries and malt-black irises, it is always Maelbaetha I want? That through rat-poison and zoos and bleeding feet, it is always Maelbaetha I want. And that now, now that I have the reader alone, as in a crude parody of a children's pantomime, that want is nothing without the reader. All those who believe in despondent life and illuminated manuscripts shout yes. Brave Taha. Stubborn Taha. I am so tired. I have worked so hard. I would so love to have someone to tell me what to do.

And of course I am presumptuous. But the doctor who tells us we must die is a Ciceronian and a bore because he means I, you and that other individual must not fuss and that my Maelbaetha is like countless other persons. What do we owe the dead? A degree of care, surely. A degree of mutual kindness. Stop. Join with me. Let us wage wart on simplistic dreams and gratifications. Let us forsake grandeur, however romantic, however flattering, and concentrate on awkward, humble precisions. If we were to plant a sapling for each corpse, what a landscape we would have, what a weight of tree and shade against the cruelty of insipid forgetfulness!

MacBeth was to live for another three years. I have taken time over that verb form. But it stands. He died after suffering a stroke. I understand he spent some five weeks utterly speechless, partially if largely paralysed. He never recovered the ability to speak but, the paralysis slackening somewhat, his eyes became in the words of an unsuspectedly vivacious correspondent 'powerfully if obscurely expressive'. My old secretary also told me MacBeth died in rehabilitation, 'still refusing to manage chalk and slate' and, it is comforting to think, in a furious heave and outburst of dissent. Comforting but not necessary. I have a nice vague sense of lap, lap, lapping; lives, pages and various fingers, that one mouldered and here from hairless youth to liver-spotted age, a quiet process on a shelf, home to a silverfish, some ignorant dusting, yet the pages opening and your eyes picking up the name. Maelbaetha, Maelbaetha, Maelbaetha.

Careful, Taha. Appeals for pity usually sicken. Still. To recount. I babbled, I gibbered, I twittered, all within the confines of my heart. I was not, you see, about to beg. That is clear. The great strut and tringle of my life had been removed and I sat, coy, bemused and quite hopeless.

What bitter despair there was in me! Such cruelty! Such

hate! I'd . . . what? Nothing. Hard nothing. And even my pro-
tests sank. And everything was in a blinking, a shuttering in
my lids. I was obliged to sign certain papers terminating my
employment. Generous terms on the whole. But I could not
speak. Is it strange that when insulted I have often had nausea-
ting visions of my own cruelty? A means of preservation only.
Dried skin. A terror of innocence. Bitter air. Well? Blot that ink.
What's to waddle? Taha. No swaying. A residual shame (from
what?) as I scurried down the corridor. And even the new
porter had left his cubbyhole. Then out. Weak sun, chill air,
nothing. A stony stillness, a what now?

Ah, I know how Adam swallowed!

Stop. What now? continued much less aboriginally. And
alone. I sat. I felt a perverse elation. There were plans I had –
were there not? – activities always hankered after. These sank.
Well, well. I had rather a problem with running mucus; I mean
my nose expressed what my eyes did not. I never felt less like
weeping. Monkish, mawkish and irritable. But in fact how
easy it was and how little I had accumulated to hinder my
going. Solid possessions faded. The roof flew. Walls melted.
No friends called. The little I took – too little and far too few
books – I packed up and accompanied on the sea voyage, a
piece of not so pure sentimentalism. I wanted to be sick by
rusted rivets in cold salt air because I had come that way. And I
wanted to revise again my wife's accident in her bath, that
quarry water and vole, that cramped garden pond and, yes, a
seashore nightmare so convincing it was barely night, scarcely
more than exiguously lit shadows.

But somewhere in those thirty-odd years I had become an
expert sailor, had acquired an inexplicably cast-iron stomach,
rode out a storm in the Bay of Biscay without a hint of queasi-
ness. That over, the air warmed, warmed some more. And
after a few days I arrived at a squat levantine place, with a blue
blue sea but, oddly, no sea birds. The port was dusty and
listless, sheds and a few drooping palms, the harbour awash
with flotsam and trash. Small shabby men struggled with
cargo and baggage. I looked up. The evening sky was a fan-
tastical, culinary arrangement of clouds as white as lobster
meat or, more accurately, poor man's lobster, monkfish, streaks

of octopus ink, some spoonfuls of crab coral, a dash or two of saffron, all on a bed of glistening red peppers. Could I possibly be seeing right?

'Damn,' said the captain.

'Why?'

'It's the reverse here.'

'What do you mean?'

'That shepherd's warning stuff. What we are looking at now is a strong wind tonight.'

I admit, this information cheered me. I like differences. I thanked him for his attention. I watched my stuff swung out and deposited on the dockside. Taha the natterjack negotiated the gangway. Strange. I shuddered as I stepped ashore, suddenly felt an almost unbearable sensation of tergiversation, as if my life had been used to demonstrate some plausible but unforgivable trick. Oh, and why did I feel I was to be met? That someone was about to enclose me in their arms? I looked around me, over my shoulder – but there was no one. Only flat coast and weathered sheds. Yet the feeling that there was someone there persisted. I closed my eyes a moment.

Foreignness is unavoidable bad faith. I opened my eyes. I licked my lips and prepared to employ a language long unpractised. It was then I suddenly remembered that 'please' is not welcome here, can be taken as sarcastic.

'Yes, yes,' I said. 'Those are mine. And that one there. Yes, pick them up. Come on.'

Perhaps they were shocked at being addressed in their own language. Perhaps my accent had crumbled. Perhaps my tone and manner were wrong. All plaint and contempt, that little crowd of men began advancing on me, their hands outstretched, their faces wrinkled into a whining rictus. It was a reflex gesture. I jerked up onto my toes and snapped at them.

'Please!'

They halted at once. I swallowed. Calves trembling, I let my heels slowly down to the ground and spoke again, much more softly.

'Please?'

212